A Whisper of Life

A Whisper of Life

Gloria Cook

CANELO

First published in the United Kingdom in 2007 by Severn House

This edition published in the United Kingdom in 2019 by

Canelo Digital Publishing Limited
57 Shepherds Lane
Beaconsfield, Bucks HP9 2DU
United Kingdom

A CIP catalogue record for this book is available from the British Library.

Print ISBN 978 1 78863 340 6
Ebook ISBN 978 1 78863 069 6

Look for more great books at www.canelo.co

Printed and bound in Great Britain by Clays Ltd, Elcograf S.p.A.

To Ron and Jenny Cook. The very best of friends.

Chapter One

Her shoulders down, her eyes misted over, Kate Viant trudged along the lane. How could they do this to her? How could her family be so low, so rotten; so heartless? Because they had always hated her, that was why. For years they had called her useless and ugly and stupid. They were ashamed of her because she walked with a limp. Throwing her chin up she punched the air. It wasn't her fault she had caught polio at the age of five and had ended up with one leg half an inch shorter than the other. Her parents had complained every time they'd forked out for the cobbler to build up her shoes – hand-me-down shoes. She had never had anything new. Her moment of fury crumbled into torment, her affront disintegrated into defeat. For her family to be this cruel to her, as they had been a short while ago, was beyond her worst imagination.

Tears flooded down her washed-out face and she pressed the backs of her hands, reddened by much scrubbing of floors and doorsteps, against her eyes. In her blinded state she stumbled to a nearby field entrance and rested her arms on a lower bar of the wooden gate. She sobbed out her pain, her heart ripped to shreds. She had been staying in Hennaford for the last few weeks, caring for her grandmother who had taken a tumble and broken her wrist. A few days ago her grandmother had died suddenly, a tragic accident, but this didn't figure in Kate's misery. Granny Moses had been a sour, malicious woman loathed and feared by her family, and Kate had been the one forced to look after her. She had said many spiteful personal things to Kate, all designed to cause maximum hurt. Everything Kate had done for her had brought only biting criticism. The old woman had complained about her cooking, how she had made her bed, every cup of tea she had brewed. Although Kate had brought her ration cards with her, Granny Moses had accused her of eating her out of house and home. She had accused the family of neglecting her, particularly Kate's mother, Biddy. She had declared she would never forgive Biddy for deserting her on her marriage to live with her husband at Tregony. The accusation of neglect was not true. Biddy would do that at her peril. She was also greedy in the hope of getting her hands on her mother's savings, convinced that her mean lifestyle pointed to her having a considerable sum of money hidden away.

Hurtful words from the rest of her family taunted Kate as she wept. An hour ago her two older brothers had come with a borrowed horse and cart to pick up Granny Moses' possessions. Kate had helped carry the austere furniture to the cart, as well as the rest of the dreary stuff which, except for a few select items Biddy had taken away, she had been left to pack up by herself after the funeral for a whole lonely day and night. Then she had fetched her little cloth bag of belongings, sad to be going home, for despite her grandmother's constant harping there had been something good about her stay. The few neighbours she had encountered while pumping water in the nearby concrete village court seemed to have taken to her. They had congratulated her for her quiet, polite ways, saying she was a good girl to care so tirelessly for Mrs Moses – their expressions making it clear that they felt sorry for her and that the old woman was despised by all.

Her grandmother's cottage was tucked in behind a privet hedge, at the foot of the village hill. As she'd scurried to and from the court, where the cart had pulled in off the road, a couple of passers-by had called out goodbye. She had dared not linger for a word or two or it would have angered her brothers. It had been nice to be among friendly people for a while. She was kept in at home to do all the housework, and denied the opportunity of getting a job and doing the usual things girls of her age did, like making eyes at the young men. Not that anyone would want her. She was a cripple, and although sixteen years old she looked much younger. She had nothing but drudgery, ridicule and loneliness to look forward to.

As she'd made to climb up in the back of the cart, to seek a comfortable spot amid the jumble of her grandmother's things, her eldest brother, Sidney, had barred her way. 'You're not coming back with us, maid.'

'When am I then? Have I got to catch the bus?' Surely her tight-fisted mother hadn't sent her the bus fare to Truro, and then for the eight-mile journey to Tregony? That didn't make sense.

'No,' Sidney scowled. Short, testy and bull-necked, he'd glared at her with contempt. 'You're not coming back at all.'

Kate had blinked into his steely narrowed eyes. Her other brother, Tony, had sprung up on the cart seat and picked up the reins. 'What do you mean? Do you know about this, Tony?' Tony Viant kept his back to her.

3

'Me and Delia's getting married,' Sidney said. 'We'll need mine and Tony's room, so he's moving into yours.'

Kate's large grey-green eyes grew wide with horror. 'You just can't leave me behind!' She grabbed the back of the cart to scrabble up on it but Sidney wrenched her away by the wrist, squeezing brutally tight.

'No? Just watch us,' he sneered. 'You're not wanted any more.'

'But where am I to go? I don't understand.' She'd felt the strength seeping out of her body. Part of her brain told her this couldn't be happening, a bigger part said her family was fully capable of abandoning her as if she was so much rubbish.

The Viant readiness to mock showed in Sidney's every dispassionate inch. 'Rent's paid up till the end of the week so you can stay here. Should give you time enough to find yourself a job. Rich people are always looking for live-in domestics. Someone'll be glad to take on even a little runt like you.' There was no point in arguing or pleading with Sidney or Tony. She was nothing more than a disposable asset to the family. She could even imagine her acid-tongued mother making hard-done-by remarks that she was lazy and ungrateful, that she had sponged off them long enough and it was time she made her own way in the world. Her mother wouldn't miss her unpaid service. She would make her new daughter-in-law do all the housework from now on. Kate knew Sidney was about to leave without even saying goodbye. 'But there's nothing left in the cottage! You're even taking the food and I've got no money to buy anything.'

He'd glanced at her, swung round to the cart, located the box containing the meagre contents of the larder,

4

then thrust them into her arms. Then he'd plonked a battered old shoe box on top of the food as if making some magnificent gesture. 'Don't forget to hand the keys back to the landlady, Mrs Bosweld, of Ford Farm. 'Tis down Church Lane, round the corner, by the pub.' He and Tony left.

For some bewildered moments she had watched them clip-clop up the village hill, her two brothers who had inherited their grandmother's selfish and malevolent ways, while all she had got was what was in her arms.

For ages she had perched on the bottom step of the cottage stairs, her elbows on her knees and her hands supporting her face, gazing at, but not seeing the box of food, the shoe box and her little cloth bag where she had dumped them. It was frightening to be suddenly pitched all alone into the world and she fought back panic with every breath, but it was even worse to be so ruthlessly forsaken. The walls of the small gloomy dwelling had seemed to be folding in on her and she felt she couldn't breathe any more and she'd hurried outside. Without knowing why she'd started walking, branching off beside the pub, down Church Lane. She was pleased there was no one about to witness her distress.

The bar of the gate was hurting her arms. Taking her hanky out of her skirt pocket she dried her eyes. The skirt was a cut-down. The faded print blouse on her willowy form had come from a jumble sale. She looked hard up and pathetic – a beggar girl with the urchin haircut her mother insisted on giving her. She had never looked nice, although some people had said she had pretty red hair. She had nothing. She was nothing. She gazed into the field. Sheep grazed contentedly and lambs frolicked. She would never spring about like the lambs, never be that carefree. The field sloped away steeply to a stream. She might as well drown herself in it. Life had never had anything to offer her and it never would. No one wanted her or was ever likely to. She lifted the scrap of rope that kept the gate shut, pushed on the gate, which juddered over deep tractor tracks, then closed it after her, careful to secure the rope in place.

–

Jonny Harvey closed in on the outskirts of Hennaford. Strange, he was suddenly feeling emotional. He had not lived in the village since a boy, leaving when his father had remarried, but he'd always considered it his home. Although his father was back living here, in a different house, Jonny thought more fondly of another property, Ford Farm, where he had been raised for a while under the guardianship of a beloved late uncle. The farm was where he wished he could stay for this leave, with his sensitive Aunt Emilia. There would be a warm welcome at Tremore House, where he was expected, but his father had filled it with noisy adopted young children, while Ford Farm, the largest property in Hennaford, had few inhabitants nowadays and was cosy and peaceful. He needed peace right now, and time and space to think, for he was in a quandary about his future. More than that, he was unhappy, how desperately he had only just realized. When he had alighted at Truro railway station the need to be alone a while longer had overwhelmed him. That was why he was making the six-and-a-half-mile journey on foot.

From early days he had planned out his life, which had gone mostly as he'd wanted. After achieving a physics degree at Oxford, he had gone on to a brilliant career in the RAF as a flyer. His intention was to serve until pensioned off. Then he'd travel the world and explore new challenges, while keeping contact with former veterans at reunion dinners. The war, which had ended three years ago, had shown him things couldn't be taken for granted. His plane had been shot down by enemy fire over the Channel a few days after D-Day. He was thankful to be alive and not badly maimed, of course, but burns had fused together the fingers of his left hand; no longer able, as a squadron leader, to fly operations, he had been forced to become a senior training officer. The small amount of scarring to his face had added to his envied dark good looks that were so appealing to women, but his relentless pursuit of women was less satisfying now. More and more there seemed to be no particular purpose to his life. Outside of training he had nothing in common with the younger pilots. Most of his peers were married and had families, they now spoke a different language to him, they had moved on with their lives and he felt the odd one out. He viewed matrimony as dull and dreary, but even though some of his friends grumbled about their wives and the duties of domesticity none of them were lonely. As he was, and miserable, and suddenly weary. He was thirty-four years old, strong and healthy, but felt past it and valueless, and he was vaguely afraid without knowing why or what of.

He reached the first outlying little whitewashed cottage, and shortly afterwards the garage and filling station, owned by his father; resolute black lettering spelled out 'T. Harvey' on its frontage. The business was quiet with petrol rationing still in force; anyway, few round here could afford a motor car. Trade came by way of the A30 running through the village. He knew the two mechanics, a middle-aged man and a fresh-faced apprentice. They were easy-going, average, quiet plodders, as most of the indigenous people were. He'd stop and have a natter with them. News of others from Hennaford, people he was so familiar with, would ease some of his strange emptiness, he hoped.

The local bus, jarring and heaving on its ancient chassis, lumbered towards the garage. On board, a young woman sitting next to a dusty window was watching Jonny turn in towards the wooden building. Abbie Rothwell liked to pick out details and form opinions about others. There was something striking about this tall RAF officer, striding along powerfully, a canvas holdall slung over his wide shoulder, his hand reaching out in greeting to the man and boy who hurried in greasy overalls, wiping their hands on rags, to greet him in return. The officer might be a Harvey, one of the bigwigs who resided round here. Her mother had tried to tell her something about the family she was about to stay with, and although Abbie had barely listened, for her mother tended to ramble on, she recalled something about a pilot war hero. So the officer was likely the son of the chap who owned the garage. There was nothing subservient in the workers' approach to him. There was mutual respect between him and the two.

The Harveys were, apparently, good sorts. Her stay among them – although not with the branch the RAF officer came from, if he indeed was a Harvey – should be pleasant enough and hopefully non-invasive; Abbie liked to go her own way. Her hostess Emilia Bosweld, formerly wife to the late squire, now remarried, had been her mother's childhood friend. 'If you're going down to Cornwall to find inspiration for your artwork, darling, you could do no better than to stay at Ford Farm,' Honor Rothwell had enthused. 'It's huge, so you won't feel squeezed in. I'm sure Em would be delighted to have you.'

'I'd rather be on my own, Mummy.' Abbie had screwed up her nose, glancing away in an attempt to cut the conversation short.

'Yes, I know you would, but I don't want you to be all alone and fretting over Rupert.'

'I wouldn't be doing that.' Abbie had employed her melodious voice softly to soothe her mother. She was an only child born many years after her parents' marriage and both of them worried over her for the slightest thing. Abbie felt this strongly, particularly as her father was often bed-bound with weak lungs. 'I mean, Rupert wouldn't want me to do that. Honestly, Mummy, I'll be fine. Actually,' she frowned, 'perhaps I should postpone the trip. Father had a bit of a cough on him over breakfast.' Now that she no longer had a husband and household of her own to consider there was no reason for her mother to bear the burden of nursing her father alone.

'There's nothing to worry about. Your father's toast simply went down the wrong way.' Her mother sounded confident and she should know. She diligently watched over former naval commander Archie Rothwell, badly injured from the torpedoing of his ship in the Great War. They had met and fallen in love at Ford Farm. Abbie suddenly thought it would be a poignant place to visit.

'But we don't think it's a good idea for you to be on your own yet,' Honor had persisted. 'Rupert has only been dead for six weeks.'

'I know. But you'll feel better, won't you, if I go to your friend's? I'd intended to call on Emilia Bosweld anyway. You've spoken a lot about her over the years and I feel I know her.'

'Good. Em and I always intended to visit each other but neither of us have got round to it.' Honor had sped to the telephone and made the arrangements.

Abbie was on her way to Ford Farm, free to be herself again, free from Rupert and his dreary ancestral home, and his surname, Goodyear, which she would never use again. It was dreadful that Rupert had died though. She would have divorced him eventually, not least because he was tenaciously unfaithful. She had loved him at the beginning, or rather loved him as she'd thought he was, a strong-minded high achiever, honest and good-humoured. She had been right only about the last thing and that had quickly disappeared. Rupert had been shallow, fluffy and irritating, and given to tremendous sulks if things didn't go his way. He had been useless with his family business of publishing. He would have brought it down if not brought down himself first, literally, over the edge of a bridge into a swollen river by the drunken female driver he was with. It seemed inevitable that he'd suffer some sort of tragic end. Perhaps it was better that he'd died young, instead of lingering to become, in all probability, a lonely, bitter, ageing failure.

She would always have a link with Rupert. She had met him at a book launch. She was a watercolour artist but also worked as an illustrator of children's books for the

Goodyear publishing house. She had come down to this county of popular holiday resorts to paint beach scenes for a series of adventure stories. She'd paint the countryside too. There was countryside enough back up in Lincolnshire, but what she saw here through the rattling window was just as lush and green and charmingly broken up into smaller fields and shorter hedgerows. There was never far to travel before arriving at a hill to be scaled or descended, and the engine of the antiquated bus chugged valiantly to reach each summit. She got the impression that the driver, a chuckling sort in sagging jacket and well-worn flat cap, and smoking a pipe, enjoyed each challenge. The two other passengers were housewives, wearing dull scarves over swept-back hair, chattering about everyday matters like how best to stretch a few ounces of meat ration to feed their families. Ordinary people living ordinary lives. They made Abbie feel secure, assured her that everything was normal. She lit a cigarette, leaned back against the worn, marked leather upholstery and relaxed. She was free and her life uncomplicated. All she had to do was enjoy it.

–

As Kate made her way down the slope, Jill Harvey entered the field from one adjoining it. She had come to check if any more ewes had lambed or were lambing. Yesterday she had carried home an abandoned lamb, the weakest of a pair of twins, to be bottle fed and nurtured in the farm kitchen. No other nursing ewe could be coaxed to foster the lamb. The lamb wasn't sick, its mother had merely rejected it in favour of the stronger sibling. It should grow to be healthy. Saving this lamb had been more than a normal job for a farmer's wife. It had taken on a new significance for Jill. She was twelve weeks pregnant. She and her husband Tom had been longing to have a baby. They had been married nearly four years, and although tests had revealed nothing was apparently wrong with either of them it had taken all this time for her to conceive. Now she was blissfully wrapped up in plans to knit baby clothes, choosing names for the baby – a boy would definitely be named Thomas after his daddy. Should they buy a new pram or use the huge, ivory-handled carriage affair that had transported Harvey babies for at least four generations? A smaller pram would allow easier passage along the narrow winding lanes. She would be sure to follow the district nurse's advice to the letter and take plenty of vitamins, get lots of rest and have no late nights. Nothing foolhardy would she attempt, she would keep her baby safe and well. This evening she and Tom were going to draw up the colour scheme and decide on the furniture for the nursery.

There would be another generation at Ford Farm, something the older inhabitants of Hennaford would welcome. There had been so many changes in the village since the war ended that some pensioners were feeling unsettled. After years of long service both the shopkeeper and the schoolmaster had retired. The pub landlady had died, and so had Tom's dear old grandfather who had lived at the farm. People had moved away, one young family had uprooted to Australia. The village's most astringent gossip, Mrs Moses, had been buried two days ago, although that was one change people didn't really mind – few had bothered to pay their respects at her funeral. Her family, as mean as she had been, had not held a wake. There was a granddaughter whom Jill had heard owned a pleasant nature, and was a 'poor little soul', much unappreciated for seeing to Mrs Moses's care and who had unfortunately witnessed the dreadful event of her choking to death on a large mouthful of food. 'Served her right,' a passerby at the time had stated. 'I heard she tearing into that little maid just a minute or two before. Choked on her own venom, if you ask me. Caused a lot of trouble over the years, the Moses woman did, with her evil tongue. It's been silenced for ever and a good job too!' The village would be a pleasanter place without the frightful Mrs Moses.

Movement further up the field caught Jill's eye. A girl was shambling down towards the stream, her head bent to watch for safe passage over the uneven surface of springy pasture, but it was easy to see she was thoroughly dejected. With the evidence of her limp, her unflattering haircut and grim clothes, she could be none other than Mrs Moses's granddaughter. It was natural for her to be distraught in the circumstances but there was something about her that worried Jill. She seemed overshadowed by some crushing burden, as if lost in the depths of something she couldn't cope with, as if living itself was almost too much for her. Jill picked up her pace in the girl's direction, putting up a hand in a friendly wave. 'Hello there!' The girl didn't seem to hear so Jill called again.

Kate heard a shout and the shock made her wobble. It was a strain to keep her balance. When she was stable she froze like a lump of iron. A young woman was striding up towards her. She had been caught trespassing and was in for a telling off. Was there no end to her miseries? 'I'm sorry, honestly I am,' she blurted out before the stranger reached her. 'I know I should have asked permission to be here, but I was careful to shut the gate. I won't do it again, I swear.'

'It's all right. Everyone is welcome to wander across Bosweld land as long as they follow the country rules, as you have just done,' Jill reassured her with a smile. There was a dimness about the girl, not because she seemed unintelligent, but through living a life impoverished of all joy and never knowing a simple pleasure. She kept her head down but Jill looked up. 'It's Kate Viant, isn't it? I'm Jill Harvey. Mrs Bosweld is my mother-in-law. I'm sorry about your loss. How are you bearing up? Is there anything I can do for you?'

Faced with unexpected kindness and sympathy while at her lowest, Kate was unable to keep back a fresh surge of tears. 'Th-thank you, I'm fine…'

'You obviously are not. Would you like to come to the farm with me and have a drink and a chat? Perhaps I can do something to help. Tom and I have our own part of the house so no one else will be there.'

'You mean it?' Kate sniffed into her hanky. She felt guilty for thinking about ending her life. She wouldn't have done it, but what she would have done, God only knew. She wasn't going to shun the chance of a little hospitality.

'Of course.' It would be quicker by way of the fields, where they could reach the farmstead round at the back, but Jill led Kate out to the lane where it would be easier for her to walk. As she closed the gate a sharp pain stabbed at her lower abdomen. Instantly worried, she rubbed there.

Kate noticed. 'Are you all right, Mrs Harvey?'

Jill waited a moment, concentrating on where the pain had been. 'Yes, I think so,' she answered, although she was worried and prayed the pain would not recur. 'Call me Jill. Would you like to tell me something about yourself as we go along, Kate?'

Kate gazed down at the dusty road as they moved off. 'I come from Tregony. My father and eldest brother are coalmen and my other brother does odd jobs.'

Jill walked slowly to compensate for Kate's inevitably slower gait but even so Kate was keeping slightly behind her, as if she had no right to be on a par. Jill shortened her steps to Kate's pace. 'And your mother is a housewife?'

'Yes,' Kate said in a breath of a voice. She had spoken about all those who had just rejected her. Her family. There wasn't even a suggestion that she keep in touch with them. There would be no invitation to attend her brother's wedding. The hedgerows were dotted with primroses. She had picked bunches of the creamy delicate flowers for her mother every year in the hope of appeasing her, of gaining her approval, even a touch of her love. Her gifts had either been ignored or scorned. 'You can't get round me with silly gestures. You're up to something, aren't you? Get on with your work. Bleddy girl!' This was the most common reference to Kate. She had nothing but bad memories and no future to look forward to. A cry of despair was just under the surface and she didn't know how much longer she could keep it under control.

Jill sensed her heartache. 'Kate, what's wrong? You don't have to tell me, of course, but if you want someone to talk to I'm ready to listen.'

Kate looked into her face and saw only genuine concern there. This woman, who by her well-toned voice didn't originally come from a farming background, and with soft youthful fair looks, her long rolled-under hair the colour of honey, was the kindest person she had ever met. Jill saw the hurt and torment in Kate's avid expression and made to put an arm round her shoulders. 'Don't worry, I'm sure—'

Suddenly an agonizing pain ripped up through her stomach, echoing throughout her body and flooding her with fear and alarm. 'Arrgh!' She doubled over, gripping her middle and falling to her knees.

'Jill!' Kate screamed, stooping to her, hands reaching for her. 'What's happening?'

The panic rising in Jill for her baby made it impossible to speak. She felt wetness between her thighs. She yelled and gripped her stomach tighter and tighter, instinctively trying to protect her child.

Kate beat down her own panic. Jill was writhing on the ground, curled up and making horrible groaning noises. Something was dangerously wrong with her. It might be her appendix. A youth in Tregony had suffered a burst appendix. He wasn't taken to the infirmary in time and the septicaemia had killed him. She had to get Jill to Ford Farm where someone could ring for an ambulance. She had never been there but from what she had heard the ford couldn't be far ahead and the farm was reached by the short hill up above it. She tried to get a hold under Jill's shoulders but Jill refused to let herself be unfurled and lifted. 'Jill! You've got to let me help you!'

It was hopeless. The more she tried to touch Jill and attempt to lift her up the more Jill screamed and fought her off. Kate straightened up and stared down the lane in desperation. How on earth could she get Jill to the farm?

She looked back the way they had come. A woman of about Jill's age, carrying a suitcase and something folded under her arm, was ambling towards them. 'Help!' Kate screamed to her. 'Please help us!'

'I'm on my way!' Abbie dropped her things and ran up to them.

Chapter Two

Jonny was on his way to Ford Farm. He was down in the dumps, but heaven alone knew what Tom and Jill were going through. Why did bad things happen to good people? It didn't make sense. Somehow the war had made sense, the world fighting off dictators and evil regimes, but these little personal tragedies were always hard to accept. Tom and Jill had lost the baby they'd wanted so much. They would make perfect parents. It just wasn't fair. Their marriage was a love match. In Jonny's experience there weren't many of those about. His own parents' marriage had come to a bad end – although if his mother hadn't embarked on a disastrous affair his wonderful half-sister, Louisa, who lived in Truro, would not have been born. He couldn't ignore that his father had married again, very happily, until his wife had died in an accident, and he was now blissfully in love with his third wife.

All was quiet as he turned out of Back Lane into the main street of the village. There were usually people about, arms folded in the way of those involved in chitchat. The blacksmith's, the butcher's, the shop and sub-post office, and the farm shop were all shuttered up, as if closed down for good. There weren't any children out playing or even a dog taking a wander. It was as if the population had decided to stay indoors and quietly mark the sadness that had come among them. Homes were set on either side of the main road, singly, in pairs, or in short terraces, some at odd angles. All seemed to have assumed a shadowy greyness, the picturesque or quirky sacrificing their character, the drab even more drab. Taking a lengthy puff on a cigarette, Jonny sighed and kicked a stone into a short stretch of hedge. He hated seeing Hennaford deserted. It was unsettling, foreign to him.

After several yards he'd passed the shops, the village court, and the little Anglican mission church planted by thoughtful Victorians to compensate for the parish church being two miles distant down Church Lane. The pub, the Ploughshare, came into view across the road. The new landlord had painted the walls pale pink. The usual half barrels of spring flowers on the courtyard had been replaced by long terracotta troughs. 'Bloody cheek,' Jonny snarled. People had no right to come in and make changes. The window displays of the shop, he had noticed, were rearranged in unrecognizable order. Roughly across the road from the pub was the redoubtable grey Wesleyan chapel, rightly shorn of its iron railings for the war effort, now with the addition of a small hole high up in one of the plain window panes. Sacrilege! Damn the perpetrator, probably some ignorant youth throwing a stone. Jonny balled his fist. How dare someone sully *his* village? But he must shake himself out of this grimness. He had no right to be selfish. Tom and Jill were the ones who really had something to be depressed about.

A moment later he was surprised to see Tom, in the company of a young blonde, emerging from Church Lane. 'Tom!' He ran to his cousin, grabbing his hand and placing a grip on his shoulder. 'I'm so sorry. You and Jill must be devastated. I was horrified to hear the news when I arrived at Tremore. Thank God Jill came through the operation OK. I was on my way for an update.' All the while Jonny jabbered away, his heart was wrenched over Tom's stricken expression. Tom was usually a blend of quiet resolution, dignity and laughter. Now he displayed the emotion of one who had lost an essential dimension of his being. He chewed his lip when troubled; now it was red and raw. 'Oh, were you on the way to Tremore?'

'Thanks for coming, Jonny.' Tom's voice was thick with unshed tears. He clung to Jonny's hand. 'Actually, we're on our way to the Moses place. This is Abbie Rothwell, by the way, Honor and Archie's daughter. Abbie, this is my cousin, Jonny.'

'How do you do, Miss Rothwell.' Jonny treated her to the well-practised smile he used on women, but he didn't linger over her as he'd normally have done, but returned to Tom.

'Why are you calling there? Father told me about the demise of the Moses woman. What's the latest news on Jill?'

'Um.' Tom shook his head and pressed his fingers above his eyes to call up the dreadful facts. In the last few hours he'd been tossed back and forth between fear and horror. He was numb and confused. 'They're keeping her in for a few days. It was what they call an ectopic pregnancy. The baby was growing outside of Jill's womb, in a fallopian tube. The tube ruptured. The surgeon had to operate swiftly. Thank God, Mrs Moses's granddaughter happened to be with her when she collapsed, and then Abbie came along. I could have lost her, Jonny.' Tom sniffed, gulped and tossed his head away, no longer able to hold back the tears.

'Steady, old man,' Jonny whispered, taking Tom in a hug. Tom brought himself under control. His voice stayed watery. 'I saw her when they brought her out of the theatre. She was so pale and grey. Her whole body had gone into shock, you see. They had to remove the damaged tube. Jill doesn't fully realize what's happened to her yet, and that it means it will be even harder for her to conceive again. I can't bear it, Jonny. I can't bear to think of her suffering.'

'I know,' Jonny soothed. 'I'm so sorry. I'm sure Jill's quite comfortable now, out of pain and being well looked after.'

Abbie had moved away to give Tom space. Poor man. What a day it had been. She had only been in Hennaford a few minutes before being faced with the traumatic scene of Jill Harvey on the ground in terrible pain, blood staining her trousers and her heavily sweating face an unearthly pallor. And the girl, Kate Viant, frightened and bewildered, but bravely trying to help her. Abbie, who was never easily fazed, had taken charge, while Kate, after explaining who the casualty was, had gratefully followed her orders. Jill had passed out. 'We must get her off the road. You stay with her and I'll run on to get help and tell them to ring for an ambulance.' Emilia Bosweld and her husband, a former Army surgeon, had rushed back with Abbie to the scene. Perry Bosweld had tended Jill. Tom had been fetched from the fields in time to go to the infirmary with Jill. After Jill had been loaded into the ambulance it was realized that young Kate Viant had slipped away.

Tom had not long ago arrived home with the news that Jill had recovered consciousness and was fussing about Kate. 'She was very groggy but also insistent,' he'd told those in the spacious kitchen in his mother's half of the house, the usual gathering place at the farm. 'I couldn't make out all that she said but it was something to do with the girl being upset and needing help. I reassured Jill that I'd go to see her. I need to thank her properly anyway. I hope she wasn't too distressed. It's not long since she witnessed her grandmother's horrible death.'

'Would you like me to come with you?' Abbie had offered. 'I think she trusts me.' Abbie had soon realized she had come amid a close family who cared about the community. Her mother had stated that the Harveys and Boswelds were a fascinating lot, and although Abbie hardly knew them, she was already sure this was true. With an unfulfilled marriage behind her, Abbie had believed all the love and romance stuff was nonsense until seeing the fear and panic in Tom Harvey for his adored wife. His mother, still an earthy beauty in her middle years, and her husband Perry, exuded the same affinity. Unwittingly they touched each other as they talked and gazed into each other's eyes. Abbie should have known such a deep sensual and abiding love existed. Her own parents shared it. They automatically finished off each other's sentences, answered each other's unspoken remarks.

She sensed Tom to be perceptive and genuine, one who saw no point in ceremony. The Harvey males had powerful physiques, of the sort that drew admiring looks from women and envy from weedier men. Tom had an attractive face, but Jonny Harvey's was gorgeous, a stunning piece of sculpted maleness, with strong lines, cheekbones in just the right place, and divine dark grey eyes. Suave in his uniform, he looked as if he had been born to be a warrior and looked even more the part with his slightly marred face and ruined hand, yet she sensed in him a loss of spark and direction. The way the wholly masculine cousins gave and sought comfort, unembarrassed to do so in public and in front of her, a relative stranger, touched her soul. These were real men, as opposed to Rupert whose flashy faġade had hidden a shabby weakness.

A moment later, Jonny said, 'I'll tag along with you to the Moses place.' Knowing Tom needed to be alone in his thoughts, he joined Abbie during the short walk. 'I knew your parents well, Miss Rothwell, as a boy when I lived at Ford Farm.' He was taking her in. She was a 'looker' and totally at ease under his appreciative gaze. She was open and satisfied with herself, with no secrets to keep and no particular struggles after her recent widowhood. Very good company too, he was sure. He liked women for company as much as he enjoyed bedding them. Abbie Rothwell had something of Honor's sweet femininity and Archie's vibrant watchful eyes. Archie had been his friend and he wanted to start off with Abbie as a friend, so he adjusted his manner appropriately.

'Really. I'd like to hear all about that.' Out of interest and to enjoy the chat with him. From the way he'd swept his eyes over her it was obvious Jonny Harvey was a dedicated woman-chaser. She didn't mind. She could handle that sort of attention and she had no inhibitions about enjoying sex. He was a charmer, he kept women guessing and hoping, but she didn't figure him as a rat. There was something going on, however, behind his potent bearing, something new to him – for he didn't have the grimness of one long dragged down. This enigma made him a perfect subject to paint. Few people needed persuasion to sit for her. She usually picked out those who would not be compliant but she had no idea which way he would react.

'I'll look forward to doing so when we get the opportunity.' It would be good to relive old memories of when Uncle Alec was alive. 'The Moses place is just here.' A few steps back along the way he had come and he was pointing to a narrow weedy path through a break in the high privet hedge. 'I'm glad not to be facing the old woman. Her tongue was like a poisoned dart.'

'I took little notice of her granddaughter,' Tom said, after coughing in a bid to clear the husky emotion from his throat. 'But she seemed the opposite to Mrs Moses. A little mouse, in fact.'

'She's very young,' Abbie said, as they trooped up the path. 'She might be nervous to see all of us at once. She's a little used to me. I think I should go first.'

'Good idea.' Tom stepped back.

Jonny glanced through a window. There were no curtains up at the sparkling clean glass. 'Good Lord. There's not a stick of furniture in there. It seems she's packed up and gone.'

'Her family must have been here,' Tom frowned. 'But if the key had been handed in Mum would have said so. Abbie, try the door.'

Abbie lifted the latch. 'It's not locked. I'll knock and call to her.' She opened the door a crack and tapped on it twice. 'Hello! Kate? It's Abbie Rothwell. Can I come in?'

Through the gap in the door she detected sounds like a little scampering creature. Then there were light irregular steps. 'She's coming,' Abbie whispered.

It had startled Kate to receive a visitor. She recognized Miss Rothwell's firm bright tones – she might have come with news of Jill Harvey – but she went warily to the door. She gazed at the older woman through the newly forming twilight, then retreated from the doorstep at spying the two men. 'I'm sorry. My brother Sidney said the rent was paid up for a few more days so I thought it would be all right to stay here.'

'It's all right, Miss Viant,' Tom said. 'We haven't come to take issue with you about anything. My wife was concerned about you and I promised her before I came away from the infirmary that I'd see if all were well with you. The other chap here is my cousin. Do you think we could come in, please?'

Kate was relieved at his friendly manner but wouldn't dream of disobeying someone older, let alone one of her betters. 'Of course.' The door opened straight into the living room and she limped into its middle. It was bleak and cheerless – as it had been before it was stripped of its furnishings. Beside the empty hearth was the kindling chopping block, which she had carried in from the back garden to use as a seat. Kate had been huddled down on it trying not to cry over her fate, or what the kind Jill Harvey's might be, while trying to form a plan about how she might get work and a more permanent roof over her head.

Abbie went inside and approached Kate, all smiles. Tom followed but kept back a little. Jonny stepped over the threshold but stayed thoughtfully near the door. The place was uninviting and smelled of stale liniment. The linoleum, so well trodden its geometrical pattern was blotted out in most places, had been brushed clean of the last speck of dust. Kate had been an excellent housekeeper for her grandmother.

Abbie thought she should reassure Kate again. 'Mr Harvey has only come to thank you for helping Mrs Harvey this morning.'

'Yes, absolutely,' Tom said. 'We'll both always be grateful to you, Kate.'

'How is she? Will she be back home soon?' Kate was praying it would be so, hoping she might get the chance to open up her troubles to Jill, who might be able to point her to a job.

'Not soon, I'm afraid,' Tom said. He explained why, watching the girl's eyes, which were so like a kitten's, stretch wide in horror and become wet with tears.

Kate looked down at the floor, too inexperienced in life to know what to say except, 'I'm sorry.'

The simplest statement, yet the sincerity in it was profound. Tom understood why she had brought out the protective side in Jill and it stirred him in the same way. It was evident Kate had known a lot of misery and had been put upon, probably all her life. 'Thank you. Would you like to tell me why you've been left here all alone? Is someone coming to fetch you?'

Kate shook her head, her wretchedness almost palpable. 'No. They don't want me no more. My parents or my brothers. They said I've got to fend for myself from now on.'

Abbie's jaw fell open in outrage on Kate's behalf. Jonny, glancing between the little mouse of a girl and the older woman, saw that Abbie could be something of a lioness. He liked that strength in a woman.

Tom gasped. 'Well, we can't have that,' he said firmly.

It was not lost on anyone how Kate responded to the edge of authority in his tone. Some of the misery cleared from her drawn features and she adjusted her stance, as if coming to attention. She was reaching out in hope. She was like a sad, neglected child. It was easy to want to gather her in close and swear to look after her for the rest of her life. She said nothing, waiting in that pitiful hope that things might be about to change for the better.

Tom glanced at the forlorn cloth bag and the tatty shoe box. 'I see you've got your things together. Good. How would you like to come with us, Kate? To Ford Farm? Miss Rothwell has just come to stay but there's plenty of room. My mother, Mrs Bosweld, will be glad to welcome you, and my wife will be pleased to know you haven't been left to remain all alone.'

'You mean it?' A glow filtered into Kate's pallid complexion and chased away the shadows, but the lightness eased off quickly. She was too used to having any kind of hope snatched away. Was Tom Harvey, the heir to Ford Farm, as genuinely kind as his wife? Was it possible for so many good pepple to live in one place and to be gathered here in one small room? Miss Rothwell had rushed to her aid in the lane with concern and had given orders without snapping. The RAF officer, whose amazing good looks she found a little daunting, was aiming the most pleasant of smiles at her.

'Absolutely,' Tom replied. He had the urge to ruffle her auburn hair. He wouldn't dream of actually touching her but she shouldn't be treated like a child anyway. She deserved respect and needed careful interaction or she'd retreat into herself. He picked up the bag and the shoe box. 'Shall we go?'

'Yes. Thank you,' Kate said. She had proper shelter for the night, perhaps for a day or two, perhaps even until Jill got out of hospital. It was enough for now.

Chapter Three

Jill stared up at the ceiling high above her head. One more day and she could leave behind this immaculately tucked-in bed, the clinical smells, the hushed bustling efficiency of the infirmary staff, and the rigid routine. She was counting off the minutes until she was back at home and surrounded by her own things, in a more restful atmosphere, in the security of being with Tom. To see for herself how Kate was. But it also meant leaving her baby behind, the scrap of humanity that had barely formed and had died inside her, too soon to tell if it was a boy or a girl. Not enough of anything to be given a funeral. To face the numbing fact that her hopes of becoming a mother were slimmer now a vital part of her body had been cut out.

The beginning of the regimented visiting time was rung in. The double doors down the end of the surgical ward were opened and people filed in, doused in church quietness, assuming encouraging smiles, bearing the usual sort of gifts for the neat rows of the sick and the recovering. Jill's fellow patients were envious of the number of visitors and well wishers she received. Every evening Tom came alone. Usually, it was someone from the family in the afternoon. Yesterday, it was Jonny, not knowing what to say, bluffing his way through, talking about nothing in particular. She'd got the feeling he had something on his mind. Jill's ready ear and non-judgemental nature meant she often found herself a confidante, but Jonny had not shared his deepest thoughts with her. She was glad of that. She had her own miseries and she was concerned about Tom, he was being brave and positive for her sake but losing the baby was just as heartbreaking for him. Focusing a little on Kate for a moment or two helped her cope with her aching loss. Today, it was Jonny's half-sister – a long-time family friend before the secret of her true identity had been revealed to her and Jonny – who had come to see her.

'Hello Jill. You look a little brighter today.' In her unpretentious manner, Louisa Carlyon kissed Jill's cheek and patted her hand to convey she knew she must still be feeling devastated, despite looking better. Slender and fair, invariably gentle, in a neat utility suit, small felt hat and white cotton gloves – her clothes were always easy on the eye – she rarely failed to uplift the recipient of her care. She had a ragged birthmark, the size of a half-crown, on her right cheek, but it did not spoil her attractiveness. While smilingly glancing at Jill, she added the daffodils she had brought from her garden to one of the overflowing vases of flowers on the bedside cabinet. 'Is Tom bringing in your things tonight?'

'Clothes to go home in tomorrow, you mean? Yes. He'll get Mrs Em to pack them. He's so afraid he'll bring the wrong things. I wish I could have been there for him all this time. He's got that little boy lost look, you know, that he gets when he's terribly upset. At least he's got young Kate Viant to take his mind off things.'

A wealthy war widow, fully occupied with charity work here at the grey-stoned infirmary and elsewhere,

Louisa was curious to meet Kate Viant. She pulled up a chair. 'Jonny's filled me in on what he knows about her. What a dreadful affair, but the Lord works in mysterious ways. If you hadn't been taking her home you would have collapsed in the field and, well, the end result doesn't bear thinking about. And if not for your kindness, no one would have known about her problem and something bad might have happened to her.'

'She wrote me a letter of thanks.' This brought a hint of a smile and an inkling of colour to Jill's blanched cheeks. 'It's written well so she's obviously a bright girl. It's in the drawer. Read it, if you like.'

Louisa read aloud the words in careful big lettering on the Harveys' headed stationery. *"Dear Mrs Harvey."*

'I told her to call me Jill, but I suppose she thought she should keep to formality in the letter,' Jill interrupted. 'Tom says she seems happy and relieved to be at the farm but is very unsure of everything. That's understandable after what she's been through, the rotten life she must have had. I'm eager to find out if anything really dreadful happened to her. I'll never forget how upset she was that day.'

'It will be good for you to have something to think about, but don't take on too much and risk your recovery, Jill.' Louisa went on with the letter. '"I hope you are getting well. I would visit you, but Mr Tom said it's family only. I like being here at the farm. Everyone has been very kind to me. I like playing with Mrs Em's little boy, Paul. I take him for walks. Miss Rothwell is a very nice lady. I am looking forward to seeing you again. Yours sincerely, Kate Viant." It's a very sweet letter, Jill. She comes across as rather childlike.'

'I'd like to make sure she gets a better chance in life. I owe her that. I've got Abbie Rothwell to thank as well. I didn't even get a glance of her. Have you met her?'

'No. I haven't been to the farm for a while. Jonny seems to like her. He's not chasing after her in the usual way. Actually, I'm worried about him. He's told me he's feeling restless and he seems really down. Oh well, there's always something, but I expect he'll sort himself out soon.' Louisa put the letter away in the drawer then lifted out a new 'get well' card. 'From Mark and Jana. Who are they?'

'Mark Fuller. The chap who moved to Hennaford two years ago, the one who's gone into partnership with the builder, Jim Killigrew, just down from the farm. Jana is his little girl.' Jill felt a stab of heartache and jealousy as she thought about the seventeen-month-old child, who, having been abandoned by her mother, was being success-fully brought up by her doting father. With a sense of despair she knew how anguished she would be when next faced with a child. She wanted her baby. She wanted time to wind back and for her baby to have been safely conceived inside her womb. The baby she would never see, would know nothing about. She couldn't even picture it. Part of her felt she had let her baby down. She didn't want to answer any more questions about the Fullers. She wanted to be alone and hide away. But she couldn't do that for ever. Panic rose up in her.

'Oh, of course. He survived as a Japanese POW. Then his wife did the dirty on him. I've not met him yet either. Well, I really ought to go. I don't want to tire you.' Louisa had sensed Jill becoming distant but her curved eyebrows shot up at seeing Jill turning red. 'Jill, are you all right? Shall I fetch a nurse?'

'No.' Jill took a deep calming breath. 'I keep getting moments where reality hits home, that's all.'

Louisa reached for her hand. 'Dear Jill. I won't say the usual things, I'm sure you'll not want to hear them. I'm always available if you need me.'

'I know. Thanks, Louisa. Life goes on, they say, but not for my baby. Its life was no more than a whisper.'

Kate was cleaning the room she was staying in. She wouldn't allow herself to think of it as 'her room', as people usually did when temporarily resident somewhere. That would make the wrench harder when she had to leave. It was marvellous to sleep on a gleaming brass bedstead with a sprung mattress, with plump pillows, fine linen and a soft wool blanket, all covered with a coral-pink watered silk bedspread. At home she'd had a narrow musty mattress on the floor of a bleak cupboard-sized room, where her family had barged in invading her privacy. Now she had a double bed all to herself, in a house which altogether seemed the size of a manor. One of the main sources of awe to her was having the use of a proper bathroom. No need for a chamber pot pushed under the bed here, no trips necessary down an ash path to the bottom of the garden to a tiny, draughty, spider-infested, stinking privy. There was actually hot water on tap, unimaginable luxury. The household never had to fetch water from the well. The dreaded job of trudging journey after journey to fetch heavy buckets of water from the well at home had used up a big chunk of each day, leading her ungrateful mother to snap down her ears, 'Get a move on, damn it, bleddy girl!'

Another wonderful thing here was the lack of unpleasant smells. The odour of farmyard manure filtered inside when the windows were open but it was an unavoidable smell and one the nose quickly got used to. At home her mother and the men had been careless of hygiene and their offensive body odours had permeated every dark and dingy corner. Her father and Sidney had never washed the coal dust off themselves thoroughly and it had been impossible to launder their blackened shirts, the towels and sheets back to whiteness.

She was in the corner of the Boswelds' wing, with its refined Victorian facings. The front window of her room looked over the lane and she could see ploughed and planted fields, and fields of cattle and sheep, and neighbouring farms and the church tower in the distance. The view at the side window fell away into a meadow and the woods. Ford House, once Harvey property, now owned by the local builder, could be glimpsed, and further up the hill was a new house, built on traditional country lines and belonging to Jim Killigrew's partner. The man who lived there, Mark Fuller, had a beautiful infant daughter, who he'd brought over to play with three-year-old Paul Bosweld.

People were always dropping in at the farm. Kate tended to keep her distance from them. The visitors were curious about her and often kind, but she didn't want to make any friends. She didn't want to get to like it here too much. At some point she would have to leave. Most of all, she mustn't get to rely on anyone. Dreams and hopes were all too easily crashed. Although she didn't believe the people here would simply turn her out, she couldn't risk one day soon pining for Ford Farm and the security she now enjoyed. The emptiness might be unbearable.

She dusted and polished the walnut furniture and used the carpet sweeper in here every day. There was no need, the room sparkled like diamonds, but she was used to being busy and she wanted to show the family her gratitude. It was lost on her, despite their constant reminders, that they owed more to her than they'd ever be able to repay. Putting the cleaning things back in their wooden box, she opened the wardrobe and looked into the full-length mirror on the door. She smiled a wide smile. It was what she did every time she saw herself in the glass. Each time she could hardly believe it was herself. She was wearing a blouse with a pretty scalloped edge and a pair of trousers. Mrs Bosweld, known by all as Mrs Em, had gone into town and bought them for her. It was wonderful to have trousers to take the emphasis off her disability and cover her ugly shoes. She had a new dress too. She had tried it on in stunned excitement. Mrs Em, who was tall and beautiful like a statue, with volumes of shiny reddish-brown hair, had offered to fasten the buttons at the back of the neck, but had sensed Kate's embarrassment and kindly waited outside the door. Kate was shy about her softly moulded figure and ashamed of her underwear, made from any old scraps of cotton. Jill, who although taller than Kate was roughly the same size, had asked Mrs Em to take some items from her own wardrobe, and now Kate had proper underwear, another dress, two skirts, and two cardigans which were not knitted from unpicked garments. Tilda, the housekeeper, who fussed over her like a broody hen, had showed her how to use the sewing machine to take up the hems. It never occurred to her to consider if she looked attractive in her gifts. Having something fine and pretty on her spare frame was a joy and her only concern.

'Kate! Are you up there?' came a shout from below. It was Mr Bosweld, at the foot of the stairs.

'Yes! Coming right away!' She snatched up the cleaning things and hurried out to the long landing. She felt an empathy with Perry Bosweld. He too was crippled; he walked with a limp, aided by a prosthetic, having lost a leg in the Great War. He was cheery and good-hearted, and wore clothes more colourful and stylish than other men. Miss Rothwell termed his dark looks as classically handsome, and said he was 'one of those men who gets better with age'. And she wanted to paint him. He was just the sort of man Kate would like as her father. He gave her twinkly-eyed grins and his posh voice had soft tones. Apart from Jill, he was the one person she wasn't at all shy of.

When she reached the last two steps, gripping the handrail tightly – climbing up and down was tricky for her – Perry Bosweld held out one hand to take the cleaning things from her and the other to help her alight.

Kate didn't realize that she responded to him with shining eyes, or that he was thinking how pretty she was when her face fit up. She was an engaging little thing. Abbie wanted to paint her too. Abbie had a long list of portraits she wanted to do, starting with Emilia. Quite right, there was no one more fascinating and beautiful in the world than his beloved Em. 'Kate, my dear, do you fancy a stroll down to the shop? My monthly rose-growers' magazine should be in and I don't want to wait for the paperboy to deliver it. Would you mind, please?'

'Course not, Mr Perry. Anything you say.' Kate was pleased to do little jobs for the family. They stressed she was a guest among them but she felt she must pay her way somehow and not become a burden; she dreaded that happening, for then surely they would want her out.

'Thanks a lot,' Perry beamed back in his friendly manner. Kate was always eager to please, and his little ruse to encourage her to get away from the house for a while had worked. Apart from exploring the farmyard and short trips down to the ford with Paul, she had barely poked her nose out of doors, wanting instead to haunt the kitchen and help Tilda with the housework. Admirable of her, of course, and Tilda Lawry, in her mid-sixties, was glad to have someone willing to fetch and carry for her, but it wasn't what Kate was here for. The family had taken her under their wing, not as a charity case but because they genuinely liked her. Hopefully she would prove a focus for Jill when she came home tomorrow, help her come to terms with her heartache. And, more personal, the terrible sadness and put-down aspect that clung to Kate reminded Perry of his daughter Libby. Bullying had cost fourteen-year-old Libby her life. Some years ago, unable to bear returning to the boarding school where her life had been made hell, she had walked into the sea and drowned. He handed Kate a ten-shilling note. 'Keep the change as a thank you for going. Treat yourself, if you like.'

Kate stared at the note as if she had never seen such a thing before. Only on rare occasions had she acquired a few pennies of her own. 'But it will be a lot of change.'

'You deserve it, Kate.' He closed her small rough hand over the money, for she seemed about to hand it back. 'You've done a lot for all of us. Take it, to please me.'

What else could she say but a grateful 'Thank you very much.'

Emilia had been listening further along the passage. She'd slipped away to a cupboard in the kitchen where discarded items were kept and hurried back with a small brown leather handbag with a gilt clasp. It wasn't fancy but it was smart, and had belonged to her married daughter, Lottie. 'There you are, Kate. I've been having a bit of a turnout and I was wondering if you'd like this. It'll be just right for you.' Just right for her to carry the ten-shilling note in. 'It's got a little purse compartment inside and a mirror.'

'I can really have it?' It was a gift beyond Kate's dreams. None of the girls her age that she knew had a grand handbag like this and she didn't think she'd ever possess one. It would make her feel quite grown up. Mrs Em was so kind. Kate eased into feeling completely comfortable in her presence. There was no reason not to. Mrs Em had explained she had been the dairymaid here before marrying the squire, Mr Tom's father. If only she could be taken on as a worker, Tilda's assistant perhaps, even in a smaller, less well-furnished room, and stay here for ever.

'Off you go then,' Emilia laughed, resisting the urge to hug the girl in case she didn't like it. 'And take your time. It's a lovely day out there.'

Emilia opened the front door for her, then she and Perry watched, arms linked, at the hall window as Kate started off, her limp not as obvious as usual. She was swinging the handbag round and round by the handles to get the feel of it, bringing it up to her eyes to get a good look at it, then opening it up and using the lipstick mirror to gaze at her reflection. Finally, she held it still by her side and carried on with her head up in the air.

'Dear of her,' Emilia said. 'It doesn't take much to make her happy.'

'It's good to see her with a touch of confidence at last. Em, darling, can't you do something about her hair? Kate doesn't deserve to go round looking partly like a guttersnipe. It seems everything was done to her to keep her down.'

'Abbie and I are going to do something with our hair tonight. I'll suggest to Kate that we wave hers too.'

'That's the ticket. It's nice having people in the house again. It's been too quiet since Lottie moved into her own place, and your father died. Such a terrible shame we won't be getting a new grandchild and a playmate for Paul from Tom and Jill.'

Emilia gave a hefty sigh. 'That's the trouble with life. It never takes long before sadness comes round again. At least Jill meeting up with Kate when she did means there's better times ahead for her.'

–

Jonny and Abbie were up in the foothills of Perranporth, amid pyramids of sand crested with marram grass. They were facing the sea, above the two miles of fine pale yellow beach, with military-occupied Penhale Point a little way upcoast. They had formed an easy, trusting friendship, the sort when two people feel they have known each other all their lives. Without saying so, they admired each other's achievements, were comfortable about their differences, and both were sure there was nothing to find out about the other that they wouldn't like. It was as natural as daylight that they went about together. The regulars in the Ploughshare had assumed Jonny had brought his 'young lady' with him on this leave to meet the family. The couple's amused denial had brought out the opinion, whispers they'd overheard, that 'even so, something will come out of it'.

Abbie had gone over to Tremore on the north side of the village and met Jonny's thoroughly pleasant father and attractive, ordinary young stepmother and little stepsister, and the three former evacuee children under their guardianship. Jonny grumbled mildly that there was too much noise and commotion in the house, but Abbie saw he was somewhat envious of the slightly muddled, boisterous order there. She had painted him in the garden at Tremore. His father, Tristan, had insisted on buying the picture, which had been hung in the library. Jonny maintained he valued his independence above all things and could never enjoy the 'wife and family thing', but she wondered about that. Why keep bringing it up if it was so unimportant to him?

Jonny was stretched out on a red tartan rug, his arms comfortably supporting his neck, wearing just shorts. He'd been on edge for months and it was great to relax for a while. In good company, enveloped in nature, the soft warmth of the sand underneath him, his lungs filled with the evocative tang of salt air, his ears charmed by the sounds of gulls screaming overhead and the rollers of the Atlantic Ocean beating in on the shore. 'You'll have to go along to the south coast as well, Abbie.' He broke the long meditative silence. 'It's not as untamed and rugged as it is here. Everything is formed more softly but it's equally as beautiful and inspiring.'

Abbie had a small sketch pad perched on her raised knees. To speed things along she had painted on some washes the previous night, enough to add contrast and subtlety to the monochrome sketch she was making of Gull Rock out at sea. 'I intend to do the very thing,' she said in a voice removed from his company, her eyes flicking to the flat horizon of the boundless expanse of blue-green water on which sat lazy puffed clouds and a distant sea-going ship.

Jonny leaned up on his elbows. Abbie was with him and yet she wasn't. She was deep inside her creativity. She had brought the manuscript of the book she was illustrating down with her – kept safe in her room – and she made notes on her work where figures and dwellings and pirate ships and such things would go. It amazed him how fast she worked. When she used colour from the miniature paint box, dipping the brushes into the small bottle of water and mixing tints with a graceful flourish, she'd allow one sketch to dry and start another.

They had moved about, starting under the cliffs, which were honeycombed with little caverns, at the Droskyn end of the beach, parts only accessible while the tide was far out. Abbie had drawn everything from rock pools brimming with several species of green, brown, orangey and pink seaweed, to the various dark formations of the weather-hewn granite rocks, to driftwood and scraps of rope and netting washed in from fishing boats. And tiny whitewashed cottages high up on the cliffs. Every living being she encountered she captured. The local children playing barefoot, some in makeshift bathing costumes cut down from old jumpers. Early holidaymakers, the elderly mainly, in lightweight clothes, sandals and sun hats. A lady in a long dress with an elegant parasol, who looked like a screen siren. Dogs scampering in and out of the waves and two riders on horseback.

Jonny took out his cigarette case. 'Want a gasper?'

'In a minute. I've nearly finished this. Then we can tuck into the picnic Tilda packed for us. Sorry if you're ravenous and I've kept you waiting.'

'Don't worry about me. You're the one who's working. It's fascinating watching someone so talented and absorbed in her work.'

When she was satisfied with the sketch she gazed down on him. 'Aren't you?'

'What?' Jonny said, passing the picnic hamper to her. He took it for granted that she as the female would dish out the grub.

Anyone else doing this would have greatly annoyed her, but Jonny didn't in the least see her in a lesser role, in fact he was honouring her with the responsibility. He was a strong thrusting sort, but at that moment he looked lost and vulnerable and she was happy to wait on him, to seek a way to encourage him. 'Are you having a few problems with your career?'

'Not with the force, but I am with myself.' He twisted his mouth as he struggled to uncork a bottle of hock. 'Oh, I don't know... I don't even know what I think or feel or what I want any more. Pathetic, isn't it?'

'I wouldn't say that.' When he'd won the battle with the wine bottle and poured out two glasses, she handed him a plate with two potted beef sandwiches, a slice of apple pie and a tiny wedge of cheese on it and a check linen napkin. 'Perhaps your inner self is prompting you to seek an entirely new direction. I suppose you'd always intended lifelong service in the air force but there's nothing to say you can't allow things to change. I get the idea you're fighting with yourself, Jonny. That's the worst sort of battle of all, you know.' Jonny stared at her. She was right. He saw all his ambitions and plans as if they were inside a closed box. He had been free when he'd set out in life, the skies and horizons seemed endless, but now everything had closed in on him. If he didn't do something about it he might end up in chains of his own making. He'd thought he'd owed it to all his dead comrades, the young men and women who had not made it through the war, and to the survivors horribly maimed and disfigured, to stay in the force and serve no matter what. But he was not paying real homage to their sacrifice and their memory if he ended up a dried-up fossil with little more to show than a chest laden with service medals. His friends wouldn't have wanted that for him. They had fought not just for freedom from tyranny but for their hopes, for the ability to go on to seek contentment and fresh experiences. Tears sprung along his curling dark lashes and he couldn't speak, only nod.

'It will be all right, Jonny. You'll make it so.'

Her confidence in him meant everything. 'How?'

'That's not for me or anyone else to say. You'll know. It will just happen if you let it.' She left him to eat and drink quietly, giving him the opportunity to allow some of his old thoughts and values to fade and be replaced by new possibilities. She packed up the hamper.

Just let it happen. He'd try not to fuss and fret but to be still inside and let fate take its course. Fate had ordained that he'd survive the fighting and now it seemed it might be prompting him to do something new with his life. Life away from the air force was scary. Of course he was as free to stay on as he was to leave, perhaps he merely needed to see things in a different light. 'More sketching here or shall we move again?'

'I think I've done enough today,' she said, packing away her materials.

'Back to Hennaford then?' They had ridden the three miles or so here on borrowed bikes and left them by a gift shop down in the little town.

Abbie let her eyes wander over him. All the way up from his bare feet and long legs, his firm stomach, his broad chest sprinkled with crisp black hair, and his throat, always a sensuous part of a man to her. She reached his gorgeous face, his wide delectable mouth. She closed her eyes for a second and imagined kissing him. She knew Jonny would be a dream of a kisser, and not just on a woman's lips. He would be masterful and devastating with his hands. He would be expert in every way there was to send a woman wild during lovemaking. His body shouldn't be allowed to remain lounging and redundant.

Moving on her knees she went up close to him. 'I'd like to make love to you, Jonny. Would you like that too?'

His eyes turned a smoky grey. In a rush he was consumed with sexual hunger, yet he examined whether it was a good time to move on from just being Abbie's friend. He decided it was. She wasn't seeking commitment any more than he was and it wouldn't spoil what they had. He put his uninjured hand along the side of her face and bent forward to kiss her waiting parted lips. 'I know a nice little hotel where we can go.'

'Let's stay here.' She ran searching fingers up and down his hot skin. 'There's no one about and I don't want to wait.' Neither did Jonny. He enjoyed making love in the open air, best of all with a knowledgeable partner. He pulled her into his arms and let himself go with the moment.

Chapter Four

The first sensible place to ask where Kate might have gone was in Hennaford's general store. Some busybody probably knew what had happened to her, and gossip circulated best in places where people gathered. Sidney Viant found himself the only customer as he strode up to the long mahogany counter. To the short shapeless woman in a plain apron over a brown spotted frock behind the counter he painted on a cheery smile. 'Morning.'

'Yes, young man?' she intoned, keeping her attenuated face taut and humourless.

'Eh? Oh, yeh. Box of Swan Vestas.' Receiving pursed lips and a frown, he tagged on quickly, 'Please.'

Nora Grigg half turned to the shelf behind her for the matches, but rather than put the box on the counter she kept it in her hand.

Sidney disguised a scowl. Bitch! The shopkeeper, with pinned-up greying hair, spectacles hanging from a chain round her neck, was a prim and proper sort and didn't trust him for some reason. He knew he was hard looking but he didn't believe he came across as a thief who would run off with the takings. He stuffed his fist into his jacket pocket and scavenged for some change, then offered the requisite money in farthings. 'I was wondering if you knew anything about my sister. Kate Viant is her name.

46

She looked after our gran, Mrs Moses, till she died a short while ago. Do you happen to know if she got work locally?'

Nora Grigg pulled in her sagacious features. She wouldn't tell him anything, except perhaps for lies, about the girl who'd been in here only yesterday, looking pert and a little confident for once. She had seen this character driving a horse and cart past the shop the day his obnoxious grandmother's home had been cleared out and she had taken an instant aversion to him. No wonder, considering what he'd done to that poor young maid shortly afterward. It was disgusting. He and all his family should be weighed down with shame. It was unlikely there was a good reason for him wanting contact with the sister he had abandoned. Nora had taken over the shop a few months ago and had found no trouble fitting in with Hennaford. She had formed a loyalty to the villagers, especially the landowning Boswelds and Harveys, who had given Kate Viant a home. 'As far as I know she moved on somewhere. Don't know where exactly, but someone said she left on the next bus for Perranporth.' He looked annoyed rather than disappointed. Nora gleefully rubbed his nose in it. 'Some upset she were, apparently. If some of the good people round here had known she'd been cast aside on her own they would've given her a bed for a night or two at least. Would have done it myself. I hope no trouble will come to the poor little soul.'

'That's why I'm here,' Sidney retorted gruffly. 'To see if she's all right. She refused to come with me and my brother that day, and my mother's sent me to bring her home. We want to know if she's safe and sound. Mother's worried sick. If I wrote down our address, and if you was to hear news about Kate, can you drop my mother a line? Put her mind at rest?'

Slowly polishing her glasses and putting them on with distinct condemnation, Nora set her discerning eyes on him. 'You'd have me believe that you and your family care about your sister, would you?' A believer in the axiom that what someone didn't know wouldn't hurt them, she'd take it upon herself not to tell Kate or anyone at Ford Farm that her brother had been inquiring about her.

In other circumstances Sidney would have given the shopkeeper a lot of lip, but he really did need to locate Kate so he didn't risk upsetting her. 'We do actually. Goodbye.' He left the shop quietly, sidestepping a house-wife civilly as she entered, suppressing his instinct to storm out and make the merry tinkling bell shudder on its fixings. He thumped his hobnail boots down each of the four irregular granite steps outside. Across the road in the concrete court was a white-bearded old man at the decorated iron pump. Sidney sauntered over the empty road. Perhaps he'd get some information out of the old boy, who would probably be keen to chat to anyone to break up the monotony of his day. He'd try courtesy. 'Good morning, sir. I'm hoping you can help me.'

The old man didn't seem to hear. Sidney waited for him to finish filling his pail halfway and to lift it down off the crook of the pump, and then he repeated his greeting. The old man, in mismatched clothes that had been new two or three decades ago, including a long grey coat, unnecessary wear in the warmth, adjusted his bent posture, but he was unable to stand fully straight. Seeing someone there he pushed back his frayed cloth cap, revealing scratchy white hair and a thread-veined, furrowed, sallow complexion. 'Who are you?' He put his hand up to his ear to better hear the reply.

'Can I carry that home for you, sir?' Sidney thought this a good ruse.

'You saying I'm not up t'seeing t'it meself?' the old man growled.

Sidney sighed. *Cantankerous old sod.* He spoke loudly, widely mouthing the words. 'Did you see the girl who stayed a while ago with Mrs Moses? I'm a relative. I'm trying to track her down. Have you any idea where she went after Mrs Moses died?'

'I don't make it none of my business to learn 'bout what others do.' The old man made a steamy noise. 'Humph! Too many folk stick their noses in where it edn't wanted. Not me. I keep meself to meself, always have 'n' always will. Don't know nobody 'n' no more do I intend to! Ask in the shop. 'Tes what anyone with an haporth of sense would've done.' Expelling another indignant 'humph', he picked up his battered pail and shuffled away.

'Miserable old bastard,' Sidney muttered after him.

He lit up a smoke, strode back across the road and got on his bicycle, which he'd leaned against the gate at the side of the shop. There was no point in asking anyone else here for information about Kate. They'd only send him away with what his mother called a flea in his ear. His grandmother had been right, Hennaford was a place full of small-minded hypocrites. No doubt the old man gossiped his head off to the villagers. The shopkeeper seemed to have liked Kate. That wasn't surprising. She had never been any trouble – if she had tried to be, their mother would have beaten it out of her. Sidney missed having her at his beck and call and he missed her cooking. His mother made bread like rubber and her pasties were like sawdust inside a crimped case of clay. Now he was the one getting the full force of her furious reproaches and he'd had more than one hard slap across the face for making one stupid mistake. 'Why did you give your sister that shoe box? You should haven't given her nothing except the two pounds to pay for bus fare and lodging until she'd fixed herself up. Your gran ferreted away money for years, I'm positive of it. There was nothing in the old tins and things I took out of the house, and Father and I have taken everything of hers abroad, including the furniture and mattresses, and we haven't found a single penny. So if there was anything it would have been in that shoe box, with certificates and family photos and your grandad's Army medals. If that bleddy maid's got her hands on what's rightfully mine she'll spend the lot and it'll be all your fault!'

Sidney didn't admit he'd kept the two pounds to buy tobacco. He had to hand over most of his wages and there was never enough to see to his needs. He doubted if Kate would spend much of the money, if there were any. She was careful and sensible. She'd keep the bulk of it for a rainy day. If he could get his hands on the money he'd keep most of it so he could afford to rent a place for him and his new wife.

He would ride on to Perranporth. The bus route took in other villages and hamlets on the way but Kate's best chance to have found a job was where there were hotels and guesthouses. Kate would be easily recognized by the description of her hair and limp. He was determined to take the shoe box off her today. After the trouble she was causing him, she had better watch out.

Getting gingerly out of the car to avoid the soreness where her stitches had been, Jill felt a rush of emotion at arriving home. Tom guided her gently into their kitchen in the original part of the farmhouse, which dated back to the mid-eighteenth century. He knew Jill would relax more in here than in their sitting room.

His mother and Tilda were there, and there was the wonderful smell of freshly baked bread. As was thought necessary for a convalescent even in fine weather, the fire was burning away in the range to provide cosy warmth. Kate was there too, lingering in the background.

'Here we are, darling,' Tom crooned tenderly, dropping the small suitcase of her night wear and toiletries. 'Come and sit down. There's a stool all ready for your feet. We're going to spoil you.'

'Hello everyone,' Jill said, having to clear her throat, gazing to all four corners of the square room to find comfort in the familiarity of her home. The table covered with leaf-patterned oilcloth. The colourful mugs hanging from hooks under the wall cupboards. The ornaments of hens and comic pigs – wedding presents – up on the mantelshelf with a silver-framed photograph of her and Tom's wedding. Freshly picked daffodils and primroses in various pots were dotted round the room.

Emilia stooped to hug and kiss her. 'Welcome home, my love. I'll make the tea.' There was nothing like this magic elixir to fortify and to settle a person in. Ford Farm was never hard pressed to fill its teacups. From time to time in the pub, Tom met up with someone who sold stuff on the black market.

Tilda, who had shooed out the cats and Jack Russells, some of the many animals kept at the farm, to ensure the 'dear maid isn't bothered by them', sniffed into her hanky. She hadn't meant to cry and was horrified that she was unable to remain dry-eyed. 'Oh, Miss Jill. I'm so sorry… forgive me.'

'It's all right, Tilda.' Jill gazed down at her body where her baby had briefly been. 'It wasn't meant to be. Hope-fully…' She couldn't go on. Tom was beside her and reached to squeeze her hand. 'Hello Kate, dear. How are you? Tom and Mrs Em have told me you've been a wonderful help to everyone. I've been looking forward to seeing you again.' Kate seemed set to stay on the periphery and she beckoned to her. Jill had only seen her for a few minutes but Kate's anguish at that time was imprinted on her mind. She wanted a good look at her, hoping the pain and hopelessness had loosened its tormenting grip.

Kate came forward as if stepping out of the shadows. 'Me too, Jill. I'm very well, thanks. Everyone's been very good to me.'

The new lightness in Kate, the clear pink and marble of her complexion, took a little off the edge of Jill's sorrow. 'My goodness, you look nice, lovely in fact.' With delight she watched Kate swing the skirt of her new dress, a soft blue and white two-tone affair, with a fuller skirt to reflect the fashionable New Look. Her hair had been waved and shone healthily in its auburn tints, and was set back off her sweet oval face. There was a perfect symmetry to her modest features and her kitten-eyes were a stunning almond shape. She appeared like some innocent creature from a fairy tale. How could anyone be cruel to her? Jill had lost her precious baby but her need to protect and nurture someone young and vulnerable was transferred to Kate. She would make sure Kate was well cared for from now on and given the opportunity to do well in life. She didn't want to see as much as a frown on her and would protect her at all costs.

Jill held out a hand in case Kate became worried about what she was to say next. 'Have you been told of the new arrangement, Kate?'

'No,' Kate replied uncertainly. Had a position been found for her? If so, it was bound to be a good one organized by these charitable people, but she didn't want to leave here.

'Tom and I would like you to move in here with us. He'll be able to get on better with his work knowing I've got someone handy by, and I'd be glad of your company and to have someone run errands until I'm completely better.'

'Oh, I'd love to!' Kate's relief was mixed with the greatest excitement of her life. 'Thanks very much, Jill. I promise I won't let you down. I'll cook for you, if you like. I'm a good cook.'

Jill could see the energy pulsing through her. She was like a child eager for new experiences. Having been kept practically a prisoner, she had a lot to learn. Jill would shield her from the pitfalls. Having her here would help soothe her own desolation.

Emilia had poured the tea. 'Take a seat everyone. After this, Kate, I'll help you move your things across to your new room. And, my love, how would you like to learn to be a dairymaid? It would give me more time to be with Paul.'

Kate had to put her cup down, for her hands were shaking at the implication. 'Does that mean I can stay here for good?'

'Of course,' Tom said, tweaking her hair in a brotherly fashion. 'You're part of the furniture now.'

'Oh...' It was all Kate could articulate, her beaming smile said the rest.

'Is Abbie Rothwell about somewhere?' Jill asked. She was taking it for granted that Perry was staying away with Paul so she wouldn't be upset at seeing the youngster.

'She's gone to sketch at Portscatho with Jonny. Those two are joined at the hip,' Emilia answered.

'Well, I suppose that's not surprising. Jonny's never without female company.'

'He's taken to Abbie in a way I've never seen in him before. He's devoted to her.'

'Yes,' Tom contributed. 'Seems to be more than the usual thing going on with him.'

'It's time Mr Jonny settled down,' Tilda said, starry-eyed.

'Don't get carried away,' Emilia laughed. 'Jonny says he'll never marry and I don't believe he ever will.'

In the evening Jonny arrived with Abbie, and after he'd looked in on Jill, he met up with Tom in the yard after the milking. Arms leaning on the gate of the cattle yard, they relaxed with a cigarette. 'Jill's looking better than I thought I'd find her,' Jonny said.

'Having Kate here is distracting her. I'm so bloody thankful the Moses woman broke her wrist and Kate came here to care for her.'

'It's just as hard for you too,' Jonny stated. A chap in his squadron had gone through the same thing and had mentioned that no one stopped to consider what the father was going through.

'Yes. But it's Jill I'm worried about. How is she going to handle it if time goes by and there doesn't seem the likelihood of another baby? She so wants to be a mother.'

'Jill will be terribly sad but I'm sure she'll take it in her stride. She's not the sort to wallow in self-pity.'

'No. She's too wonderful for that.' Tom tossed his cigarette down. 'Damn it, Jonny! She didn't deserve this. It's not bloody fair.'

Jonny pressed a hand on his shoulder. 'I know.'

They both stayed silent for a minute in honour of the lost baby, then strolled about the farmstead, hands in their pockets. Tom said, 'Tilda's expecting an announcement concerning you and Abbie.'

'There's no chance of that,' Jonny grinned. 'We're compatible in every way, but Abbie no more wants a second marriage than I want one at all. We'll be going our separate ways soon. We'll keep in touch. I'll make my way up to see Archie and Honor some day.' He travelled back thirty years, he a nervous boy after his mother had run off with her lover, finding security only with his Uncle Alec. He ran his eyes over the barn, duck pond, stable block, animal and storage houses, picturing himself as a small boy, helping his uncle build ricks and driving back from the market with him on the old trap. He'd made a friend of Archie Rothwell after his mysterious arrival, living as a tramp and looking for work. A very tall figure in a greatcoat and billycock hat, his fair hair and beard long like a wizard's, walking on war-crippled feet with the aid of a tall stick. Psychological damage had caused him to disappear from an officers' nursing home without contacting his family in Lincolnshire. Honor Burrows, insightful and tender, from a genteel family down on its luck, had nursed an ailing Archie back to health. After a tangle of relationships had been resolved, one could say, 'and the rest is history'. Jonny felt like that small boy now, but he didn't have Uncle Alec or Archie to advise him.

'Mum reckons you're restless. Uncle Tris has said as much to her too. Is everything all right?'

'Oh, I don't know, Tom. I don't know what I want any more. It's as simple and as awful as that.'

'I'm sorry.' Except for a child, Tom had everything he'd ever want. His father had chosen to leave the farm to his mother, but one day it would be his, back under the Harvey name again, sadly perhaps for the last time. 'Do you feel the need to look for a new direction?'

'I don't even know that.' The admission heaped misery on Jonny's bones. Jill had a distraction in the Viant girl – he'd noticed she was turning into a pretty little thing – and he had a distraction in Abbie, but what after he got back to Biggin Hill? He pushed the thought aside, determined to make the most of his last few days of leave. 'I've been taking snaps of Abbie, and scenery for her to take back to Lincolnshire. I thought I'd develop them in Uncle Alec's darkroom, if Aunt Em wouldn't mind.'

'Of course Mum won't mind. I'll go in to Jill now. I hope the snaps come out to your satisfaction.'

Although no one but Jonny used the darkroom it was a source of sadness and pride to the family. Alec Harvey had been a passionate photographer and so had Tom's older brother Will, an aerial reconnaissance officer in the RAF, killed when his plane had been blown up. Jonny had enjoyed the peace and glories of nature while taking photographs when out with Abbie. Good studies would be useful if she needed to make any finishing touches to her illustrations when she got back. He'd taken on the challenge with the same concentration and enthusiasm for perfection required when piloting a plane. He was eager to get into his uncle's domain. He always felt a sense that Uncle Alec was there. Hopefully, he'd receive a sign or something to point the way out of his confusion.

—

Kate lay in her new bed. The room didn't have the Victorian grandness of the old one, it was half the size, but she was deliriously happy in it. The single window was small but the view down over the back meadow and woods was just as pleasing. The ceiling sloped, giving old-fashioned character, and the walls were papered in a simple floral design. Paintings of a buttercup meadow, the local church, and a picture of pressed wild flowers hung from the picture rail. Miss Rothwell had kindly given her a sketch done on Perranporth beach, of little children making a sandcastle near the seashore. Mrs Em had found a frame for it. Kate had hung it up with pride.

She stretched out her arms and legs, luxuriating in the sensations of sweet-smelling fresh linen. Her mattress at home had only had the rough scraps of her parents' old double sheets. Her mother would begrudge her these wonderful things, and the fact that she had a permanent home with good-hearted people. Biddy Viant had done her the best of favours by ordering Sidney not to bring her back. This was her own little place. She had everything she wanted – she was going to be paid two pounds, fifteen shillings a week, a princely sum, with all found – so she would be able to fund all her personal needs and start a savings book at the post office.

She had put her clothes and belongings away but had forgotten the shoe box. It was scruffy and made the room untidy and she didn't want to look at it because it was associated with bad memories, yet she couldn't bring herself to throw it away, at least for a time, it was her only link to her past. In a way it was an inheritance from her grandmother, and she deserved something no matter how valueless the contents proved to be. One day she might be able to find the inner strength to take the lid off and see what was inside. It was quite heavy. Just a lot of old odds and ends, she supposed. She climbed on the small armchair and pushed the box to the back of the shelf at the top of the wardrobe. There, out of sight and out of mind. Leaping back into bed she settled down for a good night's sleep.

Chapter Five

Friends and family stayed away from the farm for a few days to allow Jill time to settle in at home, then it seemed they all came at once, for a little while. Bringing flowers, and any little luxury procured despite the rationing, each saying what they thought was best to cheer and encourage her, and being introduced to Kate if they had not already met her. Then they gathered with Emilia and Perry in their sitting room. Abbie, who was currently sketching and painting about the farm, was taking time off as the day was overcast. Jonny was there too.

'Jill's putting on a brave face but you can see how devastated she is, the poor love,' Jonny's father Tristan said grimly, fingering the ends of his neat moustache. He was cramped up in an armchair, having the Harvey trait of being far taller than average height, but unlike Jonny and Tom, he was thin and rangy. His black hair was sprinkled with silver, making him appear scholarly, and because he was astute and kind, people tended to seek his advice. Jonny wondered why he hadn't spoken to his father about his restlessness and the vague feeling of bleakness he couldn't shake off. Goodness knows, his father had prompted him often enough to.

'The girl with her seems a nice little thing,' Susan Harvey remarked. As she always did she glanced at her husband for his opinion. Tristan nodded and smiled at his wife, nearly thirty years his junior.

Their mutual adoration and passion was plain. Somehow this annoyed Jonny. When she'd become his father's housekeeper Susan had been a struggling war widow, expecting little of life, with an eight-year-old daughter; his father had been comfortably easing into middle age. Then they'd fallen in love. They had fought against the differences in their age and background and had allowed themselves a new beginning. While he, himself, was… what? 'A miserable coward clinging to your first intentions,' a little voice of his own whispered inside his head. But what else was he to do? What could he do? What did he want to do? If only he knew. Perhaps if he stopped the feverish whirl of thought after thought the answer would be right in front of him.

'Kate is devoted to Jill. It's a relief having her here,' Emilia said.

'She's a darling,' Perry added fondly.

'And quite fascinating. I'm trying to get her to agree to sit for me,' Abbie said, picturing Kate in various costumes, arranged in dreamy places, like the bank of the stream. Her feet could be painted in as perfect and bare or in dainty slippers. 'She'd be the ideal model for fairy queens or sprites.'

'That's a thought.' Jonny was seeing Kate behind a camera lens, in her own clothes, just as she was – the epitome of unflawed maidenhood. Trouble was, she seemed overawed by him and he was sure it would prove a hard task to get her to pose for him. The others in the room assumed he was referring to Abbie's remarks so didn't question what he'd meant. Abbie caught his eye. She never failed to feed his base desires. She was an energetic lover, their bodies fitted together in fantastic union and they complemented each other's adventurous spirit. He gave his brows a certain lift and she answered with a brief lowering of her lashes. She was eager for him too. As soon as they could get away to some secluded place they would make love for the rest of the day.

Another of the visitors was Elena Killigrew from nearby Ford House. Having had a surprise baby at the age of forty-six, fifteen months ago, and because she was perceptive and wouldn't dream of upsetting a soul, she had inquired first if Jill would want to see her. Jill did, saying the quietly religious woman, who could be trusted to come up with just the right thing to say, was welcome.

'I'm so glad Jill and Kate have each other,' Elena said. 'They've both had a major blow to come to terms with. Kate is content in her new home at the moment but I noticed the way Jill kept watching her. She knows that issues may well come up for Kate in the future. It's hard to believe the girl's family could just turn her out in such a heartless manner.'

'There's some right rotters in the world,' Jonny observed. He wondered if he could get some good pictures of Kate unawares rather than approaching her directly and frightening her off. She'd be more natural that way.

The latest visitor to look in on Jill joined them – Mark Fuller, joint partner of the Killigrews in the local building business. When not at work he was rarely seen without his infant daughter, but he had, of course, not brought her with him today. 'All right if I join you for a few minutes?'

'You don't have to ask, Mark. Come in.' Emilia motioned for him to sit beside Abbie on one of the plush sofas. She had a large tea tray on the go and plenty of spare cups. After pouring the tea she asked Abbie to pass it to him.

'Thank you, Miss Rothwell,' Mark said. His mind was not on her but his daughter. 'Did you say you had some homemade rose hip syrup for Jana, Emilia?'

'I did. It's in the kitchen. I'll fetch it when you're ready to go, which I hope won't be soon. We don't see nearly enough of you.'

'No, old chap,' Perry said. 'When Jill's up to it, we must arrange for you to have dinner with us. You and Jim too, Elena. And you, Abbie, if you're still here.'

'I'm not planning on leaving just yet,' Abbie said, her eyes fixed on Mark. 'Call me Abbie, everyone does,' she told him. She wasn't going anywhere until she found out more about this exciting individual. The instant he'd entered the room she'd instinctively perked up her posture, which had thrust out her curvy breasts, and her stomach had done a peculiar flip. With the tan of an outdoors man, Mark had little bulk to his physique and although he couldn't be termed good-looking, he was sexy in an unconscious way, which added outrageously to his appeal. There was no animal invitation to women about him as there was with Jonny, nothing overtly beguiling, but he stirred her so much it was a hard task not to reach out and touch him. She edged along the button-back sofa for closer contact. He smelled of the wonderful fusion of subtle aftershave, exotic tobacco and sensuous man. He glanced at her and smiled; there was a velvety mesmeric quality to his light-brown eyes that drew

62

her in even more. She was terrified that the raw pleasure of being near him would show in her face.

To keep her dignity she trawled over the ordinary things about him. In the course of her stay she had been told about him. He was a former lieutenant in the Royal Artillery, a surviving Far East prisoner of war. He'd still been recuperating from near starvation and the injuries received from brutal beatings, a scarecrow of a man, when he'd come down from Surrey to Hennaford to look up the orphan evacuees living with Tristan Harvey; a promise made to their dying father, a corporal. Medically discharged, he had started a new life in Hennaford. He and his wife had agreed to an amicable divorce, but unknown to him she had given birth to his daughter. Rather than giving the child up for adoption without telling Mark as she'd intended, she had brought the girl down to him. Mark had been delighted to take her. His daughter, it was stressed, was 'his life'. Proof of this was a new batch of photographs he was passing round. A doting father, yes, but surely he had room for some female company?

'I'd like to take a bash at a portrait of little Jana,' Jonny said, feeling he could make a better job of it than Mark had with his photos. Mark had got the light wrong and the focus should be softer. 'I quite enjoy wielding a camera.'

'Take as many of my little princess as you like.' Mark was pleased.

Jonny reached across from his chair and passed the photos to Abbie. She enthused over them, wrenching as much eye contact as she could from Mark. 'She's absolutely divine. You simply must let me paint her.'

'That would be lovely,' Mark said, pointing out Jana, of golden curly hair, toddling in the garden, eating a crust of bread, playing with the family dog, making a cute funny face, in her nightgown, with her nanny, and lots more, all of which held no real interest for Abbie.

'Good. We must make a date of it.'

'I'll sort out when I'm free. I'd like to watch while you work.' He couldn't bear to miss out on one little moment of Jana's development or a single important event in her life.

Jonny noticed how engrossed she was in the other man. He didn't know whether to feel slighted, annoyed or unconcerned at being forgotten so quickly. He shrugged to himself. Abbie was a lovely woman, a good sort and soothing company, but that was as far as it went between them. Good luck to her if she thought she had met someone she really liked. He was suddenly keen to get back to his camera. He'd go home with his father and step-mother and take some up-to-date snaps of them and the children to take back to base with him.

There was another newcomer and he leaped up to greet her. 'Louisa, darling! How wonderful that you're here.' He embraced his half-sister, clad in a feminine dress with a narrow waistline and matching bolero. Her light blonde hair sat in perfect curls on her shoulders under a discreet hat tipped jauntily to the side. She had waters of grace and exuded a gentle fragility, which inspired men of all ages to dance attendance on her. The other men had got to their feet out of politeness and were darting their sight all around her, as if checking she was entirely whole and not needing protection in some way.

'How wonderful to find you all here,' Louisa said, beaming around the room. 'I was wondering if Jill's up to a visit.'

'She's had quite a few visitors today but I'm sure she'll be pleased to see you,' Emilia replied. 'All the support she's getting will mean a lot to her.'

'I'm so glad. I'll pop along in a few minutes.'

She was introduced to Mark. 'I'm pleased to meet you at last, Mrs Carlyon,' he said, keeping hold of her hand for a moment after he had shaken it.

Louisa gazed at him. 'Yes, indeed, Mr Fuller. It's a pity we've kept missing each other. I've heard all about you and your little girl. I'd be most interested to meet her.'

'I'll make sure you do.'

Jonny saw the immediate rapport between them. He threw his eyes on Abbie. She seemed to be squaring up in her inner self, obviously seeing Louisa as a rival. She must be hating Louisa's understated but exact grooming; she, until a minute ago, had been lounging like a tomboy, and she wore formless trousers, flat unpolished shoes and an old blouse, and had given little attention to her hair.

Everyone sat down, Louisa in the armchair Jonny had vacated, he on the piano stool close to her. While people considered what to say there was a brief silence. Elena broke it. 'I must go soon, but while I think of it, Emilia, I'd like to mention the village play. The headmaster, Mr Patterson, has approached me with the idea of putting on something he's written himself. It's a different leaning on Robin Hood, with mythical creatures, dragons, and our own Cornish piskies and spriggans visiting Sherwood Forest. It's time to drum up actors, backstage people and musicians.' She looked around hopefully. 'Anybody?'

Emilia and Elena jointly arranged nearly all the village events. Emilia began making mental lists. 'I'll get cracking on it. If we could get Jill involved it could be the very thing to take her mind off her loss.'

'Tremore will provide a good contingent, as usual. Eh, darling?' Tristan said.

'I'm sure we will,' Susan agreed. 'I'll run up some costumes but please don't expect to see me on stage.'

'Kate would make a perfect fairy princess or wood nymph, although I doubt she could be persuaded to act,' Jonny remarked.

'I could send off my work from here and stay on a bit longer, if that's all right with you, Mrs Em, and help paint the scenery, if that would help,' Abbie offered graciously, twinkling her brilliant green eyes at Mark. And lingering on him with a sweet, coy smile. He was too polite not to respond and she wanted him to see her in a different light. To see she could be as calmly devoted to all the womanly qualities as the damned Carlyon woman was. Abbie wasn't afraid to fight for something she wanted in any way it took.

'Of course it would. Thank you, Abbie. We'd be very glad to have a professional help out,' Emilia replied.

'I'm sure you could organize the carpentry, Mark,' Abbie purred at him, edging that little bit closer to him again.

Louisa glanced at Abbie Rothwell and saw the possessive observation she had clamped on Mark. So the artist was taken with Mark too. Too? Was she taken with him herself? Having others on her mind these last few years, she had given up pursuing her own private life, but yes, she had been deeply attracted to Mark the instant she'd set eyes on him.

Abbie returned the glance with lips pressed into a smile that was not a smile, and Louisa read the silent signals and the smugness in them correctly. 'Back off, I saw him first.'

Louisa retained her composure. *Think I'm weak and helpless, do you, Abbie Rothwell? Too ladylike and sensitive to fight my corner and perhaps too prudish to know passion? You'd be surprised to learn I had a raging affair with Tom before Jill came on the scene.*

Mark nodded in agreement to Abbie's suggestion. His attention was only in one direction. 'Will you be taking a hand in it, Mrs Carlyon?'

'I don't usually, but I definitely will this year, Mr Fuller.' Louisa lowered her tone huskily, pouting her lips in a gesture of triumph at the woman beside him.

Everyone except Jonny was oblivious of the war that seemed to be about to break out in Amazon proportions.

Chapter Six

'How did you get on?' Jill asked Kate as she came in from the dairy. Kate had blown into the kitchen like any typical young person, swinging the stable door wide and letting it bang behind her. It pleased Jill that she was displaying such new verve and that her shyness was easing away.

Kate proudly placed on the table a round pat of butter, in its distinctive pale yellow Ford Farm greaseproof wrapper stamped with a buttercup design. 'I made this all by myself. Mrs Em said I'm getting better every day, that I'm a natural and an asset. I'll put it in the refrigerator.'

Each of them had the habit of looking the other over to make sure she was well. Kate had come quickly to Jill on two occasions when she'd been overcome with grief and had needed a pair of comforting arms. She made sure Jill was eating enough, getting plenty of fresh air and not overtaxing herself. 'Oh, you've put your walking shoes on,' Kate said. 'A stroll will do you good, Jill. Do you want me to come with you?'

'Yes. I feel ready for my first outing. Mrs Em and I are going to the schoolhouse for the first meeting about the village play.'

'Oh, I don't want to be dragged into acting.' Kate hunched up, on the defensive. She avoided anything that might draw attention to her out-of-true legs and her ugliness. She still thought of herself as ugly, believing her family's unvarying description of her. They'd implied she was stupid and she was sure others thought the same. She couldn't bear to be on show and have people whispering about her.

Jill was quick to reassure her. 'Don't worry, my love. I wouldn't ever let anyone try to badger you into doing anything you don't want to. I've got no intention of acting on stage either. I thought we could volunteer to make the tea for the rehearsals and take charge of the refreshment on the night of the performance. Just come for the walk and to listen. It will give you the chance to see some more of Hennaford and meet a few people. Please don't back out, Kate. I do still need your support.' She was using a little emotional bribery but she really did need Kate to be there, her presence was helping her work through her grief. When she'd collapsed in anguish having come across the few rows of white knitting she'd started for a baby's matinee jacket, Kate's immediate care had acted like a balm. Now she was knitting a bolero cardigan for Kate to wear with her summer dresses.

Kate's fears fell away. Jill had that effect on her. She felt shielded from the nasty things in life, and that she was wanted, and utterly snug. She belonged somewhere where her company was actually sought. She had a proper home. She could say to herself that Ford Farm was home to her without a scrap of feeling she was presumptuous or wrong. 'I'll do anything for you, Jill. I'll slip up and get changed.'

'Good girl.'

Jill set off down the hill towards the ford with Kate and Emilia protectively on either side. Kate trailed her fingers over stalks of long grass and the crowns of lacy cow parsley, yellow coltsfoot and creeping cinquefoil that crowded the hedgerows. More than a month had passed since Elena Killigrew had first mentioned the play, and Kate was falling in with Hennaford's meandering rhythm. Humming softly, she listened as Jill and Mrs Em mulled over last year's play. It hadn't been much of a success owing to the freezing harsh winter before it. No one had shown much heart for it. Like the rest of the country at the year's start, Cornwall had suffered greatly and come to a total standstill during what was known as the Big Freeze.

Kate remembered that terrible time when all movement had been perilous, when water had iced up in the pump and even in the buckets already drawn indoors. Villages had been cut off for days in the snow blizzards, milk had frozen on doorsteps, meat and bread had been almost impossible to come by. Electricity had been cut for several hours a day. If people couldn't get to work, like her father and brothers, they didn't get paid. Kate had shivered throughout the day and night, forced to sit outside the reach of the wood fire in the slab and denied an extra cover for her bed. She had got chilblains on her hands and feet, cracked skin and lips, but not a jot of sympathy. There had been many accidents resulting in broken bones.

Worst of all had been the disappearance of a child who had slipped out of her bed to play in the snow. A frantic search for her had failed, and it was only after the thaw, which had wreaked more havoc with flood waters and burst pipes, that she was discovered beside the next door neighbour's shed, having been buried and frozen by a fall of snow from the roof. Kate recalled her mother talking about poor little Millie Weeks. 'Serves her parents right. They couldn't have been looking after the maid properly and that's what they got.' Kate shivered to recall the cruel words, at the thought of freezing to death like Millie. Although she was safe, memories of her family were beginning to plague her with inexplicable moments of dread, as if something had happened to her but she didn't quite know what. Thank God, she was far away from them. She pushed her family out of her mind, hoping to keep them out.

They reached the ford. Just an inch or two of water trickled across the road over its stony bed. An old man with a lavish white beard and crooked walking stick, accompanied by a little white terrier with one black paw, was weaving a stiff path up to the other side. Gaily wagging its thin tail, the dog shot through the water and ran up to Kate. Laughing, she stooped to pat and stroke it. Emilia led the way over the wide slab of granite that acted as a bridge, lying tight against the hedge. She knew Andy Trevean wouldn't go any further than here on his daily constitutional. 'Patch, get back here!' He waited until the three women and the dog were on his side of the ford, his wrinkled face in its usual, decidedly grumpy state. He was never inclined to speak first.

'Good morning, Mr Trevean,' Emilia said brightly. There was no one as grouchy hereabouts as Andy Trevean but no one really minded. It was just his way, people said, he was a nice old boy underneath it all. And occasionally he did show a friendlier side.

'Mornin' to 'ee, Missus Bosweld. Good to see 'ee up and about, Missus Harvey. I was mighty sad to hear about your loss.' He stared at Kate from yellowing eyes. 'Hello, maid. You're young Kate Viant, aren't you? I must say you're looking a sight better than the last time I spied 'ee. Well, I won't say much about your late grandmother, mustn't speak ill of the dead, even though she had a tongue like a viper and a heart as dark as a coal house. A relative of yours was lurking round here backalong, one of your brothers what left you behind, I reckon. Didn't like the look of him at all. Drawing water, I was, when he crept up t'me asking if I knew where you was. Didn't tell him nothing mind, thought you wouldn't want him to know where you were. Hope I did the right thing.'

Kate went rigid. It had probably been Sidney. Was he seeking her out to demand she go back to do the housework, or for some other horrible reason? Or was it Tony? He was a little kinder than the rest. He might have sneaked away to inquire if she had set herself up somewhere and was well. That was unlikely. Tony was lazy, weak-willed and too afraid of their mother for such a venture. 'You did the right thing, Mr Trevean.' She tried not to show how this unnerved her. She couldn't bear the thought of being dragged away from Ford Farm, from Jill and Tom and all the others there. 'I'm really happy where I am.'

'Don't 'ee go worrying, maid. No one round here's going to let anyone make trouble for 'ee. Here, my handsome.' Mr Trevean put his gnarled brown-spotted hand into his overcoat pocket and after a bit of rooting about pulled out a silver shilling. 'This is for you. Spend it on what you like, and God bless 'ee.'

'Thank you, Mr Trevean.' Kate accepted the gift with a bright smile. After the anxiety of learning that Sidney had been looking for her she was delighted.

'Mr Trevean was right,' Jill said as they carried on, taking the left fork for the village where the lane branched.

'No one will allow your family to hurt you again, Kate.' She exchanged a dry look with Emilia. Both were troubled to hear that a Viant had reappeared asking about Kate.

'Will there be many people there? At the schoolhouse?' Kate asked, increasingly apprehensive now they had turned into the village, had passed the shops and were climbing up the hill on top of which rested the school. There was a large chapel window in the side of the squat stone building. Its top panes were open and the sound of children singing *'I'll give you one-o'* floated out on the mild air. She wasn't used to mixing with crowds and she tended to feel trapped in a confined space where she had to stay for an uncertain length of time, where others could get a good look at her ugly shoes and wonder what her feet were like. She always avoided seeing her slightly withered lower right leg. She never glanced in a mirror when her feet were bare in fear of seeing her lopsided balance. She wished she hadn't come, wanted to be back at the farm, playing with Paul or chatting with Mr Perry. Allowing Miss Rothwell to do a painting of her would be preferable to this. Or even finding herself alone with Mr Jonny and feeling painfully overwhelmed by everything about him.

Sensing her disquiet, Jill and Emilia linked their arms round her. Emilia said, 'There will only be Elena Killigrew and Mrs Patterson, the headmaster's wife. Mrs Patterson knows all about the play her husband has written. We'll just be sharing notes about who has signed up to do what and when. Will you feel comfortable with that, my love?'

'I think so,' Kate murmured. It didn't seem too bad knowing there wouldn't be a crush of strangers, some of whom might be overbearing, or nosy about her.

'You've got us, remember.' Jill gave her a little squeeze.

An hour and a half later, Kate was back home. While Jill put her feet up with the latest *Woman's Weekly*, she went up to her room. Her reflection in the dressing-table mirror smiled back at her and she wasn't a bit surprised because she was basking in a sense of achievement. She had enjoyed the time in Mrs Hilary Patterson's front room. It had small windows and was dark, but Mrs Patterson, a bubbly young mother and a bit scatty, had furniture that was lightweight and simple and chintzy. Coffee had been served straight from the kitchen in vivid-coloured mugs. In sandals and socks and a 'make-do-and-mend' skirt made up of two old garments in breezy colours, her dark hair tumbling carelessly about her neck, Mrs Patterson had giggled a lot. Kate learned afterwards from Mrs Em that the pupils liked Mr Patterson's firm, encouraging form of teaching.

'My headmaster was a tyrant. He terrorized me,' Kate had said. He'd also ridiculed her over her crippled leg and stressed she would never do well in life. That didn't matter now. She couldn't have done better for herself and she was accepted just as she was. From her time in the schoolhouse she had realized she was able to mix with others and to offer her opinion, as Mrs Patterson had heartily roused her to do. She had actually made a suggestion. The organizers had said they wanted the play to be uplifting after last year's so-so event and Kate had piped up, 'There could be community singing at the end of the evening. Most people enjoy a good sing-song.'

'What an absolutely spiffing idea!' Hilary Patterson had clapped her hands, making the many bangles on both wrists jangle, music in themselves.

The meeting had been a success and no one could take that away from her. It had been a good day. She had met kind old Mr Trevean. She would put the shilling in her post office savings account. She liked going to the shop. Miss Grigg was friendly and easy to chat to. Suddenly her mood plummeted. She tried to prevent it but the blight that stole her joy held sway. Her mind refused to block out Sidney's reappearance in Hennaford. Why had he wanted to see her? Not because he or her parents were feeling guilty about deserting her, that was certain. They had exiled her. Why couldn't it be left at that?

Her eyes were drawn to the wardrobe. In there, up on the shelf, was the shoe box Sidney had thrust into her arms. Could there be something in there that was wanted? She got up on the chair and pulled the box out, then sitting on the bed she prised off the lid. A musty smell filled her nostrils, making her cough and shy away. Nothing of value seemed to be in it; just a lot of old papers, gone rusty-coloured at the edges. Lifting the top half she discovered family certificates, payment receipts, letters in envelopes, old rent cards for the cottage, postcards and sepia photographs. A man of about fifty with a walrus moustache stared back gravely at her from one photo, her grandfather. She couldn't remember him, he'd died when she was an infant; his name was on the back of his likeness. Older photos showed forbidding Victorian forebears posing in studios. Her mother would want these, she supposed, and the birth, marriage and death certificates. And some old Army medals. This must explain what Sidney was after. She sighed with relief that it wasn't her that the family wanted back.

Out of curiosity to learn something about her grand-father, Hubert Moses, she read a letter addressed to him. It surprised her to find it was a love letter from her grandmother during their courting days. It wasn't very loving or the remotest bit sentimental, but Kate would never have believed the miserable old woman capable of such emotions. She detected bossiness in the tone of the square-shaped words. Hubert would have definitely been henpecked. Like mother, like daughter, she thought grimly about her grandmother and mother.

While taking out the rest of the contents she was pondering what to do with the shoe box. Keep it hidden away as part of her past or wrap it up and post it to Tregony to break the last connection with her mean family? The final item was a large brown envelope. She pressed her fingers around it, trying to guess its contents. More of the same, it seemed. She shook out its secret on the bedspread.

'Phew!' She clapped her hands over her mouth to forestall a cry of exclamation. Money. Lots of it. All in ten-shilling and one-pound notes. Now she had the full truth. Her mother must have suspected her grandmother had hoarded away savings and guessed they were in the box. She must have been livid with Sidney for giving it away and had sent him to get it back.

'Well, I won't make it easy for you, Mother,' she told the carping image of the sour woman inside her head. There had been some old blank paper and envelopes festering in the shoe box. She'd write her mother a letter. One she never intended to post.

Chapter Seven

Abbie was on her way to Keresyk, the home of Mark Fuller. He had been elusive since their first meeting, never at home when she'd called there and hard to get even over the telephone, but she had at last managed to pin him down to a day and time to paint his daughter. This morning he would be at home to organize Jana for the occasion.

Abbie had questioned herself as to whether Mark was worth bothering with. She had never pursued a man before. She was used to them making the running. It wasn't as if there would ever be anything permanent with Mark and she was sure she wouldn't be at all interested in his daughter beyond painting her. She didn't particularly like children, she didn't have the overwhelming desire and need to have a family like Jill did. And although she was delaying her leave-taking from Ford Farm out of a moment of stubborn jealousy to win something with Mark, she had no intention of staying there again. So why go to his house now? She was a free agent. She could go anywhere she wanted. Why not pack up, visit her parents, and then travel extensively overseas as she'd intended after this? She wasn't one for letting people down though. Mark was excited about getting a portrait of the child he adored. And there was something about him. It was why she had taken the bother of putting on her most feminine dress, a mid-calf, full-skirted Dior that her mother had bought for her, its nipped-in waist and sloping shoulders accentuating two of her best features. She had pinned on a diamond cluster brooch with matching earrings and added a single-row pearl necklace – not her usual choice of jewellery but presents from her parents, packed by her mother in case she attended a formal dinner. Instead of comfortable walking shoes or sandals she wore low heels.

After crossing the ford she turned right and climbed the next short hill past Ford House, and here she was at Keresyk again. One corner of the house peeped out tantalizingly from behind the hedgerow. A few feet along the drive the house was in full view and Abbie did as she had done before, paused to peer and stare and absorb a masterpiece of sensitive workmanship, which never failed to stir her creativity. With the woods as backdrop, gently swaying in their dressing of summer foliage, Keresyk itself was worth painting. It made discerning use of old brick, stone and timber. The gardens at the front and sides were so cleverly schemed that they might have been the dedicated work of former times. The house seemed to be dreaming in profound thought; then, as sunlight sparkled on its windows, it was as if it was waiting expectantly to welcome its visitors. The only thing missing at the moment was a wealth of rambling roses creeping up the walls, but clever forethought promised that future joy. This was how Mark had seen his home in the planning stage: a cosy retreat, a soothing paradise that reached out a cherishing greeting each and every time he returned to it. A nurturing nest to lovingly compensate his daughter for the lack of her mother's love. If he cared so very much for Jana he must be a truly amazing man. One worth getting to know, at least.

The simple carved oak door was opened and Mark appeared in the doorway, holding Jana in his arms. A retriever cross appeared at Mark's side. The breath caught in Abbie's throat with a yearning sob. He was tall, commanding and appealingly attractive in a casual shirt. Jana wore an unaffected white dress with a pale green sash, her feet bare and her hair the same dark sandy tint as his, curly and shiny without the unnecessary addition of slides or bows. They made a matchless picture in the perfect setting.

'Welcome.' Mark waved to her.

She went up to them with every determination. He was worth going for and she'd spend no more time hesitating about it.

'Look, darling,' he cooed to Jana, 'it's Miss Rothwell. She's come to capture you just as you are.'

Capture both of you and hold on to you. 'Hello,' Abbie called brightly. Once she'd closed in she went straight for Jana. 'Hello little one, hello Jana. You're just as gorgeous as everyone says you are.' Jana Fuller was a gently chubby child with huge contented eyes and winning smiles.

'This is Addi,' Mark said, patting the dog's broad head. Standing sideways he ushered Abbie in over the threshold. 'Put your things down. I hope they weren't heavy to carry.'

'Not too bad,' she replied softly and as if a trifle out of breath, setting the tools of her trade on the long hall table. Normally she would have shrugged off the suggestion, saying, 'It's only a bag of paints, brushes and a watercolour board.' But Mark had responded to Louisa Carlyon's soft femininity and she wanted him to see her in the same way.

She took a swift look round, summing up the place. Daylight gleamed through the open doors of the downstairs rooms and down the pale oak staircase, indicating the existence of lots of windows with no fussy curtains up at them. The furniture was either in pale oak or pine, in clean uncomplicated lines with brass military handles. There were just a few ornaments – scientific instruments and plainly decorated pottery which appeared to have been chosen carefully as items that particularly appealed to Mark.

She smiled her most charming smile straight into Mark's eyes. 'I really like your house inside and out.' Then she took Jana's tiny hand. 'And I really like your little girl. She's adorable. Aren't you, Jana?' She put on the silly jolly voice grown-ups used on children. 'Oo, I could eat you. I really could.'

Mark laughed, gazing at Jana with fatherly worship, and kissed her pink cheek. 'Come through to the sitting room, Miss Rothwell. Would you like some tea or anything else before we proceed?'

'I'd love some tea, Mr Fuller. Do call me Abbie.'

'Of course. I'm Mark. Take a seat, Abbie.'

The sitting room was delightful, nothing crowded or gloomily old-fashioned or annoyingly modern, just a tasteful union of uncomplicated mouldings and Art Nouveau. There were ferns and spider plants in decoupage pots. Abbie stayed on her feet and reached out her hands. 'Shall I look after Jana while you slip off to the kitchen? Would she come to me? Or we could drink in the kitchen. I don't mind at all.'

Mark's expression showed he approved of an easygoing woman. 'Fine, follow us then, Abbie.'

Except in grand houses a kitchen was usually the inner sanctum of a home, into which only one's friends were at liberty to wander. This couldn't have been a better start. Mark's kitchen had the usual cooking range, but instead of a dresser stacked with china there were simple, white-painted shelves and shapely enamel storage jars. Marble slabs on a rudder-leg table were used for preparing food. She approved of the tonal graduations of ochre colour wash on the walls. A tray with a linen cloth on the break-fast table had been already set, with a plate of shortbread fingers standing by. 'Miss Mills, my housekeeper-cum-nanny, prepared this before she took her afternoon off. She does fuss over us, doesn't think I'm capable of cutting a slice of bread. And she doesn't actually approve of me being in here unless I'm eating breakfast.'

He put Jana down. Abbie crouched to her level and set about amusing her. A child steeped in love, Jana was perfectly confident with a stranger. 'Our cook is like that. My father is more or less an invalid, chest problems among other things, a legacy from the Battle of Jutland. And my dear mother is a fragile-looking woman but really has a strong constitution. You hail from Surrey, I understand, Mark. Have you parents there?'

'Long dead, I'm afraid,' he said, lighting the primus under the kettle. 'Jana doesn't have any doting grandparents.'

'That's a shame. She deserves everything life can offer.' She was saying these things to impress Mark but she was taken with Jana, who readily responded to her while chirruping away in the sweetest voice. 'But I'm sure you more than make up for it.'

'How will you go about the portrait?' Mark said. 'You can get an adult to sit still, but not a child.'

'Watercolour lends itself to swift, spontaneous work. I'll watch her for a while before sketching on the board. I don't like formal poses in young children. If Jana does what she normally does I'm sure I'll capture her just as she is. Has she got a favourite toy?'

'She has a furry grey rabbit she likes to trail about. I think it's in the hall. We haven't discussed your fee, Abbie. Do you want a cheque before you begin?'

'I wasn't thinking of a fee, Mark. It was I who offered to paint Jana.'

'Oh, but I insist, and on paying your full rate.'

'Well, I'll think of something when I've finished. I want you to be absolutely happy with the final portrayal.' The tea was ready. She carried Jana to the table and dared to sit with her on her lap. Jana was fine with this but turned her eyes on her daddy. He tickled her under the chin and she chuckled. Mark had removed the biscuits.

'I've hidden them away. Hope you don't mind, Abbie. Don't want Jana dribbling crumbs on her dress.'

'Very wise. You couldn't have chosen a better dress, rather than some froth of nonsense that would detract from Jana's true self.'

'Louisa designed it for the occasion and had her dress-maker run it up.'

'Louisa Carlyon? She's been here?' Abbie had to keep the disappointment and the sharpness out of her voice.

'Yes. Louisa's very good with Jana and Jana loves being with her.' He laid a tender touch on his daughter's cheek. 'Don't you, darling? You love being with Aunty Louisa.'

'You and Louisa Carlyon are walking out?' The jealousy and fury that raged inside Abbie unnerved her. She had never felt this way concerning a man before.

'Yes, we are. We've had dinner together several times and Louisa spent last Sunday with us.'

It was not surprising she had been unable to get hold of Mark before today. Louisa Carlyon must feel very smug about that. Jonny had probably known about his half-sister's dalliance with Mark before his leave ended and had kept quiet about it. Damn him! She could have made an enormous fool of herself by making a pass at Mark. 'How nice.' Abbie took a sip of her tea, then, sounding thoroughly professional, 'Well, we'd better get on before Jana becomes restless.'

'Righty-ho. Where do you want us? Nursery?'

'Not that sort of setting. The sitting room, I think. Can you fetch the toy? I'd like to see how she responds to it.' Abbie let him take the little girl. Pushed out of Mark's life before there had even been a chance to build something with him, she thought she'd lose interest in Jana, but she found her to be just as appealing. At least portraying her would be a worthwhile challenge.

She worked silently, studying Jana until her expressions and manner were imprinted on her mind, until she had the essence of her. She dashed off some sketches in her pad, of Jana toddling, hugging Addi's neck, trying to capture the way she played with the toy rabbit and plonked it on her daddy's lap. How she smiled at him and returned the terrific bond of love they had. When Jana managed to climb up on a low chair and sat, half sprawled, talking to her rabbit in baby gibberish, Abbie worked on the watercolour pad with pastels and brushes.

Time went on and, lost in her skills, she forgot Mark was there. Jana blinked and her eyelids fluttered to a close. Moments later she was sleeping soundly, sweetly floppy in the way of a slumbering child, all her little limbs relaxed and her head comfortably to the side. Mark left the room, but Abbie was unaware of it until she heard him talking on the telephone.

He crept back after a few minutes, and whispered, 'Everything all right, Abbie?'

She nodded.

'Sorry, I didn't mean to disturb you.'

'You didn't. I've just about finished for today.'

'You've hardly moved for over an hour. You must be thirsty. You didn't really drink your tea before. I'll make us a fresh pot.'

Abbie thought to refuse but then couldn't be bothered. What did it matter? He was going to be no more to her than a client, so she might as well accept some refreshment. No man was worth getting in a tizzy over. 'OK.'

She was studying what she'd done when he returned with the tray. He said, 'Can I see?'

'Not until I've finished. Just the finishing touches to do now.' She stretched up her arms and rolled her shoulders to ease the accumulated stiffness. Her feet were hot inside her shoes. She would never work in anything but her usual comfy casuals in future.

'That was Louisa on the phone,' he remarked, pouring the tea.

'Oh really, I didn't hear it ring,' Abbie replied in an offhand manner. She wasn't interested.

'Turns out she's worried about Jonny. Says he's been very down in the dumps for some time, which isn't at

84

all like him. So she's decided to go up to him at Biggin Hill and stay locally. See if she can get him to come to terms with whatever is on his mind. Strikes me he's a strong character. Everybody gets downcast at some time or other.'

Abbie sensed the tension in him. Was he annoyed with Louisa for deserting him so soon in their budding relationship? 'Jonny is a very strong character. He accompanied me on many a painting trip and he was relaxed on every occasion. And when he's got a camera in his hands he's really chipper. I haven't had the chance to get to know Louisa. I've heard she's very caring and only happy when she's got a cause. I do admire people like that, never thinking about themselves. Jonny's the only family she has. I expect she'll always be anxious over him and want to make sure she's always there for him.' She hoped Mark saw Louisa as an over-fussy do-gooder, an interfering type. 'Did she say how long she'd be away?'

'For as long as it takes, whatever that means,' Mark frowned over his teacup.

'Oh, sounds like she won't be here for the first reading of the play. I've had a meeting with Mr Patterson and we've agreed on what we want for the scenery. It should all be a lot of fun. I find the locals a friendly enough bunch.' As far as Abbie was concerned, Louisa Carlyon leaving Mark on his own before anything really firm had been established between them meant he was up for grabs.

'They are.' Mark smiled now. 'Will you need another sitting for Jana's picture, Abbie?' He looked fondly at his peaceful daughter.

The answer was no, that was only required for unsatisfactory work or oil painting, but she said, 'As many as it takes to get it absolutely right, Mark. When I can come again?'

Chapter Eight

Biddy Viant inspected the two steep slate steps that led down to the narrow passage inside her cramped home. A heavy-boned woman with droopy jowls like a basset hound, she thumped along in her slippers to the minute kitchen. 'Can't you do any better with them steps, Delia? Kate used to scrub 'em up fit enough to eat your dinner off.'

'I do my best,' retorted Delia Viant, three months married and five months pregnant. Her mother-in-law only cared about the state of the steps in case the neighbours looked in. Although she demanded a lot of sweeping and dusting to be done, neither she nor the Viant men bothered to keep the place tidy. They all tapped cigarette ash on the floor and their terrible table manners meant crumbs and gravy went everywhere. If Sidney hadn't got her into trouble she would have thrown him over. He was moody and aggressive, and because his cowardice allowed his bitchy mother to rule him, the resentment had made him worse. More than once he'd said he wished his mother was dead.

Delia despised her mother-in-law. She couldn't draw a breath right for the sour-faced mare. What did she want out of her? Blood? She never got off her spreading back-side herself to do a stitch of work. The family wouldn't get a decent square meal if she didn't put her own cooking skills to use, and never did she get a word of thanks. Young Kate had suffered all this before her. She had been a nice little thing, undeserving of the cruel treatment meted out to her. Whatever she was doing now it couldn't be worse than this. Delia got on with the ironing, performed with heavy irons heated on the slab, the articles pressed on bed linen spread over the tatty blue oilcloth on the table.

The table took up a lot of space and Biddy eased past her, none too gently, to her ragged horsehair easy chair at the hearth. She flopped down and lit a cigarette. She got Tony to roll up her twenty-a-day habit each evening. Delia thought sarcastically, 'Sure you can manage to strike the match yourself?' She caught sight of her offended reflection in the little square mirror beside the heavy stone sink. Why had she made such a mess of her life? She had been quite pretty, there had been more young men than Sidney pursuing her, but now she was already slipping into frumpiness, the glossy dark hair she had been proud of was dull and lifeless, most of it hidden under a square wool scarf tied as a turban. She was going to end up with a brood of brats all crushed in here if Sidney didn't have the gumption to find something to rent of their own. There was plenty of room at her parents' smallholding but she had disgraced herself, they had disowned her and she would never get any help from them. So now she must moulder in this dark, dank and airless place.

She didn't wish ill on Kate and hoped she was faring well, but if only Sidney had found her and got his hands on that shoe box. He'd have rifled through it and removed any money. He might be less surly and she might have got a home to be proud of. His hag of a mother, breathing like a blocked-up chimney as she puffed away, had been suspicious he'd retrieved the money and thrown the shoe box away. It had taken a cowering and begging Sidney all evening to convince her that he'd looked all over Perranporth and had failed to find a sign of his sister. He had even asked at the other villages and hamlets on the bus route.

Biddy was also thinking about the shoe box. It was never out of her mind. It ate away at her and tormented her. She was sure her mother had squirrelled away some savings, she'd hinted about it, crowed about it, on the occasions Biddy had pleaded hardship. 'That's what you get for marrying someone away from Hennaford and for abandoning me. Was a time when a daughter stayed close to her mother to look after her in her old age, but not you! Met a bloke in Truro at the fair and that was it. From that day forward I vowed I'd look after myself and that's what I've done. You should learn to be thrifty like I am.' Her mother had rarely bought new clothes and had gone without a good supply of coal and logs in winter, and rather than use the electricity installed by her landlady she had used the cheapest candles for light. So over the years she must have been putting money away. It would have amused the mean old bag to know she was sitting on a small fortune while her daughter and grandchildren were going without. Biddy cursed herself for not searching more thoroughly through her mother's home on the day of the funeral.

Kate must have that money, she must. She wasn't a curious girl but she was sure to have looked through the shoe box by now. Perhaps she'd found the money the first day and rather than look for work at Perranporth she had gone there and stayed in a guesthouse or hotel. No proprietor or receptionist would have divulged that sort of information to someone of Sidney's lack of refinement. Kate wasn't artful, but if there had been a lot of money she might not have used her real name. She may not have actually gone to Perranporth, she might have lied about her destination. Or, if the shopkeeper in Hennaford was as unhelpful as Sidney had said, she too might have lied. Kate had seemed to be popular there. According to the shopkeeper, she would have been given a bed for a few nights. Perhaps some do-gooder had taken the girl in. She might never have left Hennaford. Sidney couldn't be trusted to take another try at finding out the truth. It would mean stirring her stiffening bones but Biddy knew what she would do. 'Nothing ventured, nothing gained.'

'What was that?' Delia sighed, sweating and getting a headache, longing to get off her weary feet as she wielded another hot iron.

Biddy barked, 'You're making a pig's ear of that shirt! Do it again.'

–

'Why are some men so stupid?'

'Pardon?' Kate lifted her brows at Jill. It was a surprising statement to come from her. Jill loved Tom and cared for all the men in her life, including her only uncle, who lived at Falmouth.

'Oh, nothing. I was just thinking aloud.'

Kate chased after the direction of Jill's eyes in the Methodist social rooms, where there was a gathering for the first reading of the play. Jill was glaring at Mark Fuller, who was taking measurements for scenery. He was up on the stage, a platform three steps high and permanently in place, with Abbie Rothwell. She was holding the end of a builder's tape measure in place for him several feet away. Kate and Jill had parked a couple of canvas iron-framed chairs as if sitting at the back of an audience. They had brought two shopping bags, one filled with Thermos flasks of tea and the other with mugs. 'Has Mr Fuller done something to upset you?'

'Not him,' Jill replied grumpily, folding her arms.

'Who then?'

'It's her, Abbie Rothwell. Haven't you noticed the way she's all over him? He's courting Louisa, but the minute she left to be with Jonny, madam there has been trying to dig her hooks into Mark.'

'Oh.' Kate watched the pair on stage. The instant Mark Fuller had taken the measurement and was jotting it down on a scrap of paper Miss Rothwell shot to him as if drawn by a magnet. She stayed very close to him, gazing into his eyes, smiling and smiling, hanging on to his every word. Kate knew little about romance but it was obvious the artist was hankering after the builder. It was also clear that he was oblivious to her ploy. She recalled Jill mentioning that Miss Rothwell had spent a ridiculous amount of time painting little Jana Fuller and was now painting Keresyk. Now they knew why. 'Doesn't look as if it will come to anything.'

'No it won't, she's wasting her time, but Mark's going to be so embarrassed when it finally dawns on him what she's up to. Look at her, she's like a vamp. I only hope she doesn't come between him and Louisa. Louisa will back off if she feels compromised in any way, which would be a terrible pity, she and Mark are perfect for each other.'

Although Jill was grateful to Abbie for coming to her rescue, she didn't approve of her behaviour. Abbie was only after excitement and sex, she enjoyed the chase. She had soon had enough of Jonny and had moved her sights on to Mark. She could prevent an ideal marriage and all for nothing.

'What are you two looking so glum about?' Emilia asked. She was there with a script of the play in her hand.

'We're not. We were just saying it's a bit cold and musty in here,' Jill replied, circling her toe on the planked floor, which no matter how tirelessly it was swept always looked dusty.

'Well, it always is. Big buildings tend to be if they're not often used. Put your cardigans on. We've got nearly all the cast members here. I'll place some chairs in a circle and we'll have the reading. Kate, would you like to help me? Jill, you stay put. If Tom finds out you've been lugging chairs about he'll tell us both off.'

'I'll turn my chair, then stay still like a good girl.' Before she did so Jill aimed a look of reproach at Abbie, who was stepping down off the platform. Abbie had full make-up on, something she only did when in the vicinity of Mark.

Abbie was startled to be the recipient of such frostiness and she paused on the spot. Jill had been off-hand with her recently and she had put it down to depression after the loss of her baby. But now she saw that Jill actually disapproved of her, and Abbie knew the reason when Jill transformed her annoyed glance to Mark. *So, she's noticed I want Mark and doesn't like me stepping on goody-goody Louisa Carlyon's toes. What a silly attitude to take. Wouldn't she have gone after Tom, who she loves so much, in the same way?* If such an occasion had arisen and she had held back and lost him, too bad. And too bad for Louisa Carlyon if she didn't fight to keep hold of Mark. Louisa couldn't mean that much to Mark anyway. After the first sitting with Jana he hadn't mentioned her. Abbie gave Jill an expressionless smile and decided to ignore her.

Mark was waiting to follow Abbie down the steps. He put his hands on her shoulders. 'Artistic moment?'

'What?' She was thrilled to feel his touch. She wanted to close her eyes and revel in it and fool Jill they had a closer relationship. If only they did. Mark was friendly and polite but no more. She didn't even know if he found her attractive. This was a hopeful sign.

'Have you seen something in these rather bleak surroundings to give you inspiration or have you had a brilliant idea about the scenery?'

'Well, I'd like to be ambitious with the scenery and I was just thinking that I can't do it all alone. I'll draw the outlines and fill in the details but I need someone sensitive to help who wouldn't just slap on the paint. Is there anyone here I could trust?'

'Jill would be a good choice but she mustn't do anything too physical yet. There's Mrs Em, but she's already got enough to do. There's Tristan Harvey. And me, of course.'

This was what she was hoping to hear. 'You'd help me?'

'Certainly, be happy to.'

'Excellent,' she smiled to herself. 'That's settled then.'

More than a dozen people took seats in the circle, most rustling scripts. Kate was discomfited at who had parked on her side. Alan Killigrew, the adopted son of the Killigrews, a manly twenty-one-year-old. She was shy and uneasy with men of this age group. She'd heard him referred to as a 'wag', and according to the noise he'd made as he'd larked about and the laughter he'd evoked he certainly liked to joke. She kept her eyes down but knew he was looking at her, and a hot path of scarlet burned up her neck and face. She wanted to die when he said close to her ear, 'Aren't I the lucky one to be sitting next to the prettiest girl in the room?' Thinking he was mocking her, she wanted to disappear for ever.

Putting an arm behind Kate, Jill poked Alan and hissed, 'Pack it in, you.'

'I was only telling the truth,' Alan muttered, manoeuvring to produce his rolled-up script from his trouser pocket.

Kate feared she was about to combust. Alan Killigrew must hate her now. She wanted to go back to the farm and cry out her shame and degradation and never leave it again.

'Don't mind him,' Jill whispered to her, putting her arm round her waist for a moment. 'Alan's harmless.'

'Right then,' Elena began the formalities. 'I'd like to thank you all for coming this evening and working so hard to start to get this show on the road, and I'd like to offer my particular thanks to Miss Rothwell who has kindly volunteered to do the scenery. The play will have a really polished look this year. We've got nearly a full cast here to begin our first reading of *Maid Marian's Secret*, the secret being that Maid Marian is really a good witch and it's she who gets the better of the Sheriff of Nottingham with her magic, rather than Robin's guile and brawn. Martha, my daughter, sends her apologies. I'm afraid she can't come this evening. Now I'll hand over to Mr Patterson who wrote this splendid play for the village.'

Dale Patterson, of decisive features, with a deep resonating timbre in his voice and the habit of leaning back with an arm hooked round the back of his chair, got stuck straight in. 'Let me see if I've got the cast list right. Alan Killigrew, Robin. Martha Killigrew, Maid Marian. Mrs Bosweld, lady- in-waiting. Mr Bosweld, the Sheriff. Mr Tristan Harvey, Little John. Myself as Friar Tuck. Mrs Louisa Carlyon, she's not here, is she? A peasant mother.' *That's about right for her,* Abbie thought maliciously. 'The schoolchildren will play the piskies, et cetera. We'll have a goodly number of Merry Men, soldiers and peasants, but we have no one for Will Scarlett. Any takers?' His sight homed in on Mark.

Mark shook his head. A part in the play would take too much time away from Jana.

'What about me?'

No one had heard two people steal in, Jonny and Louisa.

Mark shot to his feet and was on his way to Louisa. 'Darling! What a lovely surprise.' He kissed her cheeks and she did the same to him. They followed with a peck on the lips. Abbie folded her arms in poor grace. Jill smirked at Kate. Kate was glad to have the newcomers take everyone's attention, she had been sure they had all been staring at her.

Tristan had risen at the same instant. 'Jonny, what are you doing here? I'm pleased to see you of course, but I don't understand.'

'I'll talk to you later, Dad.' Jonny, in civvies, appeared the exact opposite of how he'd been before, effervescent, his handsome face a healthy colour, and Tristan was content to wait for the promised explanation. 'Sorry to interrupt everything, Mr Patterson. I'll fetch a couple of chairs and we'll squeeze in.'

'So you'll be Will Scarlett, Squadron Leader, excellent!' Dale Patterson jotted down his name in the cast list. 'Right, we'll begin. Scene one, Robin and Maid Marian in – will someone read in Miss Killigrew's place? How about you, young lady?'

Kate quailed at the inquiry. This was terrible. She wouldn't be able to get a word out. She went blood red. 'I... I...'

Jonny gave her an encouraging wink. He was thinking how she had turned into a captivating swan since he had last seen her.

'I'll do it,' Jill offered quickly.

'You can share my script, Jill,' Emilia said, on her other side.

The reading went well, although hesitantly and with a certain amount of giggles and apologies over mistakes. Kate was relieved when it was over. Handing out the tea was another trial. She was sure everyone thought she was stupid for stammering at the headmaster's request. If possible she would get out of coming again.

When she collected up the mugs, Alan held on to his for a moment. 'You'd have made the perfect Maid Marian, Kate,' he said, with no silly banter in his voice, just serious intent. 'I was thinking, would you like to go to the pictures with me sometime?'

Chapter Nine

'You don't know me well enough yet. I'll wait until you do then I'll ask you again.' Alan Killigrew's unexpected invitation was echoing inside Kate's head long after the event. She had reacted with mortified silence, and he had done nothing more than smile at her during the following week's rehearsal, an occasion she had agreed to attend only after a lot of persuasion from Jill. 'Don't worry about Alan. He won't become a nuisance. He's not like that. You're far too young for dating anyway. I'll take you to the pictures myself. Did you consider going out with Alan?'

'No, of course not,' Kate had replied swiftly, afraid Jill would think her 'fast'. Her mother had warned her that if she ever caught her 'behaving like a whore' she'd take a horsewhip to her.

Out on her own and wandering along the top of Long Meadow, watching the tall grass parting for her from behind a pair of sunglasses, a straw sun hat pulled down low on her forehead, she mulled over Alan's invitation. It was frightening and exciting to be asked out, she had never believed she would be. If she did go out with Alan some time in the future, allowing for the fact he hadn't met someone else and was still interested in her, she would have the worry of him trying to do things to her that he shouldn't. She knew what that sort of behaviour led to, she had spied Sidney with his hand up Delia's skirt and Delia hadn't liked it. And what if Alan tried to kiss her? Even a simple peck was far beyond what she wanted yet.

Alan wasn't bad looking. He had a good build and nice buttery-coloured hair. With his jolly sense of humour he never failed to lift the atmosphere when the rehearsals got too serious. Along with Mrs Patterson, he was helping Miss Rothwell paint the scenery and was doing a brilliant job of it. He was clever and talented. Her mother would never have dreamt she'd be asked out at all, let alone by someone with prospects – Alan having a father who was a partner in a business. Part of her would like her mother to know about this, she would like to say to her, as her mother had often put it to someone she felt she was one up on, 'There you are. Put that in your pipe and smoke it!' She wished she had not thought about her mother. It reminded her of her grandmother, of her bawling at her and insulting her, and of the horrible choking noises she had made as she died. It was hard not to think about those in her family, to leave them in her past for good.

After days of steady rain, which had pleased Tom by thoroughly irrigating the crops, it was a lovely sunny day, the air fresh and warm and a little balmy. The long hedgerow was adrift with bushy hawthorn trees, their clusters of dainty flowers long gone rusty and died off, promising a wealth of bright red haws late in the year. The hawthorn may have lost its profusion of lacy whiteness but lower down was the radiant mist of cow parsley. Jill had picked a large bunch of the blossoms, also known as Queen Anne's lace, as a pretty alternative to garden flowers. A wren, likely the inhabitant of a domed nest somewhere in the protective hedge, trilled from its hiding place, inspiring Kate to break into a blues song. Tom had introduced her to jazz with his gramophone records. She was experiencing so many new things. Brambles were forming and she was looking forward to picking black-berries for Jill and Mrs Em at the summer's end, to being able to take her time with the pleasing task rather than have to hurry back and slave for her mother.

'Hello Kate. Out for a stroll?' It was Abbie Rothwell, roosting on the summit of the meadow with her painting gear.

Kate pushed back her hat and pulled off the sunglasses. She blinked in the bright light. Jill had given her the sunglasses and she'd been thrilled to wear them, she'd only seen them before on the well to do or in pictures of film stars. 'Miss Rothwell. I didn't see you there. Hope I'm not disturbing you.'

'Not at all. It's all right to call me Abbie, you know, Kate.' Abbie put her easel aside. She hadn't formed a single stroke of pencil or paint. 'I'm really not in the mood to do anything today.' She patted the picnic rug. 'Want to sit down? There's plenty of room.'

Kate knew why Abbie was looking so glum – the engagement of Mark Fuller and Mrs Louisa Carlyon had recently been announced. Kate lowered herself down carefully on the edge of the rug. She pulled her hat down over her brow and replaced the sunglasses on her nose. Abbie had the discomfiting habit of gazing deeply at her and she wished she were wearing trousers instead of a skirt.

Abbie had come here to be alone but she didn't mind Kate's unobtrusive company. She had felt a fool in front of Jill over Mark and Louisa Carlyon's decision to marry – Jill hadn't kept up the antagonism, she wasn't a spiteful sort.

Abbie had thought she'd stood a chance of winning Mark's interest but she was merely the artist who had depicted his daughter. He had fallen in love with Louisa and, honest and sincere, he had stayed faithful to her. Abbie was left appalled at her own lack of integrity. Rupert had been shallow and conniving, leaving her hurt and humiliated, yet she had tried to steal Mark without a thought about how it might have affected Louisa. She wanted to get away from here but was staying as a penance until after the performance of the play. After that she would start her travels, as Jonny was also planning to do.

She glanced at Kate, who was waiting silently and respectfully for her to start up a conversation. She admired the girl. Treated as an unpaid skivvy and rejected by her family, she was understandably timid in feeling her way through her new life, but at no time had she uttered one resentful word about those who had cruelly abused her. She was like a child seeking and accepting and gladly returning affection and care, an innocent, deserving the very best in life. And she was growing ever more pretty in an ethereal way. Her naiveté and angelic sweetheart features made her attractive to men; trustworthy as Alan Killigrew seemed to be, sadly she would also inevitably be a target for those who'd enjoy exploiting her. It was a good thing Jill and Tom and the Boswelds kept a close watch over her. It would be a terrible tragedy if Kate were defiled in any way.

She would be perfect, as Jonny had said, for a portrayal of a fairy princess. Abbie's creativity was stirred. She longed to paint a series of Kate in various spots in the countryside, which could be used for books, postcards or stylized as separate studies, but she wouldn't dream of taking advantage of her. 'Lovely here, isn't it?'

'Yes. Peaceful.' From up here there was a sweeping view of the large meadow and the rambling stream below and the fields that sloped up gently beyond with infant crops or grazing cattle. The woods emerged from the direction of the farm. Away in the distance was the smaller acreage of Druzel Farm. Jim Killigrew's twin sister, Sara Eathrone, was the farmer's wife, and having a fine singing voice she was to lead the community singing at the end of the play. She had a sixteen-year-old son, who according to a giggly Tilda had given Kate 'the eye'. Could she really be attractive to boys?

'You feel really settled at the farm, don't you?'

'Yes. I never dreamt I'd be living there the day I met Jill.' Kate was hunched over her knees and rubbing her withered leg, which had grown hot and chafed sore by her built-up shoe.

'Kate, I hope you don't mind me mentioning this.' Abbie dropped her voice to a motherly tone. 'Aren't your feet uncomfortable in those shoes? You could take them off. I promise I won't stare.'

The usual wrench in her gut when the subject of her legs was spotlighted made Kate shudder, but Abbie meant her suggestion kindly. If she could steel herself to expose her feet to someone perhaps it wouldn't matter so much. No one outside the family had seen them, not even Jill. But Abbie was leaving Hennaford soon and would quickly forget all about it. 'It would be good to let my feet breathe. They get very tender.'

'You do that. I've brought some Coca-Cola. You can use the cup and I'll drink out of the bottle.' She half turned away to give Kate privacy, listening to the unlacing of the shoes and Kate's sighs of relief as she eased off the inflexible leather and her socks. When she handed over the drink Kate had curled her legs to the side with her feet tucked in under her cotton skirt. Abbie knew Kate had won a mental battle by relinquishing her footwear, the mark of her disability.

'Thank you.' Kate took a couple of long sips. 'I like this. I never had Coca-Cola until Jill gave me some. I had sherbet made up into a drink occasionally.'

'What else do you like, Kate?' Abbie wasn't merely being nosy. She was genuinely interested in her former life. How different it must be compared to her own. She had been lovingly given everything a child could want.

Kate took on a contented expression. 'Oh, animals. I like the dogs and cats on the farm and the horses.'

'You should learn to ride.'

'Mr Tom is going to teach me, when I pluck up the courage to try.'

'Just go ahead. You'll be fine. How would you like to learn to draw and paint? I'd teach you.'

'Really? But aren't you too busy?'

'I finished the illustrations for the children's books a while ago and I've sent off some land and seascapes to my agent. I can afford to allow myself some free time and I think it would be nice to spend it with you. Kate, dear, don't think I'm being pushy but I'd so like to start on a painting of you. What do you think?'

'Well…' Some of Kate's doubts about this were fading after the woman's kindness and she wanted to cheer her up. 'As long as it doesn't take me away for long from Jill, and as long as other people aren't watching and you don't paint my feet.'

It felt natural for Abbie to give her a quick hug. 'Anything you say. I want you to feel absolutely comfortable. We could come here or go down by the stream. Perhaps we could start tomorrow.'

'I'll see what Jill says. We might be going into town.' Jill had suggested that they go to watch an afternoon matinee of *The Ghost and Mrs. Muir.*

'As soon as you're free then.'

Kate finished the drink and reached for her shoes, not worried if the difference in her feet was seen. It was a wonderful liberation. 'I'd better get back to Jill.'

'I'll walk back with you.' On the way Abbie asked Kate more questions.

–

Jill was preparing a lunch of potato and watercress soup for herself and Kate. There was a knock on the door that connected the two separate homes and Abbie peered round it. 'Hello, all right to come in for a minute?'

It counted to Jill that Abbie had made no further attempt to try to come between Mark and Louisa. It meant Abbie wasn't as designing as she had appeared. Jill noted how downcast she was. It seemed there had been more than a blow to Abbie's pride when her hopes about Mark had been dashed. 'Of course. Would you like to eat with us?'

'Thank you, no. I've just had a sandwich with Mrs Em and Perry. Is Kate about?'

Jill paused from cutting potato into cubes. 'Just slipped out to the washing line. Why?'

'We walked back from Long Meadow together a little while ago. Did she tell you she's agreed to let me paint her?'

'Yes. Kate tells me everything.'

'So you know it's her birthday next month? I was thinking about a surprise party for her. Or a meal out.'

'*You* were thinking?' Jill narrowed her eyes, peeved that she didn't know Kate had a birthday coming up, that she hadn't thought to ask her when it was. 'If Kate is to have a party then Tom and I will see to it. As for eating out, it would be too daunting for her. I know what's best for her.'

Abbie frowned. Jill had taken exception to her suggestion because she jealously considered herself Kate's sole mentor. 'There was no need to be sharp, Jill. You should allow Kate to make up her own mind about things. She isn't your property. You're not her mother.'

'How dare you!' Jill slammed the knife down on the cutting board. 'I'm not anyone's mother and I don't know if I ever will be. Get out!'

Horrified with herself, Abbie reached out imploring hands. 'Jill, I'm so sorry. Please believe me, I didn't mean to imply... I'd never seek to hurt you like that... I just wanted to... Oh look, please forgive me.'

Jill thought she probably was really sorry but it didn't stop the horrendous pain once again taking hold of her shattered heart. Tears burned her lashes then gushed down her face in large scalding drops. She was racked with sobs and trembling.

'Please, Jill...' Abbie was weeping too. She had wanted to do something nice for Kate but instead had succeeded in clashing with Jill and, worse still, distressing her unforgivably. She made to go to Jill but Jill thrust out a hand to ward her off. Abbie fled through the stable door, unable to bear facing the Boswelds by returning the way she had come. She ran through the farmyard, scattering the poultry and making a couple of Jack Russells bark at her heels. 'Get away from me!' She had no idea where she was going, only that she must leave Hennaford for good.

Pegging up a white damask tablecloth on which Jill had spilt elderberry juice, Kate hesitated with a peg between her teeth. She thought she had heard a cry, then the dogs and poultry had started up a commotion. The dogs were probably chasing the cats or geese, not an uncommon occurrence. She was pleased their barks were heading away into the distance and they weren't likely to come tearing round here to the back garden and leap up at the tablecloth. She pushed down the last peg. She'd pull up the line then go in and enjoy lunch with Jill. She'd tell her about her birthday and that Abbie had said she'd 'do something for her' as part of the celebration. Perhaps she would give her a little present. She had never got anything much for her birthday, or at Christmas; a pencil, a handkerchief, once a rag doll made from scraps of cloth and old stockings; a tangerine and a few nuts before the war. It was wrong to hope to be given anything, but well, she was only human. Tilda said that a lot when excusing someone's little failings.

'Hello there.'

'Oh!' She leapt back at seeing a face and shoulders suddenly appear above the tablecloth. Wrong-footed, she fell backward on to the path.

Jonny ducked under the tablecloth and knelt beside her. Kate was leaning back on her elbows, stunned and blinking. 'My dear Kate, I am so very sorry. I didn't mean to make you come a cropper. Are you hurt?'

Her bottom was hurting but she wasn't going to tell him that. Her stomach was jarred and her heart was racing with the shock. She shook her head. She was annoyed with him, he had flustered her, but more than that it was disturbing to have his handsome dark face just an inch away from hers. Why on earth had Abbie preferred Mark Fuller to him? He was just as nice as Mr Fuller and didn't have a child as a possible issue. She had overheard Jill and Tom talking about Abbie and Mr Jonny. They had become 'more than just friendly', which Kate had interpreted as having 'done IT' together. Mr Jonny was what people called a ladies' man. Had he tired of Abbie or was she flighty for wanting another man? Kate hoped the truth was that Abbie had fallen in love and had hoped to become the second Mrs Fuller.

'Up you come,' Jonny said. He put his hands on her waist, and while lifting her to her feet he rose on his own as if she was as light as a drift of thistledown. Kate's face glowed scarlet while he looked her all over. 'You're not too badly dishevelled, thank goodness, or I'd have Jill reading me the riot act. Are you sure you're not hurt, Kate?' He stood back to gaze at her; a camera was slung round his neck. What a sweet little treasure she was. Lovely and adorable. It was partly due to her that he was a civilian after sixteen years and about to start a new career.

He had been having dinner with Louisa at the hotel she was staying in near the base at Biggin Hill and he had showed her all the snaps he had taken on leave.

'They're very good, you know, as good as any that dear Will and Uncle Alec used to take. I especially like the ones of Kate. She's not looking at the camera in any of them. She's not shy or intimidated and she has a lovely smile in the one that Jill's also in. Jill looks so much better too; they're good for each other. Kate is quite bewitching. She didn't know you were taking these, did she?'

'No. I didn't want to make her feel compromised. I hope she'll agree to pose for me at some time. I suppose I'll have to mention it to Jill first, she's fiercely protective of her.'

'So are all the family. Now what about you, Jonny? I sense you're still in a dither. I'm not going home until you're fully settled again.'

He'd made a wry face. 'You are good to me, Lou. What about Mark Fuller? He might not like it if you keep him waiting.'

'He will.' Louisa had smiled the coy shining smile of one involved in a trusting love affair. 'I've every faith in Mark. Now back to you. What would you like to do?'

'What do you mean?'

'Let me put it another way. What do you really like doing?'

'Flying, of course. Women…' That had made him grin. 'Um… photography.'

Louisa had gazed at him for some time. He knew that what she said next would be the result of a lot of deep thought. 'You could take up photography in a bigger way. I mean it could be the answer you're looking for, a new direction, if you can tear yourself away from the air force. Perhaps it's time you moved on.'

Two days of intense soul searching and anguished vacillation had led him to believe Louisa was probably right. She had come to him because she knew he would never have come to a decision on his own. One thing was certain, his career had lost much of its appeal. With some trepidation he had resigned his commission, but had quickly felt as if he had emerged from under a heavy shadow. He would give himself a month or two at home. He would take pictures all over Cornwall, submit some to local newspapers, the holiday industry and travel magazines and enter them into competitions, and see what came out of it. Whether he succeeded or failed he would travel the world.

Kate was eager to get away from him. 'I'm all right, Squad—'

'None of that. I'm plain old Jonny Harvey now, and I insist you don't call me Mr Jonny. I hate that sort of thing. And if you call me Mr Harvey I shall call you Miss Viant, but I'd rather not have us do that because I want us to be friends.'

She didn't know how to answer that. It would not be easy to be a friend to him. She had never had a friend at all until she'd met Jill. How should she treat him? She didn't even think of Tom as a friend but as an elder, paternal and brotherly, worthy of respect. Jonny Harvey was smiling right into her and she couldn't bear to stay here like this a moment longer. 'I have to go in for lunch. Jill will be wondering where I am.'

Jonny strolled along with her, whistling gaily. 'I'll scrounge a bite to eat with you.'

Oh no, why couldn't he just go away? They rounded the house, arrived at the door and wiped their feet on the bristle matting.

'Kate! Oh, Kate, my handsome, I've found you at last!'

It sounded like her grandmother's voice and Kate froze on the spot. Had the old woman come back from the dead to taunt her? It couldn't be, anyway; Granny Moses had never been pleased to see her. She turned round and gasped in dread and disbelief, 'Oh, no.'

Jonny positioned himself slightly in front of her. 'Don't worry, Kate. We won't let her take you away.' Jonny had never seen Biddy Viant but she was recognizable from her sharp, prune-skinned resemblance to her mother. 'Mrs Viant, what brings you here?'

Biddy, in stout lace-up shoes, wool stockings, and her Sunday-best dark blue coat and felt hat, a slash of red lipstick on her drooping lips, waddled the last few yards towards them. The dogs formed a restless half circle behind her, ears pricked back in suspicion, glancing at Jonny as if hoping they'd be ordered to see this stranger off. Biddy was panting. For a woman who regarded exercise as anathema, it was a long walk from the village where the bus had stopped. She astonished Kate by exposing her yellow teeth in a horrible horsy smile. She clapped a gloved hand to her drooping bosom. 'Phew, I'm out of breath. I'm here to see my daughter, young man… my little girl. When she wouldn't come home with her brothers I was mortally upset.' She turned her eyes on Kate. 'I know I wasn't much of a mother to you, Kate. I don't blame you for wanting to start a new life, but me and your father couldn't just leave it, not knowing if you was all right.'

Hearing voices outside Jill listened at the open window. Red-eyed from crying, distraught beyond measure over the loss of her baby and the dispute with Abbie, she feared she had visitors and was ready to disappear upstairs, but realizing who was there, she hurtled to the door and thrust it open. Biddy Viant's declarations aroused in her the worst fury of her life. 'How dare you come here!' she screeched, marching at her, throwing her arms about wildly. 'How dare you accuse Kate of not wanting to go home, you evil witch, when it was you who ordered your son to dump her! Not once in her entire life did you give her a moment of mother's love. You can only be here now for your own ends. What do you want? To drag Kate back to be your slave again?'

Jonny tried in vain to take hold of Jill and calm her down. 'Come along. Quiet now, Jill. You're not well and you need to rest. We'll send for the doctor.'

By this time Emilia and Perry had come rushing out of the house. 'What's going on?' Emilia cried, although she had already guessed the situation from the evidence before her. Kate had backed up against the wall, small and hunched, and was staring at her mother with dread-filled eyes. While Perry went to her, Emilia turned on Biddy Viant like a tigress protecting her cubs. 'What have you said to upset my daughter-in-law so badly? What have you done to Kate? If you've hurt her…'

Biddy had never shied away from a confrontation. She thrived on differences and enjoyed causing trouble. She had come prepared to lie and grovel until she left with what she wanted. Meeting this unexpected madness confused her and all she could do was stare from one to another with her mouth hanging open.

'Mrs Viant arrived saying she was looking for Kate, Aunt Em,' Jonny said, hating to have to admit it. 'And that she didn't throw her out. I don't trust her, least of all with Kate so frightened of her, but I think we ought to listen to what she has to say.' He was sure something must have happened to Jill before this to bring her to near hysterics and now to be sagging in his arms, and he was worried that Kate's hideous reaction meant she had suffered some appalling secret abuse. He lifted Jill up in his arms and carried her inside, wishing he could comfort Kate too.

'I'll ring the doctor for Jill and get Tilda to sit with her. The rest of you had better come inside to my kitchen.' Emilia spotted a farmhand striding into the yard. 'Denny, go and fetch Tom. Tell him Jill's not well.'

When all were assembled inside, Emilia set hard eyes on Biddy. 'Right, let's get to the bottom of this.'

Chapter Ten

Ushering Kate to the carver chair at the head of the table, Emilia stood beside her. She placed Biddy Viant at the foot and ignored her looks of longing at the teapot sitting under a crocheted cosy. Unless she became convinced the woman had told the truth about the reason for her arrival the only hospitality she would be offered was the chair she sat on. In view of Kate's grim recoil she was almost certainly lying. Perry also remained on his feet, grave and alert, his arms crossed and hands placed on his upper arms to convey that he would suffer no nonsense. Jonny came through from Jill's side of the house and stationed himself behind Kate. There was a tense silence. Everyone was waiting for Biddy Viant to give a full explanation.

'What a lovely kitchen. I've never been in one so big.' Biddy was at her most ingratiating but she was truly amazed and envious. Kate had obviously told these people how she had been treated, so it wasn't unexpected she was at the receiving end of suspicion and hostility. The young woman who had screamed at her, though, must be mazed in the head. She leaned forward to get a better view of her daughter. Kate was well dressed and her hair was longer and wavy, and she was pretty, very pretty indeed. There had never been good looks in the family and this was something of a shock. Kate had also had a shock at seeing her, but why was she looking so scared? Despite the warm day – and Biddy was sweating and her throat was woefully dry – Kate was shivering, and the Bosweld woman had taken a lacy cardigan slung over the back of the chair and put it round her shoulders. 'You're looking well, Kate, my handsome, I'm glad to say. Do you work here?'

Kate was frozen in body and mind. Only her eyes were wide and alert, never straying from her mother. Despite receiving back little smiles she was wary of suddenly being verbally attacked. She saw the scene all around her but felt as if she wasn't really a part of it. She was praying her mother wouldn't insist on her going home. It was nearly another four years before she could legally do things without her parents' consent. She was scared she'd be forced away from her wonderful new home and friends, but why was she almost scared out of her wits? She could barely keep her panic in check. Mrs Em nudged her and smilingly offered her a hand. She grasped it, clung to it, and somehow forced out a whisper of a voice. 'Yes. I'm a dairymaid.'

'Well, that's good. After Sidney failed to find you I decided to come here myself and ask if you'd said where you were going when you handed in your gran's keys. So you got a job here the very same day. Where do you live?'

'Here,' Kate murmured.

'Didn't you know Sidney came to Hennaford a few weeks ago? He asked the shopkeeper if she had any idea of your whereabouts and she said you'd got on the bus to Perranporth. He asked an old man too but he refused to offer one civil word. Your brother went all over Perranporth looking for you, he did. No wonder he didn't find nothing. 'That woman shouldn't have lied.' Biddy was affronted and it showed.

It was this that made the inexplicable fear in Kate recede and rile her to indignant anger. 'Sidney's a liar! I didn't refuse to go with him and Tony. Sidney said you lot didn't want me any more. That he and Delia were getting married and Tony was to take over my room. I was dumped! Don't deny it. If not for the good people here I could have ended up dead in a ditch and you wouldn't care at all!'

Biddy had expected some sort of outburst and she was ready for it. She put on a shamed face. 'Your father and me didn't kick you out, Kate. If that was true we would have sent your things along.' It was a good thing Sidney had forgotten to take them. 'It must have been Sidney's idea. P'raps he thought it would make things easier because Father and I were worried how we were to squeeze everyone in, and we were angry with Sidney because he'd got Delia into trouble. You're going to be an aunty, Kate. I shouldn't have believed him when he come back and said you wouldn't get up on the cart no matter how much he argued with you. Tony backed him up, but you know Tony, he does whatever Sidney says. I'm sorry, Kate. Sorry you thought you'd been made deliberately homeless and sorry your brother behaved in such an unchristian manner.'

'Do you want to take Kate back with you?' Perry asked sternly, moving closer to Kate. 'I'll have you know that we are all appalled at the way you and the rest of your family have treated her. It's unforgivable.'

Tom joined them, having seen the doctor out and left Jill asleep from a sedative, in Tilda's care. He exuded enmity. 'Your arrival here distressed my wife, who has not long suffered a traumatic event. Kate saved her life. Your daughter is brave and as honest as you are despicable. She has a permanent home with us and we won't let her go without a fight.'

For a moment it looked as if Biddy wanted to spit in his eyes. She struggled to her feet and searched for a handkerchief in her handbag, then brought it up to her fleshy thread-veined nose and gave a sniff and a sob. 'I can see the way things are. I wouldn't dream of taking her away from where she's happy. She can hardly be expected to dwell under the same roof as her brothers after what they've done. None of us will ever bother her again. But she's still my daughter and before I go I'd like a private word with her alone.'

'Kate might not want that,' Jonny said gruffly.

'I only want to say goodbye,' Biddy wailed. Damn these people! She had to get the girl alone. She couldn't ask for the shoe box with this lot acting like sentries. 'Surely that's not too much to ask.'

Emilia asked Kate, 'Do you want to say goodbye to your mother alone?'

The relief that she was staying here rushed through Kate like a calming river. 'No, Mrs Em.' She stood up. 'But there is something I want to say to her. Mother, is the reason you've come here the shoe box? I've peeked in it and there's only old photos and receipts inside, but I don't suppose you'd even want me to have them.'

Biddy could have smirked with triumph but she pulled on her gloves with a sanctimonious air, as if she was the one now being shunned. 'If you never want to speak to me again, then so be it. I would like to have the photographs of my family. After all, they're no use to you seeing as how you're cutting yourself off from us. As I'm not welcome here I'll wait outside.'

Perry opened the door for her. 'I'm sure you don't want to linger in Hennaford for the bus so I'm prepared to drive you back to Truro.'

Biddy wasn't going to turn the offer down. With the money she was so sure was in the box, be it ten pounds or a hundred, she would have a wonderful time shopping for herself in the West End Stores. 'As you please.'

Kate went up to her room and fetched the shoe box. Tom returned to Jill and the others went outside to witness the leavetaking. She advanced on her mother, whose grasping arms reached out for her treasure. 'Here you are, Mother.' The shoe box was seized from her hands. 'You were right about me not wanting to be part of the family. I don't want to see any of you again. I pity poor Delia. She doesn't deserve to take my place.'

With a smug grin, Biddy looked her up and down. Before turning away, she said, 'Bleddy girl.'

Half an hour later Biddy was sitting in a cafe in Cathedral Lane, slurping down tea and dolloping jam and cream on scones then stuffing them into her accommodating mouth. After glancing to either side to see if she was being watched, she took a jubilant breath and started the assault on the shoe box.

Bolting down the last of the scones and smoking a rollup, she sifted through the ancient photos and documents without interest. She wanted only the money – please let it be a tidy sum. A stack of keepsakes and paperwork built up at the side of the shoe box, threatening to tilt over and slip to the tiled floor. Biddy didn't care, nor if the few other customers and the waitress disapproved of what she was doing. Bit by bit she searched inside yellowing envelopes, sniggering at her parents' love letters. She wasn't worried as the contents of the box grew less and less; any money was probably down at the bottom. She got to the last item. An old envelope, and it had her name on it. Bridget, her real name, and what her mother had always called her. She frowned and disappointment filled her stomach with acid. There seemed to be no hidden savings. Her mother had left her a letter; it wasn't likely to be money. Biddy glared at the envelope, which could only contain her mother's last wishes. If she had been buried in the wrong manner, too bad, served her right.

Biddy drained the last drop of tea out of the pot, wishing it were Guinness. She needed something stronger. Hold on a minute though. The envelope was stuffed with something. She picked it up and prodded and squeezed. It felt as if it could be a wad of money. Clenching her false teeth in hope she ripped open the envelope and shook the contents out into the box. What was this? Not money, not luscious pound notes. It was blank paper, old saffron-edged paper, folded over to the size of money. A hoax! 'You old devil!' Biddy cried.

She ignored a snort of outrage from a rotund, bespectacled man at a nearby table. There was another sheet of paper folded in half and this too had her name on it. It was several moments, while her anger and bitterness churned up more acid, before she lifted the sheet of paper out of the box. She had always been afraid of her mother and the fear returned. The old woman had always got the last word and no doubt this communication was precisely that. Her coarse thick fingers shaking, she opened the letter out into a full page, and read. '*Bridget, I'm not daft. I know you have been waiting for me to die and hoping to get your greedy hands on my money. Ha ha. I spent it all, on what doesn't concern you. You never were a good daughter to me and you deserve nothing for going off and leaving me alone. You made your bed and you can lie on it. Your neglected mother.*'

Biddy could have screamed and screamed. She felt the walls crowding in on her. Her mother had never stopped accusing her of neglect and the saying about the bed was her favourite one. In her seething mind Biddy berated the malicious image of the first Bridget Moses. *I married the first man who could take me far away from you, and no wonder, you vile old bitch! I hope you rot in hell.*

She gulped down the last of her tea and motioned for the bill. She paid it without leaving a tip. She put on her gloves and headed for the door with just her handbag.

'Madam, what about your box and papers?' The waitress shot after her, appalled.

'Do what you like with them,' Biddy growled with bitterness. 'I've no further use for them.'

Chapter Eleven

'Hello, Aunt Em.' Jonny put a holdall down on Emilia's kitchen floor. She was making up Thermos flasks and packing up the mid-morning crib for Tom and the rest of those out making hay. 'Got room for a refugee?'

'Who?' she smiled. He was always in a jaunty mood nowadays, with the perpetual addition of a camera in hand. Jonny never took many minutes in sizing up a subject. He spent a lot of time in the darkroom and he was planning to submit his steadily growing collection for sale soon. Everyone agreed he showed a highly professional flair. His photographs showed emotion and fluidity, and stolen moments of time which aroused the imagination.

'Me. The sprogs at Tremore have contracted the measles en masse. Father and Susan suggested I stay here until the worst is over. I offered to help out but they insisted they and the housekeeper could manage. They'll ring if they need anything and I'll drop it over.'

'Are the children very poorly?'

'No. Just a bit tetchy. The doctor's not worried about any of them. I promise I won't get under your feet, Aunt Em.'

'I know that, Jonny. You're always welcome here. You can have the room Abbie used.' She glanced out of the window to check on Paul. He was tearing about on his tricycle, madly honking the horn at a straying hen which ran away squawking in alarm. He'd only been outside ten minutes but was already grimy and his thick black hair unruly. 'That makes over half the village children are down with measles now, quite an epidemic. Mr Patterson said if that mark was reached he'd close the school and the play would have to be postponed. I hope Paul gets a mild dose and gets it over with. These diseases are so much harder if you get them as an adult. Complications are more likely then.'

Jonny went to the window. 'Look at him out there. Paul's as tough as any Harvey. Measles would just glance off him. Once I know I'm not needed as an errand boy at home I shall push off for a few days, perhaps to the Isles of Scilly. Should get some beautiful pics. Fantastic gardens there. I'm hoping to get commissions up and down the country. I'll make sure I'm back for the play. Any news from Abbie?'

Emilia shook her head. 'Not a word.'

'I never thought she'd go off like that.' Jonny was stern. 'A bit selfish of her. I know she was gloomy over Mark, but it doesn't make sense. She didn't even say goodbye to me and I thought we were friends.'

Emilia paused while pushing the last flask into a second canvas bag. 'She said she would get in touch with you. She told me she had an urgent meeting with her publisher. After the upset of the day before, I admit I didn't take a lot of notice, but thinking about it now it does seem rather strange. She asked me to phone Honor and tell her what she was doing. Honor said she had always made a point of speaking to her herself before. And Abbie was very quiet. She thanked me and slipped away without popping in to Jill or Kate. Tilda had told her about Biddy Viant's visit, and Abbie said she wouldn't cause any more trouble. You could take that remark as meaning Abbie herself had caused some trouble. Before the commotion, she had gone through to speak to Jill and disappeared immediately afterwards. She didn't come back until late then refused to eat anything saying she wasn't hungry, that she was tired, and went straight up to bed. Early the next morning she was packed up and asking if she could ring for a taxi. I hope she's all right.'

'Is it possible she could have upset Jill? I thought myself that day Jill had been in a bit of a state beforehand to lose control so badly. Perhaps that was why Abbie shoved off the way she did.'

'But we don't know for certain that she'd upset Jill and we mustn't ask Jill about it. She's only just coming out of her depression and doesn't want to remember anything about that day. Kate won't want it brought up either. Apparently, she's having nightmares.'

'Oh, the poor little thing. Well, I've heard she's got a birthday coming up. Anything special happening for her?'

'Jill's planning a little tea party. She was going to ask everyone from Tremore to come but they won't be able to now. It will have to be just us.'

'I'll do something nice for her.'

'Keep it low key, Jonny,' Emilia warned. 'Kate will hate too much of a fuss.'

Jonny laughed. 'You forget I know women, Aunt Em. I'll do the right thing.'

'Mind you do. Kate may look more her age now but she's still just a child.'

'Good Lord.' Jonny was amused. 'You can't possibly think I'd try my charms on Kate.'

The telephone rang and Perry came through from the den. 'Em, darling, it's Honor for you. She's very anxious. She seems to think Abbie is missing.'

Jonny saddled a horse and took the bags of food and flasks in Emilia's stead. Going back over the good times and the amazing intimacy he'd shared with Abbie, he hoped she was simply hiding away to think things through. But it wasn't like her to be inconsiderate to her parents. Honor and Archie must be going through the wringer over this.

In a field adjacent to Long Meadow, Tom and Denny James, one of the farmhands, a happy-go-lucky, constantly whistling youth, had been cutting grass since before sunrise, when it was cooler and the grass was easier to turn. Tom was driving the tractor, pulling the finger beam grass cutter, looking back every so often to see if the half-diamond jagged blades were working efficiently. He was satisfied. The young, sweet grass would make good hay for the cattle, it was tall and perky, unlike last year's crop when heavy snowfalls and subsequent swirling winds and downpours of rain had left it flattened and almost impossible to cut cleanly. Denny was following on after him with the horse-drawn rake, to turn and separate the grass in order to air it and keep it dry.

Jill and Kate had joined them two hours later, bringing breakfast. Jill liked to stay close to Tom, and now she was up to manual work again he was glad to have her where he could keep a watch over her.

Wearing leather gloves, old trousers and shirts, their hair under turbans, they were using forks to scrape the grass out along the hedges and out of the ruts where the rake couldn't reach. An important job but a toilsome one, where blisters on the hand were quickly formed if one wasn't used to hard graft. They stopped at intervals to wipe sweat from their brows and ease their aching backs. Kate wore specially adapted boots. With thick socks they were more comfortable than her shoes. 'Soon be crib time,' Jill said, taking a breather, eyes on the gate for a sign of her mother-in-law. 'Oh, Jonny's bringing it. We'll probably get another pair of hands, in between him aiming his camera at us.'

Kate watched as Jonny swung down off the saddle, as agile as the cowboys in a film she had seen with Jill and Tom. He was heaps more handsome than the hero in the film, and the ones of the romances she had attended with Jill. He tied the reins to the gate and waved to them. Jill waved back. Kate continued to stare. Jonny had tried to coax her to pose for him in much the same way as Abbie Rothwell had done. She would feel too uncomfortable for that but she wouldn't mind if he took a snap of her and Jill together. She had overheard a woman at one of the play rehearsals call him a 'magnificent animal' and she had noticed how women followed his every movement and hung on to his words. Even Mrs Patterson and Miss Grigg became giggly and coquettish when he was near them. He was good to watch, but now he was closing in she looked down at the ground.

'Hello ladies.' He smiled his earth-shattering smile. 'Aunt Em had to take a telephone call, so I'm taking her place. Tom and Denny have seen me and are on their way.' He had brought a small rug with him, always a gallant. He spread it out on the ground. 'Sit yourselves down. You've been working hard so I'll be mother and pour the tea.' He uncorked one of the flasks.

Kate waited for Jill to lower herself down on the rug then she sat on the side furthest away from Jonny. She couldn't get used to his jovial tones, and the way he always seemed to overshadow her. He took too much interest in her. Alan Killigrew had spoken to her at the last two rehearsals, and although she didn't want to go out with him she had felt it was time to be sociable with him. Each time Jonny had edged Alan out, interrupting the conversation and showing Alan disapproval. Jonny should mind his own business. She didn't need his protection. She didn't need mollycoddling in any way. Denny was chatty with her and had hinted about taking her for a walk. Would Jonny behave in the same manner towards him?

Tom dropped down beside Jill and put his arm round her. Denny arrived and sat cross-legged at Kate's side. There was no more room on the rug but he was happy on the dry ground. Jonny frowned at Denny when he passed him a mug and a rock bun. When Denny started to whistle, Jonny glared at him. 'Do you mind? Some of us are trying to talk.'

Denny passed Kate a wry look. She smiled at him. 'How's your mother?' Denny had told her his mother had tripped over a stool and hurt her arm.

Denny's freckled face lit up, as it always did when Kate spoke to him. 'Arm's still very sore. The bruises are coming out. She put her hand out to break the fall, was lucky she didn't break her wrist.'

This brought unwelcome memories of her grandmother with her arm in plaster and a sling. Kate couldn't suppress a shudder. Last night she had dreamt about the old woman. They had been together in a dark claustrophobic cave, a witch's den. With a cauldron bubbling out an evil smell and huge spiders' webs full of tiny dying creatures, and screeching bats and hideous toads. 'Have you brought everything?' Granny Moses, in a black raggedy dress and cloak, her features more twisted and sharp and her eyes glowing red, had demanded again and again. Kate had no idea what she meant but felt if she didn't soon produce whatever it was she would be in the gravest danger. Then Granny Moses had grasped her own throat and started choking. 'Help me, help me,' she'd pleaded in more and more terror. To Kate's horror, large eels had spilled out of her mouth but still she was choking. 'Help me!' The screaming had gone on and on and Kate, struggling in her sleep, had finally woken up in a ghastly fright, sweating and burning hot. It was as if her grandmother was tormenting her from the grave and she had been left with a horrid bleakness.

Denny slung an arm round her shoulders. 'You all right, maid? You've gone all pale.'

Jill was on the alert. 'Is something wrong, Kate?'

'Are you getting tired, Kate?' Tom said. 'Jill's just told me you didn't get much sleep last night.'

Kate hated having all their eyes on her, particularly Jonny's. 'Was that boy trying anything on with you?' he demanded, glaring at Denny. Denny snatched his arm away.

Kate was angry Denny should be accused and made to feel guilty over nothing. 'No, of course not! Don't say things like that. Denny was just being kind.' It pleased her to see Jonny suitably chastened. He muttered an apology to the farmhand. 'I just felt a bit sick for a moment. I'll be fine when I've had my crib.'

'That's the spirit,' Jill said, referring to her being brave enough to take Jonny to task. He did seem to have the habit of crowding Kate. There were already enough people looking out for her.

Jonny dipped his rock bun into his tea to hide his confusion. He had deserved the ticking off but he was bewildered about how much it troubled him to have invoked Kate's ire. For some reason it was important to him that she liked him.

Tom found his cousin's red face diverting. This had to be the very first time a female had made him blush, and a slip of a girl too. Wickedly he asked, 'Are you going to take a photo of the happy band of workers, Jonny?'

'What? Yes, if you'd all like me to.'

He used up all the film, and later in the darkroom he studied every one of Kate's likenesses through a microscope. How had she responded to the boy? Was she looking into the camera or at Denny James? Tom had joked and made everyone laugh and in every photo Kate was either smiling at the lens or Jill. No obvious interest in the spotty-faced gawky boy, apparently. Next, Jonny was asking himself why this mattered to him so much.

Chapter Twelve

Delia was woken by stumbling noises and aggressive swear words. Sidney lurching in drunk from the pub was an increasingly regular occurrence. He defied his mother by doing this. Delia sighed in despair. Biddy had become even more obnoxious since returning from seeing Kate empty-handed. Another bitter quarrel would blast through the house in the morning. The last time Sidney had come in drunk he had vomited on the stairs and Biddy had threatened to throw them both out. She would too, not caring one bit about her coming grandchild. To compensate for Sidney's wages she said she would take in a lodger.

Delia feigned sleep. Sidney took all his ill-humour out on her and he demanded sex more frequently, as if his dominance over her proved he was master of his life. Every time he was rough and he hurt her, and sometimes she ended up with a pain in her stomach. She didn't mind pain there too much and prayed she'd miscarry. Then she would leave this wretched existence and get a live-in job somewhere far away.

She listened in dread as Sidney pulled off all his clothes, mumbling and cursing. He ripped the bedcovers clean off the bed. 'Lie on your back, bitch,' he muttered through the stuffy darkness.

She couldn't go on pretending. He'd get more hostile. 'Please Sid, I'm not feeling well. I've got awful cramps. Get into bed and get some sleep. You must have already roused your mother. If you keep disturbing her there'll be even more hell to pay.'

'I'm not worried about that old hag. I wish she was dead. If she complains I'll tell her so. I'll push her down the stairs. I'll throttle her. She won't go on getting the better of me.' He made threats against Biddy while tanked up on alcohol, but in the morning he'd whimper to her like a trembling mouse. He came up close to Delia's face. She could only make out his outline but she knew he was staring down at her. 'Whinging bitch. You're always whinging at me. You're my wife and you'll do your duty.' He threw himself on top of her and submitted her to fear, pain and violation.

–

As she piled the breakfast dishes into the sink in the tiny back kitchen, Tony came up behind her and whispered, 'I heard what went on last night. How badly did he hurt you?'

Tony tended to sulk and was weak-willed but he had been helpful to her occasionally, carrying buckets of water in from the pump and heavy flaskets of washing in from the line. Once when she had dropped and broken a plate he'd covered for her to save her a bawling out from his mother. His question brought on the pain of her bruises and scratches, none of which were visible outside her clothes. She didn't want to speak about her degradation, made so much worse by the knowledge someone had been listening.

'Was it bad?' Tony persisted.

She nodded.

'He had no right to do that, the bastard! You're a lovely person. I'm working round the back of Acorn Cottage today. I'll be alone. Miss Chiltern's going into Truro. Slip out, say you're going to the shop, and meet me there. I've got a plan to get us out of this hell-hole.'

As Delia went about the housework she was oblivious to Biddy's carping. Not for a second did she think it wrong to run out on Sidney, he was violent and rotten right through and did not deserve her loyalty. One thing was sure, if she stayed here she'd keep being raped and producing children, with her life becoming ever more terrible. She would be better off dead than face that. She didn't have a single penny of her own and nowhere to go. Could Tony really get her away from here? But was he reliable? It wouldn't hurt to hear what he had to say. Luckily, Biddy wanted more tobacco and a few other things, and Delia stepped out gratefully into the fresh air.

Acorn Cottage was a solitary thatched dwelling, surrounded by high hedges and tall gates, a half mile down a quiet lane. Its owner Miss Chiltern originated from genteel folk. She was fastidious about privacy and did not mix with the locals. Tony was renewing glass panels in the greenhouse and had been downing his tools every so often and looking out for Delia. He led her round to the back. 'I'm glad you came, Delia.' There was a confidence about him and he seemed taller and more manly away from home. He took her to the garden bench to sit down. 'Do you want to leave Sidney?'

She hesitated. Could she trust Tony? It might be a trick and he would tell Sidney she wanted out of their marriage.

'Don't worry.' He caught hold of her hand. 'I can't stand it at home another day either. I know a way I can get hold of some money. If you're willing, it'll set us up nicely. We could slip off and catch the bus to Truro, then the train to Penzance and set up home together. I'd find us a really nice place, Delia, I promise, better than that stinking hole we're living in. I really like you, Delia. I hate to see what Sidney and Mother is doing to you. I think we could be happy, make a real go of it. We could say we're married, you being Mrs Viant would be no lie. You only have to give me the word. I'm going on my own anyway.'

It was a tempting offer. Penzance was by the sea; she'd like that. Tony had talked about getting away, starting up somewhere far off, even London, and Sidney and his mother had scoffed at him, accusing him of being a dreamer, of being too cowardly to branch out on his own. If Sidney came after them he'd not look for them further down in Cornwall. 'Where's this money coming from?'

'Better you don't know.' At her frown, he added, 'It's underhand, it's the only way, but it's nothing for you to worry about.'

Something to do with the black market, she supposed. Rationing was worse now than during the war and there were lots of people making an extra few quid. Tony though must be referring to the riskier dealing in stolen goods. She'd turn a blind eye to that to better her life. 'When can we get away?'

'In about a couple of weeks. Sit tight. Try not to upset Sidney. I know it's horrible for you, Delia, but go along with him in everything. I don't want him hurting you so bad you get laid up. Just think about the wonderful life we'll have together, think of the baby being mine. One good thing, if it looks like a Viant no one will ever suspect the truth.'

It was something to dream about; something to give her hope. 'Thanks, Tony. I'd better get back. Your mother clocks me in and out.'

'Just one minute.' Tony put a hand on the side of her face and leaned round and kissed her lips. He wasn't rough like Sidney always was. Why on earth had she kept courting him? She allowed Tony to give her a full kiss. She didn't want to be tied down with him any more than she did his brother, but he was her only way out of her disastrous life. While she walked briskly back her mind was only on that.

Tony lit a cigarette and went to the dining-room window. He put his nose up close to the glass. The curtains were almost closed but he could see some fine pieces of old furniture, polished to a gleaming shine. Porcelain ornaments and silverware and oil paintings were there for the taking. No doubt the old lady had lots of valuable jewellery and kept cash inside. He had done many odd jobs for her. He knew her movements to the letter. He knew the easiest way to break into her home. He would wait for a couple of weeks after he'd finished this job to allow for time and distance. Then he'd relieve Miss Chiltern of as much of her wealth as he could and start a new life with Delia.

Chapter Thirteen

Douglas Goodyear arrived by taxi at Ford Farm. It was not his first visit. Emilia showed him into the sitting room and called for Perry to join them. 'Any news of Abbie at all?' she asked the visitor, chewing her lip.

'I'm afraid there's still nothing.' Goodyear was an individual of impeccable pinstripe suits, with an air of importance and an astute gaze. He was also a willing solver of problems, which had led him to offer his services to the Rothwells to come down to Cornwall and search for his former sister-in-law. An old Army officer to the core, and holder of the George Cross for valour, good looks had been determined to pass him by. He held his bearing ramrod straight, with his hands behind his back. 'All the police can ascertain is that Abbie bought a railway ticket at Truro railway station for Paddington on the morning she left here, but to the best of their knowledge she never boarded the train. My own inquiries have also found nothing significant. Abbie seems to have totally vanished. It's nearly four weeks now. I'm afraid we can only fear for her safety. She never failed to keep in touch regularly with her parents before, or with Rupert. One thing Rupert always praised her for was how she kept him abreast of her movements.'

'Poor Honor and Archie. They must be beside themselves, and so upset that Archie's not up to travelling down here himself,' Emilia said, sitting down. She felt responsible for Abbie's disappearance. She had left here suddenly. There must have been something on her mind, and she had not noticed it. Now it looked as if Abbie was in some sort of danger. There was one thing to hope for. 'Abbie could have changed her mind about going up to London. She lied about your publishing company wanting to see her, Mr Goodyear. She might simply have wanted to be on her own for a while.'

'It's a possibility, of course, Mrs Bosweld, but I don't think any of us agree it's likely. Abbie might have been disappointed over this Fuller chap you have mentioned, but I can't see her becoming a recluse to ease a breaking heart over it. No, Abbie would never allow her parents to worry about her like this.'

Perry gently gripped Emilia's shoulder. 'Abbie leaving the railway station and meeting with an accident also seems unlikely. So it looks like abduction.'

'Oh, God, no.' Emilia's voice wobbled as she gave way to tears. She had kept thrusting this terrible possibility to the back of her mind. 'Could she have left the station with someone? But who? She doesn't really know anyone outside of Hennaford.'

'We'll just have to keep digging away, try to come up with something,' Douglas said.

'What will you do next?' Perry asked.

'After the lunch you've kindly invited me to share, I shall pop back into Truro.' Douglas rose up and down on his heels, as if ready to take off for action in an instant. 'Mr Rothwell has authorized me to put a notice of a reward

133

of five hundred pounds in the *West Briton*. It's Thursday tomorrow, the same day of the week that Abbie disappeared. I'll return to the railway station and question the travellers, see if there's anyone who always takes the train on the same day, who might have seen her. I'll do the same to the buses as they come into the town. Fortunately your nephew had taken some very good recent photographs of her.'

Jill joined them. She saw Emilia's tear-stained eyes. 'All right to come in? I suppose you're talking about Abbie. I take it there's no good news.'

'Not a thing,' Emilia replied.

Jill took on a sheepish look. 'There is something that might possibly help. I couldn't see how before but now we're clutching at straws…'

'If you think you know even the most insignificant thing, Mrs Harvey, please do speak up.' Douglas gazed at her with the air of an interrogator.

'Perhaps I should have mentioned this before.' Pink in the cheeks, for she was feeling guilty now, she told them about the distressing interchange between herself and Abbie. 'She could have left because of that. I didn't stay angry with her for long. I'll never forget she helped to save my life. Dear God, I hope she hasn't come to any harm.'

'Well, that probably explains her decision to leave but I can't see how it would have any bearing on what might have happened to her,' Perry said. 'What say you, Mr Goodyear?'

'I agree with you, Mr Bosweld. It's something to bear in mind. I'll pass on the information to the police. Mrs Bosweld looked surprised by what you said, Mrs Harvey.

Why hadn't you mentioned it before? Does your husband know?'

'I didn't even mention it to Tom.' Jill spoke in hushed tones. 'I just wanted to forget about it.'

'The young girl who's usually with you, Mrs Harvey, wouldn't happen to know anything?' Douglas was brisk. 'She could be holding something back too.'

'I'm quite sure Kate knows nothing more. She had a friendly chat with Abbie before Abbie and I had words. She liked Abbie. Abbie was going to teach her to paint and she was looking forward to it.'

'Mmm.' Douglas drew together his trim brows. 'It's a pity Abbie ever came down to Cornwall.' He had a great fondness for the woman his brother had treated so badly.

The others in the room said nothing, but all silently agreed with him.

-

Abbie awoke with a high fever and a thundering headache that made it almost too painful to lift her head off the pillow. She had to strive to recall where she was, why she was here in this small, darkened room. Oh yes, she had been taken to a little guesthouse at the bottom end of Richmond Hill, just below the railway station. What awful bad luck to have contracted the measles, to be overcome by dizziness before she had got on the train. A doctor had been summoned to attend her. She didn't remember the examination but apparently he had been concerned about her eyes, blindness was a complication of measles, but thank God she had escaped that terrible prospect.

Moaning groggily she battled to prop herself up and reached for the aspirin bottle and glass of water on the bedside cabinet. She managed to swallow a couple of pills and sip some water to ease her burning throat. She was so tired. Falling back on the pillows she kept her eyes shut for some time, then opened them and raised her arms in front of her face to examine them in the crack of light at the edge of the curtains. The telltale red circular spots had faded but the virus had leached all her strength and her arms flopped down heavily. How much longer before she would be well enough to get out of this bed? Within minutes she was deeply asleep again.

She came round to noises of shuffling in the room. 'Ohah.' Her head throbbed and her mouth was as dry as dust.

'It's all right, Miss Rothwell. Do you think you can sit up? I've brought you some chicken broth and a cup of tea.'

'Oh, um…' Abbie's voice was weak and husky. She was confused. She rubbed at her eyes. The woman was big and shadowy, around middle age. The only thing that stood out about her was a string of thick white beads.

'It's Mrs Mitchell, dear.'

'Oh yes. You're looking after me. I'm very grateful.'

''Tis my pleasure to help you. Thank goodness my husband saw you coming over all poorly when he went up to put a parcel on the train.'

'How long have I been here?' Abbie needed the woman's help to sit up straight enough to sip broth off the spoon placed near her lips.

'Just over a few days, that's all.'

'It seems much longer.'

'That's what illness does to you. Try another sip, dear. You need to finish it all off if you're going to get your strength back. You were unlucky. These childhood diseases are a sight worse when you're grown up.'

Abbie's mind was a muddle but she knew what was priority. 'You did phone my mother and tell her that I'm here? I'm sure I asked you.'

'Of course you did, dear. She rings every day to ask how you are. She's ever so glad you're in good hands. As soon as you're able, Mr Mitchell and me will put you on the next train home.'

Abbie felt sweaty and sticky. 'I need to freshen up. Can you bring me up some hot water, please? And can you unpack a clean nightdress?'

'As soon as you've cleared the plate. Then you must take some more aspirin. Doctor's orders, he said it was the best thing for you.'

Getting through the broth and drinking the tea was a trial but Abbie was hungry and thirsty and she finished the meal. Mrs Mitchell coaxed her into taking two more pills and she was sleeping almost at once.

A man joined Mrs Mitchell. 'Off in the land of nod again, is she?'

'Sleeping like a baby and as helpless as one.'

'She was easy pickings. Stroke of luck me coming across she like that while out looking for pockets to pick. We've got what we wanted. When are we going to get out of here then?'

'Soon, husband, dear. I've got an idea how to get even more out of her. A hell of a lot more.'

Chapter Fourteen

Kate was in Truro. It was the first time she had been there on her own. 'Be careful not to miss the bus home,' Jill had fussed as if she were a child. 'You've got some pennies to phone me if you need to.'

Mrs Em had suggested Jill and Tom might occasionally like some time on their own, and once or twice a week she went through to the big sitting room and played board games or listened to a radio play with the Boswelds. It was really nice to be branching out.

She took a look at the cathedral, a wondrous sight with its three spires reaching up and up to the sky. She went inside, marvelling at the lofty interior and captivated by the columns and vaulting and magnificent stained glass windows, in awe as her footsteps echoed where thousands of worshippers and sightseers had trod before her. An official in a long red robe smiled at her and she wondered if she should curtsey to the dignitary.

Outside, she picked her way carefully over the cobbles. Her limp made the journey unsure. A young soldier was suddenly there beside her. 'Would you like to take my arm, miss?'

Her heart flew up to her throat. She had no idea how to respond. If he was merely being polite she should accept his offer, shouldn't she? She didn't want to be treated as a cripple. She wasn't some doddery old lady. And if he was trying to pick her up he was out of luck. 'I can manage, thank you.'

The infantryman went along at her side, nonetheless. Once on the pavement in King Street, he said, 'Are you local? My parents live at the top of Castle Hill, right by the cattle market. My name's Harry Bane. I'm on two weeks' leave. And you are?'

Kate felt her insides doing a wild dance. He seemed nice, he had a pleasant smile and he wasn't unattractive; he had a hint of the actor Montgomery Clift about him. She was getting quite used to attention from young men. Alan Killigrew and Denny James had both asked her out recently. She had not made up her mind about either of them, part of her wanted them to forget her and part of her didn't. Of the pair she felt more comfortable with Denny because she'd had more chance to get to know him, but she found Alan wittier and he had more appealing looks. As far as this stranger was concerned she wanted to get rid of him. 'If you'll excuse me.' She walked off, her face aflame.

To her consternation, Harry Bane fell in step beside her. His shiny boots tapped out a firm tread on the granite slab pavement. 'Do you have a boyfriend?'

'Yes.' She snatched at the excuse. 'I'm meeting him soon.'

'My loss and his good fortune.' Harry Bane bowed out with a disappointed smile. 'It's not every day of the week I meet such a pretty girl.'

He strode on before her. Kate crept along to Boscawen Street, the wide main street of the sleepy city, in case he was hanging about there. He had called her pretty.

So had Denny. Alan had called her 'quite lovely'. It was extraordinary and exciting to be attractive to boys. It gave her a lift, more confidence than she had ever had before, and without knowing it she sparkled, which made her even more engaging. Older men had started to lift trilby and bowler hats to her. A window cleaner up on a ladder wolf whistled at her. It was brilliant to be noticed for her looks and not ridiculed for her out-of-true legs.

She had clothing coupons and money in her handbag. She crossed the street by the war memorial and went into Woolworths, and in sheer delight bought a gift of boxed handkerchiefs for Jill and Mrs Em and Tilda. What could she get for Tom and Mr Perry? She decided on hand-kerchiefs too. She didn't like the fact that Jonny Harvey was staying at the farm, even though he was careful now not to embarrass her and boss Denny when he chatted to her. She wouldn't buy him anything. She'd never have the nerve to give it to him and she was afraid he would receive a gift with one of his condescending smiles. To her mind, he was a bighead, boasting at how he planned to see the world and would never settle in one place. What was so special about that? As soon as there was news of poor Miss Rothwell, and Kate prayed every day it would be good news, he was to leave. The sooner the better, then she would feel completely comfortable again in her home.

She made her way to River Street, to a clothing shop Jill had told her about. She didn't have anything specific in mind; she would just see what she would see, a saying of Mrs Em's. On the way was a small exclusive jeweller's. She enjoyed looking at the precious gems set in rings, neck-laces, bracelets, brooches and cufflinks, but she lingered more over the ladies' wristwatches. She had always wanted a wrist-watch. She could afford one with her grand-mother's money in her savings, deposited in the post office here when she'd got a moment free from Jill – Miss Grigg would have been curious about such a large amount. She yearned for a watch on a gold bracelet, but she would have to choose one of the cheaper ones on a leather strap or Jill and Tom would wonder how she had paid for it. It would be a thrill to wear even a less pretty watch on her wrist.

She stepped back into the path of a pedestrian. 'Oh, I'm so sorry.'

'Stupid girl!' The woman, stout and hawk-like, with a dangle of thick white beads on her heavy chest, pushed Kate then clutched her cardigan and shook her, bringing her ugly face in close. 'Look where you're going! You stood on my foot. A bleddy little cripple like you should have the sense to be more careful.'

The hostile public censure was bad enough but there was something about the woman that chilled Kate to her bones. Had she met her before? She thought not, yet she reminded her of someone, and something, something terrible, like the stuff in her nightmares. Kate wanted to shout at her to let her go. She wanted to rail against her unnecessary spite but the words refused to reach her lips.

The woman finally loosened her grip and stalked off. Kate was left white with horror and wanting to cry out her shame. She stumbled on with her eyes down to the pavement. Avoiding people, going in a straight line, she crossed over two road junctions, both leading up the steep hill where the cattle market was. She headed along Frances Street and turned up a short stretch called Ferris Town that led to Richmond Hill. No one was around and there was little traffic. Taking her hanky from her bag she wiped at the tears pricking her eyes, hoping that if she was seen it would be thought she had a summer cold. She carried on slowly towards the hill then stopped. There was no point going on. She had never been this far before and had an idea the railway station was up above and she didn't want to go there. The best thing was to go back to the jeweller's and buy a watch and do some more shopping and forget what had happened. She mustn't let that beastly woman spoil her day out or make her want to hide away for ever on the farm. She had to do something to get rid of the bleakness, the same as she was left with after each nightmare about her grandmother. She could go on to Lemon Quay and look down at the Truro River. She had been there on the odd occasion her mother had allowed her to go with her into town and she had enjoyed watching the pleasure boats coming from and leaving for Falmouth.

She raised her chin and saw Jonny coming down the hill. Usually she wished him elsewhere but now she was glad to see his confident stride and strong bearing. He waved to her and she waved back. 'Hello, Kate,' he said. 'What a surprise seeing you here. I take it Jill is about somewhere.'

'No, I'm by myself.'

He glanced at her carrier bag. 'Been doing a little shopping, I see. There are very few shops over here. Something in particular you wanted?'

'No. I was just wandering about.'

He looked at her intently. She was trying to hide it but she was terribly upset. Perhaps she had bumped into a member of her family. Or had come this way and thought she had got lost and panicked. No, it wouldn't be that.

Kate wasn't nervous in that way. 'Are you going back on the midday bus?'

'Yes.'

'Me too. I've been taking pictures of the railway station and the engines and now I'm eager to get back and develop them. Would you like some company? We could pop into a restaurant for coffee and cake.' He lifted inquiring brows. She was normally shy of him and even didn't seem to like him and he thought she would make an excuse.

'Yes, OK. Jill and I have been to Opie's. I like it there.'

Her readiness to go with him and the flush on her pale cheeks told him she really was troubled. 'Opie's it is then. Let me carry your shopping.'

Tom and Mr Perry were polite in this way. It was something none of the men in her family would dream of doing for a woman. She handed him the Woolworths bag. Would he offer his arm as Tom and Mr Perry did? She would feel protected if that dreadful woman happened to cross her path again.

'Would you like to take my arm, Kate?' he said, unsure if it was the right thing to do. She might prefer not to, and due to his reputation any young woman with him in this manner was likely to be construed as his latest conquest. Kate, in simple clothes, with a plain straw hat and no makeup, was so different to the sophisticated, fashionably clad women he usually mixed with, and would provoke a good deal of interest. For Kate's sake he shouldn't have asked her. 'OK.'

The instant she said that he didn't care what others thought. He was proud to be her escort. He wanted to get to know more about her, her true self. She was always so guarded at the farm. Now he had a chance to do so without Jill constantly checking on her as if she was an infant. It was a situation he considered unfortunate. Kate needed no more than a little gentle guidance but Jill was using her as a substitute interest for the loss of her baby. There was a danger Jill might smother her with kindness and restrict Kate's chances of living to her full potential. His main reason for going to the railway station had been to question the stationmaster and porters about Abbie. He had learned nothing new. All the town's taxi drivers had been shown Abbie's photograph by Douglas Goodyear and the police. All of them were certain they had not taken her from the station. While retracing his steps back down the hill he could only reason that for Abbie to disappear so quickly and completely abduction was certain. He couldn't bear to think of her hurt and suffering. Or dead, which was a terrible possibility because so far there had been no response to her picture in the newspapers or the reward. Then he had turned the corner and seen Kate, and his thoughts flew to discovering why she was looking so downcast.

Opie's wasn't far away, in Kenwyn Street, above a haberdashery. When they were seated at a table by the window, Jonny smiled, 'What would you like, Kate?'

'I don't mind. Jill and I usually order coffee and we choose from the selection of fancies.'

'That's what we'll do then.' He gave the waitress the order. 'So you fancied a little trip out by yourself, Kate?'

'Yes.'

'And you've been shopping?'

'Yes.' She was terribly disappointed not to have bought something for herself, and Jill would wonder why. The day had been a failure.

Jonny saw her melancholy. For some reason it cut right into him. 'Forgive me for asking, but what's wrong? It's easy to see you're unsettled.'

'A woman was horrible to me in the street.' She glanced at him and looked down at the table. 'I suppose I shouldn't have minded so much.'

'Of course you should mind. Do you want to tell me what she said?'

Until a short while ago he would have been the last person she'd have confided in, but Jonny made her feel secure and she needed to unload the horror she had undergone. When she'd finished, he reached across the table and patted her hand. 'That must have been truly awful for you. The woman's behaviour was despicable. I'm sorry you had to go through that, Kate, my dear. I'm afraid there are some really terrible people in the world but luckily they are few and far between. You were unlucky today. Now, let's think of something to cheer you up. It's your birthday in a few days. I'd like to get you a little something, if that's all right. When we've had our coffee, would you like to look at the shops for something you'd like?'

'It's very kind of you,' she said modestly, feeling better.

Everyone liked Jonny, now she could see why. He was kind and caring. She could also slip into a shop to buy something for herself to show Jill, but a watch could wait for another day.

A woman in a full-skirted suit and a hat fit for the Ascot races, with a slinky walk, and smoking from an ebony holder, entered the restaurant and made a beeline for them. 'Jonny, darling!' she trilled. 'How absolutely brilliant to see you.'

Jonny rose and she kissed the air both sides of his face. 'Cynthia. Always a pleasure to see you.' Kate could see he didn't mean it.

'I see you have that silly camera with you again. Haven't seen you at a cocktail party for simply ages.' She tapped a gloved fingertip on his chin. 'You're very naughty to neglect the ladies of the town.' She aimed a sideways glance at his companion to see if she knew who it was then turned fully and stared at Kate. 'Good heavens. Who's this? One of your father's brood?'

Jonny wished Cynthia would move on. She was amoral and had been trying for years to get him as a trophy in her bed and she hated the fact that he had never succumbed to her. A war widow, she had 'entertained' both British and American officers during the war. She was vindictive and it showed in her hard eyes. The reason she was alone was because no one sought to befriend her. 'Miss Kate Viant. Mrs Cynthia Walker. If you'll excuse us, Cynthia, we were having a quiet discussion.'

Cynthia Walker looked down over her nose at Kate with distinct distaste. 'A change of direction for you, Jonny, taking on lame ducks.'

The woman couldn't see Kate's legs under the table and the jibe at Kate's ordinariness hurt Kate more than she had intended. Angry, she returned a haughty look of her own. If this woman could only show off and issue insults then she was not a better and didn't deserve any respect.

Cynthia Walker gave a huff and slunk away like a proud cat. She snapped at a waitress for immediate service. Jonny sat down and smiled at Kate. 'You got the upper hand there. That was one horrid woman who didn't get the better of you.'

Kate ate and drank with a sense of triumph. She had summed up correctly that Cynthia Walker had failed to get her hooks into Jonny. And it was she who had his company, the undivided attention of the most handsome man for miles. The waitresses and the other female customers, one elderly, were giving him admiring looks.

Jonny escorted her to the same jeweller's she had looked at earlier. He pointed to the window display. 'Take a look and see what you like.'

'But you can't buy me jewellery,' Kate gasped.

Jonny saw it as inappropriate. 'What then?' He didn't want to go into a dress shop. It wouldn't faze him but when he paid he would be seen as her sugar daddy. Then he had a good idea. 'I could take a special photo of you. I'll get a frame to put it in. What do you think?'

'That would be very nice. Thank you, Jonny.' The words came straight out. She trusted him now and had no reservations about his suggestion.

'Well, they sell frames in here too so let's go inside and you can choose what you would like.' He smiled down on her and she smiled back. She was so lovely. It was wonderful to be doing something that made the light shine out of her beautiful eyes. It was wonderful being with her.

Chapter Fifteen

Before Tom got out of bed he placed a tender kiss on Jill's lips. 'I love you, darling.'

Tuned into him, she woke at once and murmured, 'I love you too.'

'Sorry, I didn't mean to wake you.'

'I always know when you've left my side.' She stretched out her arms. 'Stay and give me a cuddle.'

It was important to make a dawn start on the farm but he never missed a chance to shower her with affection. He got back in bed, drew her in close to his body and caressed her neck and face. 'Last night was wonderful, darling, but are you really sure we should be trying for another baby yet?'

She snuggled in against his chest, listening to his heart-beat for reassurance. Losing her baby had made her see how fragile life was, how quickly a loved one could be snatched away, and she needed to know he was strong and well. Each time they had made love since her recovery he had asked the same question. 'You don't have to worry about me, darling. The doctor says my body is healthy to carry again and I'm more than ready. The problem will be actually getting pregnant.'

'I was so afraid you'd find making love difficult but thank God you don't. How are you going to feel if nothing happens for ages? What if we can never have our own baby?'

'It will be heartbreaking, but as long as I've got you, darling Tom… We could think about adoption. Uncle Stanley mentioned it the other day. We'll just have to wait and see what fate has in store for us. Anyway, I've got something to look forward to today, preparing for Kate's little surprise party.'

'That's the ticket, darling.' He drew away reluctantly and got dressed.

Jill rose from the bed. Tom and the family still encouraged her to take things easily but there was no need. 'Now Kate's no longer overawed by Jonny I've arranged for him to take her riding after lunch. I couldn't think of another way to keep her out of the kitchen. She loves to go riding since she gained her confidence in the saddle.' Jill let out a long sorrowful sigh.

'What is it, Jill?'

'It was Abbie who brought up Kate's birthday on that awful day. I was jealous at the time that she knew something I didn't. Now I'd give anything to have her here. Dear God, Tom, it's so terrible about her. Do you think she's dead?'

'I'm afraid it's looking more like it every day. Douglas Goodyear and the police made inquiries at every door in the area of the railway station, and a housewife cleaning her windows was sure she saw a woman of Abbie's description walking down Richmond Hill with a man. It seems she may have gone off with this character, willingly or unwillingly.' He suppressed a shudder, not wanting to linger over the terrible possibility that Abbie had been abducted and murdered. He gave Jill a secure hug. 'You're not going to brood over that, are you?'

Safe in his embrace, she said sadly, 'No matter what you go through there's always someone who suffers more. If Abbie has disappeared because she wants to be on her own, what on earth can be on her mind? The poor, poor thing.'

Tilda cooked breakfast for everyone so they could watch Kate open her birthday cards and presents. Kate was amazed by the generosity she was shown. She was bubbling with joy and hadn't been able to eat a bite of food. Jill had sent her out in the lane to collect the post. 'I've got a card from Tremore, and the Killigrews, and Mrs Carlyon, and even one from Miss Grigg from the shop. I can hardly believe it!' She didn't get a card from her family and was glad. She wanted no reminders of her old life. Her presents included clothes, perfume and a hairbrush, comb and trinket jar set. Jill and Tom had given her a silver oval-shaped locket.

Jonny, who had smiled at her throughout, gave her his present last, kissing her cheek and gazing at her for a long moment. 'You look radiant, Kate. Gorgeous.' She did, even though she was in work clothes for the morning.

The photograph frame she had chosen was of electric blue frosted glass with a sculpted design in the corners. She would treasure it for ever. Jonny had asked her to wear 'something long and floaty' when he took her photo and she had been glad to be able to cover her feet without having to ask to do so. Jill had lent her an evening dress and she had felt feminine and grown up in the satin material. Jonny had taken several poses of her in the garden and had refused to show her the photos, saying he would put the best one in the frame and she could only see it on her birthday.

She was looking forward to this moment. 'Thank you, Jonny.' The others gathered round as she carefully lifted away the wrapping paper. There were gasps of astonishment. Hers was the loudest. 'Is that really me?' Jonny had portrayed her within a misty oval, sitting on the lawn with her legs to the side, the dress draped as if it was flowing away from her endlessly. Her face was in full view and she was looking slightly down at a rose he had given her to hold.

'It's stunning,' Tom said. 'You couldn't have pictured Kate better.'

'She looks like a medieval princess,' Jill murmured in wonder.

'Utterly beautiful,' was Perry's verdict, and Emilia agreed.

Tilda had to dab a hanky to her eyes. 'I've never seen anything like it in my life. You're a marvel, Mr Jonny. Kate, you're like an angel.'

'Do you like it, Kate?' Jonny asked, leaning over the table. He hadn't stopped gazing at her for a second.

'I love it. Thank you so much.' She felt she had a special affinity with Jonny.

–

Abbie could barely move a muscle. She was cold and parched and her head ached unbearably. She searched with a feeble arm for the glass but there was no water in it. 'M-Mrs Mitchell.' It was just a croak, not loud enough to summon the landlady or another guest who might be outside her room on the landing. She would have to wait for the chambermaid. Ask her why breakfast hadn't arrived and to contact the doctor. She was ill, she had never felt so dreadful.

Time passed. All was quiet. She needed to go to the toilet. Mrs Mitchell had kindly brought a commode into the room so she wouldn't have to slip across to the bathroom. With an arm over her burning forehead, she listened. Her ears buzzed, but as far as she could tell there was silence. Surely someone was around? She would lie here a few more seconds then summon up the strength to reach the commode. Hopefully, the chambermaid wouldn't come in at the same time and embarrass her. Chambermaid? Mrs Mitchell had mentioned one but she had no recollection of seeing one. Had Mrs Mitchell lied? She probably had. The room was shabby – a low class bed and breakfast rather than a guesthouse. It hit Abbie that she hadn't seen Mrs Mitchell for some time. Had she seen her yesterday? She couldn't remember.

Something wasn't right. Grunting and puffing with effort she sat up, groaning as her arms and back ached. She moved her legs. They were like lead weights. Then she noticed the smell, pungent and fetid and disgusting. It could only be the commode. Mrs Mitchell had stressed it was no trouble to see to it but she was neglectful of her duties. Once, she had said, 'Don't worry, you're paying me enough for the privilege.'

Oh God, this was misery. When first here she had thought to ask Mrs Mitchell to phone Ford Farm and tell Emilia Bosweld of her predicament, but she had decided she couldn't really take measles there. Today she would ask that someone from Ford Farm be sent to collect her. They wouldn't expect her to remain in these conditions. For the first time she studied her room, she had always been too feverish or tired before. The tiny single bed was beside the wall under the window. The curtains were never pulled back but she saw they were moth-eaten, dipping in places and held up by string. The wall had large patches of paint and plaster missing. Not what one expected to find in a guesthouse or a place offering bed and breakfast.

Alarm enabled her to struggle to reach up and pull on the nearest curtain in the hope of drawing it back. It came crashing down, making her scream as she was showered by bits of plaster and blinded temporarily by the sunlight. What on earth was this place? Battling to control her fright, she remembered asking a man at the railway station if he knew where the nearest guesthouse was. 'You're in luck, lady. I happen to be the proprietor of such an establishment. Allow me to carry your things and I'll escort you there.' He had tried to speak well but his voice had been rough and common. Where had she been taken? And exactly what situation had she been taken into?

Horror after horror slammed into her mind. The bedcovers were old and filthy. There was mould in the corners of the room and trailing across the ceiling. The floor was dirty bare boards and the furniture worm-holed scraps. Her things were missing. And some of the stinking smell was coming off her. In all the time she had been here – she had no idea how long that was – she had never been helped to have a wash or been given a clean nightdress. Her hair was sweaty and matted. She must have been drugged not to have noticed all this before. The aspirin bottle! She seized it. It was small, of brown fluted glass, with no label on it. It could not have been aspirin Mrs

Mitchell had kept encouraging her to take. There was no sign of her luggage, her things.

'Oh, my God!' She huddled against the corner of the cold wall. She had been dragged and half-starved and robbed. 'D–don't panic. I've got to get out of here.' She had to be quiet. Someone might hear her and come to the room. She would be drugged again. Or hurt. But no one had come when the curtains had crashed down and made a loud noise. The Mitchells must be out. She had to get away before they returned.

Making her feeble hands work she pushed away the bedcovers and fallen curtains and somehow managed to swing her legs over the side of the bed. Her head swam and she had to wait for the dizziness to clear. *Please let my legs take my weight.* They did, just. One gruelling step at a time she went to the door, feeling grit and dirt under her bare feet. Again dizziness robbed her of her balance and she reached out and pressed her hands against the door to stay upright. Her head throbbed and a loud ringing filled her ears. Nausea rose in her stomach and she thought she would be sick. She had to cling to her senses. With her eyes closed she felt for the doorknob. Found it and frantically turned it. The door was locked. In ever-increasing dread and frustration she tugged on it and pushed on it. 'Come on, come on. Open, stupid thing!' It was no good – she was locked in. She was a prisoner.

Desperation replaced common sense and she hammered on the door, bloodying her fists. 'Let me out! Let me out, damn you!'

There was a tremendous rushing in her ears. Her heart felt it was about to burst. Her sight blurred. Her legs refused to hold her up. She sank to the floor fighting to stay conscious, but it was no use. She was too frail and undernourished. Blackness took her into its monumental grip.

–

Tony Viant skulked home in the middle of the morning. He had to see how Delia was. Last night he had heard her begging Sidney to get off her as the bedsprings had jerked wildly in their room, with Sidney shouting insults at her throughout the assault. The sounds of Delia crying for some time afterwards had troubled Tony, and worse still had been his mother's laughter from across the landing. His grim father never did anything to stop the disharmony in the house, he said nothing to anyone as long as he was left alone. But his mother took pleasure in Delia's abuse and it sickened Tony.

He felt guilty over Delia's suffering. He had not kept his promise to take her away, not having the courage to break into Miss Chiltern's cottage and steal from her. He would never get away with it anyway, his work there would make him an obvious suspect and he would end up in jail, and if Delia ran away with him she would probably be jailed too. Her life was a torment now, but a prison sentence and her baby being taken away would destroy her.

'When are we going away, Tony?' she had implored him yesterday. 'I can't take much more of this. I'll never cope when the baby's born. Can't see your rotten mother looking after me for the ten-day lying-in period. I'll be expected to get straight out of bed and work like a slave. If I don't get away soon I'll go mad. I'd rather kill myself than go on like this for the rest of my life.' He was really worried she would do something silly.

Warily he went inside, hoping to see Delia alone, but creaking sounds above the low ceiling beams meant she was upstairs. Biddy was in her chair, reading a newspaper and smoking. 'What are you doing here?' she hurled at him. 'You better not be out of work.'

'I've got plenty of work, Mother,' he snapped. 'I told you already that I'm re-hanging the coal house door for the doctor, and then I'll be off to Tresillian. I've been asked to do some painting at the pub. Betterfit you encouraged me when I get work. You always have to grumble and pick faults. I'm back because I forgot my crib bag. Can't work all bleddy day without food and drink, can I?'

'You're not expected to! And don't you take that surly tone with me or I'll get up and slap your face,' Biddy bristled.

'Like you do Delia's?' he fumed. 'You and Sidney love to lay into her. She's pregnant, for God's sake! Do you want a dead woman and baby on your hands?'

'What's got into you? Why do you care? Jealous 'cause you can't get a woman of your own? I know you listen in on your brother when he's doing the dirty business with that little tart. Some people would call you a pervert for that.'

Tony clenched his fists, for one ugly moment he thought he would smash his mother across her hideous smirking face. He felt an urgent tugging at his shirt. Delia had come downstairs. 'Here's your crib bag, Tony. Go back to work. Leave us in peace,' she cried, desperate for him not to cause any more trouble. He had let her down on his promise to start a new life in Penzance. He was shallow and weak, and she loathed him as much as she did the other Viants, although she was careful not to show it. She didn't want Tony treating her badly too. Her life was barely worth living. She had gone to her parents and told them of her predicament and begged them to let her come back. They had refused. 'You wouldn't be told Sidney Viant was no good. You didn't care about bringing disgrace to our door, so now you can get on with it. Don't come here again.'

Now the old woman would tell Sidney about this latest set-to and he would be furious with her, as if it was all her fault. He was already suspicious there was 'something going on' between her and Tony. The other day he had grabbed her outside and pushed her against the privy wall. 'What are you and my brother always whispering about?'

'We're not! I don't know what you're talking about.' She had tried to wrench away the fingers he had tight around her throat.

'Is he trying to bed you?'

'Of course not. Please, Sidney, I can hardly breathe.'

'You won't be breathing at all, you bitch, if I find out you're screwing him behind my back. I'll kill you both, understand?'

'I wouldn't do that.' He'd squeezed and she had choked, then screamed, 'Yes, I understand.'

'Make sure you keep clear of him. You're my wife, don't you ever forget it.'

Forget it? If she ever managed to get free of this terrible place she'd never forget for a moment how cruel everyone here was, and she'd never forgive them. She would make a run for it if she weren't carrying a baby. No one would give her a job with a baby as part of the bargain. Her only option would be to become a prostitute and she'd rather be dead than sink down that far. She didn't want this baby, certainly not Sidney's baby. She hoped it would be born dead, for its own sake as much as her own. A child had no future in this family. It would be ill treated or grow up to inherit its father's and grandmother's cruel and heartless traits.

Tony took the canvas bag, his old Army bag, from her. 'Peace? You won't ever find any peace in this rotten place.'

'If you don't like it you know what you can do!' Biddy shrieked, throwing her full ashtray at him. 'You can pack your bags and leave. Not that you will, you're too bleddy scared to strike out on your own.'

The tin ashtray struck Tony on the chest and ash and butts spilled down over his twill shirt. It didn't hurt much but he was humiliated. 'You bitch!'

'Tony, stop it and go!' Delia pulled on him.

'You dare call me names?' Biddy heaved her flabby hulk out of her chair. Then, picking up the poker from the fender, she lunged at Tony.

To protect himself he swung the crib bag at her as hard as he could. The blow sent Biddy hurtling back against the little black range. It was lit for bread making and a tin kettle was simmering on the top. Biddy screamed in agony as her spine hit the cast iron and scalding water from the kettle tipped all over her. Before she came to rest on the fender the side of her head struck the protruding door lift of the oven. She was still and silent, blood gushing from her temple.

Delia had screamed at the impact, but like Tony was now staring numb with disbelief. On wobbly feet she picked up the crib bag where it had landed across the room and put it on the table. She and Tony exchanged frightened glances. 'Is she dead?' she whispered.

'I don't know.' He was white with terror. If his mother was dead he could be charged with murder and hang. There was only one thing he could do, make a run for it, and he wouldn't be taking Delia to slow him down.

Two people burst into the house, a neighbouring housewife and the fishmonger not long pulled up in his van. 'What's happened?' He thrust Tony out of the way. 'We were outside and heard shouting and a crash. Then all went quiet. Did she hurt anyone? We were feared for the maid, she being pregnant. Oh, I see…'

Tony felt his insides turn to acid and water. He was in for it now.

The housewife, in pinny, curlers in the front of her hair, edged closer to the fireplace. She spied the fallen poker. 'Coming at you with that, was she? That don't surprise me. I've been saying to my husband for weeks that Biddy Viant is getting more ferocious with every passing day and she'll end up trying to hurt someone. Take a fall, did she?'

As the fishmonger went to see if his mother had a pulse, Tony saw his chance. 'That's it, Mrs Peam. I came back for my crib bag and she was furious with me for forgetting it. She was bawling at both me and Delia for no good reason, threatening us with all sorts. I quarrelled with Mother and she was going to hit me with the poker. She was so mad she didn't get her balance and down she went. She pulled the kettle over. Is she going to be all right, Mr Glasson?'

From his knees, the fishmonger said, 'She's breathing but I don't think she's too good. I'll drive on to the doctor and get him to ring for an ambulance. Tony, get a wet towel and spread it over her scalds, and put another round her head to stop the bleeding, and grab that blanket over that chair to keep her warm. Mrs Peam, you'd better take young Mrs Viant into your house and give her some hot sweet tea. This is no place for a woman in her condition.'

'I was thinking the same thing myself, Mr Glasson.' Mrs Peam came towards Delia with sweeping hands. 'You come along with me, my handsome. 'Tis a crying shame what you've had to put up with here. I've heard one or another shouting at you every day. I nearly got my eldest boy to go for the constable last night. I wish I had now.'

'Wh–what about Sidney and Father-in-law? Shouldn't they be told what's happened?' Delia whimpered, trembling, giving way to a flood of tears.

'Never mind they,' Mrs Peam said firmly. 'Someone will send for them. You just worry about yourself and the baby.'

Delia took one more look at her crumpled mother-in-law. Her exposed flesh was red from the scalds. Blood was trickling from her temple. *Die, you old witch. Die!*

When the others had gone, Tony shut the door. His mind was deadly clear. He knew what he had to do and he must act swiftly. Once word got round onlookers would take the liberty of entering to help or gawp. If she made a full recovery she would make life even more hell. If she had suffered brain damage she would be an unbearable strain on resources. He wasn't thinking of Delia, who would have to nurse her.

He did as Mr Glasson instructed, placing a wet towel over his mother's body and then the scrap of crocheted blanket she had used to cover her knees. 'You never loved me, Mother. You never loved any of us. I bet you didn't even remember it's Kate's birthday today. You're cruel and evil. Here's your comeuppance.'

Carefully taking a light grip round her neck and chin, noting where the gash was on her temple, he let out a cry and drove her head against the exact same place on the oven door lift. He heard her skull splintering. There was a fresh outpouring of blood but he was careful none would be splashed on him. He wrapped the second towel round her head then held her against his chest as if supporting her.

A few seconds passed and he was aware his mother was no longer breathing. 'Bye, bye,' he whispered. 'Good riddance.' He had never dared to stand up to anyone in his life but he had dared to kill his mother. He felt victorious and brave. Now if only he could get his bullying brother out of his life things would be perfect.

Chapter Sixteen

Kate refused Jonny's offer to help her mount for riding and used the hipping stock, climbing up to the top step. It was no easy feat with her odd-length legs and no hand rail, but now she was a year older she was determined to become more independent. She had adopted Cully, a dapple-grey young pony, as her own and went out on her most days.

She waited for Jonny to sit astride Tom's brown mare, Star. 'Shall we ride to Idless Woods?'

'If you like, but how about wandering over Tremore land? You haven't seen any of my father's property.' Jonny was admiring her in a crisp white blouse, trousers, and her hair in a snood. He hadn't forgotten his camera.

'OK, that would be nice.'

She felt light-hearted and rather important to be sat up high, trotting through the village with a member of the former local gentry. Jill had said to stay out as long as she liked, that it was her birthday and a day for doing things her own way – yet another wonderful new luxury to her. She was sure she would remember this day for the rest of her life.

Jonny led the way along the first narrow ribbon of Back Lane, then went off the road straight ahead on to a wide short track surrounded by fields. Kate saw the hedges were flooded with brambles and green berries, a blackberry feast here in a few weeks' time. There was a stile beside the gate of the field directly in front of them. Leaning from the saddle, Jonny opened the gate and ushered Kate through into a field where his father's pedigree shorthorn herd was grazing. They trotted through the field and several after that, weaving in and out of the lanes to reach the next fields where necessary. They cantered where there were no crops or beasts, riding up and down hills, taking in the views of lonely dwellings, the occasional deserted tumbledown cottage, and the village and other farms in the distance.

After an hour, Jonny said, 'Thirsty? There's a stream just ahead.'

'I could do with a drink,' she replied. Her cheeks were rosy-pink from the exhilarating exertion and she was pleasantly out of breath.

They were at the bottom of a fallow field where there was a predominance of hazel, an old neglected coppice in the shade of the woods. The hazel was a mass of straggling limbs from old stools that couldn't be classed as trees. Kate was reminded of another of her old hurried pastimes, when she had collected hazelnuts in autumn and her mother had demanded she hand them all over, after she had cracked the shells first. A vivid scene from the nightmare she'd had last night was of her grandmother choking on hazelnuts. Why must she haunt her even on her birthday? Forget about it, she told herself, let nothing ruin today.

'We'll dismount here and walk,' Jonny said. 'It's just a short way. I'd like to take some snaps to commemorate your birthday, if that's all right.'

'Of course it is. I'm the one who should be grateful to you.'

Before jumping down, he took a photograph from the mare of her on Cully, then another from the ground. He offered his hand to help her dismount. Such a tiny hand she had, warm and a little rough. She had grown in confidence and strength at an amazing rate since he'd known her. He towered over her. It was a meeting of a man and a maiden, of someone returning to his boyish spirit and a girl blossoming into a woman. He couldn't help smiling at her and he loved it when he provoked a smile out of her in return. It was an enchanting reward. Her natural smiles were the essence of simplicity, of one who although kept cruelly a prisoner from the world was wonderfully unspoiled by its degradation.

'You lead the way,' she said.

'What?'

'To the stream. That's where you said we were going.' When he became strangely vague and seemed to be less sure of himself, she wondered why she had ever found him intimidating. She didn't put him on a pedestal of glowing masculinity, or desire him or wish him for a husband, but saw him only as caring and ordinary. She thought now that there was no need to exalt people for any reason. They were either good or bad, some shining in integrity, others at the far end of the scale horribly dark with corruption.

'Oh, yes, of course.' To his dismay he actually found himself blushing. Kate affected him in ways no other woman could. She was so lovely, exquisite and enchanting. Sunlight shimmered on her hair, turning it to shades of copper and chestnut, and her eyes were like green oceans. Her gentle looks celebrated early womanhood at its best. She should have poetry written about her. Another new thing Jonny found, something a little unsettling, was how in her naiveté Kate might see aspects in him other women didn't. The hero-god other women seemed to find totally bypassed her. On occasion she might see him as shallow and trite – she certainly had not liked it when he'd reprimanded Denny James during the haymaking. He would have to be careful never to betray her trust.

Taking the mare's reins he started off and she brought Cully along at his side, until a natural opening in the woods was reached, where a billowing of crimson rosebay willowherb danced in the light breeze like flames. Butterflies were skimming from flower to flower. Jonny was caught up in excitement. 'Perfect! I just have to take some photos of you here. Could you take off your snood and let your hair run free, Kate?'

Leaving Cully, Kate stood in front of the blaze of flowers, which tapered up to four feet high, with spirals of leaves all the way up the sturdy stems. 'Do you want me sitting down?'

Jonny was thrilled at how ready she was to pose for him. 'In a minute, my love.' He snapped her facing him and in profile, and gazing in all directions. Then he started on some studies of her sitting in various positions. 'Great. Thanks for your patience. Now let's get that drink of water.'

They entered the ancient woods, on what was not exactly a bridle path but a track just wide enough for two riders. After a few yards, Jonny pointed to the side where the woodland floor began to drop in a gradual slope. 'Down there. It's not far.'

Passing under an awning of high beech and oak boughs through which the sun shone, casting a dappled shade over them, they went down to a small clearing, to the low bank of a tiny trickling stream. The sun shone hotly on the exposed thick carpet of grass in this almost magical place, the bank curving inward in one spot and forming a little pool before the crystal water chinkled on its way. 'Oh, I love it here!' Kate said.

'I thought you would.' Jonny hitched Cully and Star's reins to a low branch.

He watched while Kate eased herself down on her knees and, leaning over the bank, cupped her hands to scoop up water. 'Mmm, it's cold and sweet.' She gazed up at him.

Jonny was transfixed, with no thought of taking more pictures of her. He just wanted to feast his eyes on her and imprint these moments in his mind. He knelt beside her, and they both eased their thirst. He dried his hands on his shirt, then pulled it free from his waistband. 'Here, use this. Don't make yourself wet.'

She laughed. 'Always the chivalrous one.' She had heard Tilda refer to Mr Perry in this way and thought the description suited Jonny. He had so many nice ways.

'That's right.' He let a deep smile linger on her. 'I'm the knight in shining armour and you're my lady.'

'A maiden in distress, you mean.'

'Not at all. You don't look at all distressed now.'

'I'm not. This is one of the best days of my life. It would be even better if there was good news about Miss Rothwell.'

'I agree, but don't think about anyone else for a while, Kate. Remember this time as perfect in a perfect place.'

'It is.' His eyes hadn't left hers and, capturing his tranquil mood, she was mesmerized by him.

'You're perfect company, Kate.'

She smiled shyly and looked down. Compliments usually made her feel reticent but she had no idea there was a deeper meaning behind the one Jonny had just given her. She sat on the grass and gazed at the water.

Jonny did the same, very close to her. 'Lean against me if you like.'

'OK.' Turning slightly side-on she rested her back against his arm. They stayed quiet, letting their minds float but conscious of the wildlife that teemed in the woodland. Rustles indicated mice or other small creeping creatures foraging for nuts, buds and insects. A wood pigeon cooed somewhere high in the trees, and chaffinches and a woodcock issued their own distinctive calls. There might be weasels, stoats, foxes, hedgehogs or shrews anywhere in the vicinity. Together they looked in the direction of the snap of a twig or followed an insect in flight. All the while the gentle song of the stream lulled them into a dreamy state. Jonny eased his arm away and wrapped it around Kate and she leaned against the side of his body, movements at that moment natural to both of them.

A plop near a weedy spot on the edge of the bank alerted them to a water vole, startled by something unknown, plunging into the water. The long, chestnut-coloured furry creature swam towards the bank on the opposite side.

'Aren't you going to take a picture of it?' Kate whispered, unwilling to break the soothing tranquillity.

'No,' Jonny whispered into her ear. Then, holding her a little more snugly, 'I'm happy to stay like this for the rest of the day.'

–

Slipping in and out of consciousness as the day wore on, Abbie knew she had to make a big effort to rouse someone to her plight before darkness fell. She was certain now that the Mitchells had absconded with her belongings and while she was in no danger from them, she could starve to death if she didn't escape from the house. No doubt they had rented this badly neglected house and owed a lot of rent. The side of her face hurt. Putting a hand there she felt a lump and broken skin. She must have struck her face on one of the occasions she had passed out. Then she remembered looking about for a missile to throw at the window in the hope of breaking it and alerting the neighbours, praying they would call the police. There had been only one thing in the room she could use. She had stood by the bed – if she wasn't so dizzy she would have climbed on to it – and thrown a bakelite ashtray at the window. Her arm weak, her aim had been poor. The ashtray had hit the window frame and bounced back and glanced off her face.

The horror and disappointment she had endured then assailed her again. She had no voice to shout and screams emerged only as a rusty croak, burning her throat. The other thing she had tried and failed at was to break down the door. She had wrapped the musty soiled bedcovers round her feet, and lying on the floor she had tried to kick it in. The wood had refused to give. Had she banged on the walls to get attention? She couldn't remember. The sickness and dizziness was coming on her again but she must try before she passed out again. She might not come to for hours. She might not wake up at all. Panic made her drag herself to the nearest wall, pulling the bedcovers with her. She couldn't recall the layout of the house and hoped it was a connecting wall to the one next door.

Wrapping the covers round her hand she banged on the wall, counting to six before exhaustion stopped her. She listened. 'Please. Please!' she rasped. There was nothing. Fear mingled with determination and she battered on the wall with every dreg of energy she could summon. 'Somebody! Help me!' she croaked, but screaming inside, desperation eating her away, threatening to consume her, to send her crazed and unfit to carry on, to plunge her into ever greater peril.

She listened. Oh, why wasn't anyone there? Please! Please God, please! Her ears hurt. There was a hammering in her head. Then her mind cleared and she thought she heard something. Thud, thud. Yes! Surely that was an answering thud, thud. She hauled up her feeble arms and thumped two bangs. She cried out in wild elation when she got back the same tattoo again. It might be the neighbour banging back in anger. If she kept it up surely someone would come round to complain. If only she knew how to tap out SOS in Morse code and let the respondent know someone was in mortal danger. She banged three times, paused, then did it again, hoping the neighbour would realize it was a message, a plea for help. She listened again, and received three thuds in return. She started a rhythm and got back the same number of thuds each time. It went on for some time. She grew anxious. Was it a child thinking it was someone playing a game?

'I'm in here, damn you! Come and get me out.' Her hands were in agony but she bashed the wall with all her might, keeping it up until exhaustion grabbed her in its wilful clutches and she collapsed in a wretched heap.

Sweating and panting, the room whirling, she could only huddle and try to control her breathing. *Oh, please, please, whoever you are, do something. Send for the police. Tell them there's something suspicious going on next door.*

There was silence. She had failed. She was shivering, shuddering, bitter cold to the bone. How was she going to survive the last of the day and through the night? She felt herself slipping away. She was losing her last fragment of strength. She was losing consciousness and would never wake up again. She would be found eventually, a mess of bones and desiccated flesh. If only she could leave her parents a note. Tell them she loved them. Tell them she was sorry. Against her will her eyes closed.

A loud sound startled her, brought her round in a tremendous jolt. A terrified scream got trapped in her throat. Bangs and thuds, different sounds to those she had received from the other side of the wall. Someone was at the front door. She could hear a muffled voice. 'Hello! Who is it? Who's there?' Her ploy had worked! Someone had come and was shouting through the letterbox. Somehow she must find the capacity to get to the bedroom door. She couldn't risk the person going away, this might be her only chance. She had to make a lot of noise. Painfully slow, she crawled across the floor. Then, easing herself in position on her back, she kicked out and drummed her feet against the door for a second or two. Her feet fell like stones. She had used up the final drop of her resources. Her eyes closed. One last thought, she could only rely on fate.

–

'What are they doing here?' Jonny eyed Alan and Martha Killigrew as they entered Tom and Jill's sitting room, which was furnished in a fascinating marriage of remnants from the farm's former days and some new but not modern pieces.

'Jill and I thought Kate should have some more young people here for the evening,' Tom said, gaily mixing punch, laced with a little alcohol. 'Her tea party was a great success, this should round off the day perfectly for her. We're going to play some music.'

'So that's why Denny is here. I thought he was gate crashing.'

'Don't be so grumpy. The occasion isn't for family only. Friends being here will help to make up for Kate not having her own people.'

'She won't want to dance.' It was unlikely Kate had ever danced owing to her slight disability, and Jonny couldn't bear to think of her being made self-conscious by one of these callow youths insisting on her jiving. He had spent an idyllic afternoon with Kate. She had been happy and relaxed and he would ensure she'd stay that way. Nothing must spoil her day.

'I know what you're thinking. Jill and I are sensitive to the same thing. It will only be some soft background music. Mum has suggested we play charades. We'll make up two teams. I doubt if Kate has been included in that sort of fun before.'

'I'll organize the teams.' Jonny would see to it that he and Kate were on the same team and that he was sitting beside her.

'No need. It will be men against women. Denny's older sister should be arriving any minute. It will make up the numbers.'

'Huh.' Jonny mooched off. He went close to Kate, pretending to focus his camera on her for more photographs, but really to listen in on what Alan Killigrew was saying to her. Denny had been bashful while handing over to Kate a small parcel that contained a plaster ornament of a ginger cat, the sort won at a fair, and then he had ambled about the room uncertainly, obviously unused to this sort of gathering. But Killigrew was older, had more status, more experience with girls, and he was flourishing his present with a confident grin.

'You look lovely, Kate. Really lovely. Congratulations. It's an honour to be invited to your do.' Alan would have been bitterly disappointed if he had not been included. He liked Kate, more than liked her. It was what kept him hoping to gain a date with her, to really get to know her and hope she'd like him too as more than a friend. He had no trouble attracting girls and had never been shy with them. There were lots of nice pretty girls about, but Kate was different to all of them, she was special. He wasn't about to give up any chance he had with her. 'This is for you. I hope you like it.'

'Thank you, Alan,' Kate said. She kept eye contact with him for a minute to be polite, but knowing Jonny was near she turned and smiled at him. She had so enjoyed the afternoon with him.

'Open it then,' Jonny encouraged her, stealing Alan's moment.

Alan made a wry face. Damn Harvey for getting in the way.

Jonny was pleased with his vexation.

Kate unwrapped the present. 'Oh, it's beautiful.' She was delighted with the long tasselled silk scarf. 'Jill, look at this. Mrs Em, see what Alan's given me. It's so soft and delicate.'

'I'd decided what I'd get for you,' Alan said, moving to look into her face in the hope of keeping her interest, 'but I asked my mother to go to the shops to be sure it was exactly the right thing. The red and gold colours match your hair perfectly, Kate.'

'It's very thoughtful of you, Alan. Thank you.'

'I'm thrilled you like it, Kate.' He smiled a smile deep into her eyes. How he'd love to receive such a warm look in return. He was getting cross with Jonny Harvey for hanging about so close. The wretched chap wasn't giving them breathing space.

'It's an excellent choice,' Emilia said, noting Alan's admiration for Kate. If Kate started walking out with someone Alan would be ideal. Tom and Perry would warn him to stay in line. Denny too was a nice boy. She felt sorry for him. It was easy to see he was feeling overdressed and gauche in his Sunday best suit, of poorer quality than Alan's casual sports jacket. He had excluded himself from the crush of people around Kate and kept glancing at the door, probably hoping his sister would soon join them and he wouldn't feel so much the odd one out. She went over to chat to him to put him at ease.

Jill gave Kate a hug. 'You've had some wonderful presents today.' The locket she and Tom had given her was shining round her neck. She was beautiful in her new dress, her hair richly waved.

Jonny wanted to be uppermost in Kate's mind. He took the scarf from her hand then swept it over her head and placed it round her shoulders. 'It doesn't go with your dress but it will give you an idea how it could look, Kate, darling.'

Alan clenched his teeth. What the hell was Harvey up to? Damned bighead. It was Kate's day. How dare he try to steal the scene?

Tom gripped Jill's arm and pulled her aside. 'What was that all about? Jonny doing that?'

'Everyone loves Kate,' Jill said, proud of her protégé. 'She touched Abbie's heart too and she wanted to do a lot for her. I overreacted and ruined it. If I'd been calmer and not so possessive of Kate, Abbie might be here now. You know, we need to be careful not to overwhelm Kate, darling. It was what Abbie clumsily tried to tell me. We mustn't put Kate in another prison by trying to run her life for her. She must be allowed to spread her wings and live her life her own way.'

Tom nodded. 'It's hard not to want to protect her from every little knock. But you're right, we must give Kate credit for being an intelligent and resourceful girl. After all, she's survived so much. Don't blame yourself about Abbie, darling. I'm sure she didn't. I believe she went off because she had problems of her own to resolve.'

Someone had let themselves in through the kitchen. 'Ah, that must be Annie, Denny's sister,' Jill said. 'We can start the game.'

But it was Douglas Goodyear who came into the room. Jill and Tom froze. They assumed the worst about Abbie. What an awful time to come with the dreadful news.

Emilia saw Douglas. Her heart lurched. He was never an easy man to read. Right now he looked serious. 'What is it? Have you brought news?'

The room fell silent. All eyes flew to Douglas. 'Sorry to intrude,' he said. 'But I thought I'd come and tell you personally. Not long ago I had the pleasure of informing the Rothwells that Abbie has been found alive.'

'Thank God!' Emilia exclaimed. A cry of collective relief echoed round the room.

'Where was she?' Perry asked.

'Well, that's where the news isn't as good. She's in the infirmary, very poorly and on a drip for dehydration. Apparently she had been abducted from the railway station.' He told the gathering where she had been taken and the appalling conditions she had been kept in. 'She has many cuts and bruises from trying to escape. A few hours ago she managed to alert a neighbour. Not having seen the Mitchells – if that's their real name – for a few days he was alarmed and went round and forced his way into the house. Of course, he called the police and an ambulance immediately. The police suspected it was Abbie, and as soon as they managed to talk to her and confirm it they phoned me at the hotel. It was a double relief for the Rothwells. They had just received a ransom letter demanding five thousand pounds, saying pay up, with no police involvement, or your daughter dies. It had been posted in Birmingham. The ransom was to be left at a railway station in Nottingham tomorrow. The Mitchells have tried to cover their tracks but the game is up for them now. Mr Rothwell is not up to the journey down, but Mrs Rothwell is travelling down on the train as we speak. The doctors say Abbie was found in the nick of time. She couldn't have lasted much longer.'

Emilia had her hands to her face. 'Poor Abbie. Douglas, what time is Honor's train due in? Perry and I will meet her.'

Absorbing this news, and because her emotions had been running wonderfully high all day, Kate couldn't prevent herself bursting into tears. Alan reached for her, but Jonny had made sure he was closer to her and he took her into his arms. 'It's all right, darling. Abbie's safe and will soon get better.'

'I know,' Kate sobbed, pressing her face into his chest. 'It's the best present I could ever have had on my birthday.'

And this is mine, Jonny thought, relishing the sweet sensations of cradling her, comforting her. Then it hit him like a gale force wind, why he had sought this so eagerly, why it meant so much to him. He had never thought it would happen to him but the impossible had occurred. He had fallen in love with Kate. And it wasn't a good thing, it was wrong, horribly wrong. He was twice her age, old enough to be her father. He was worldly while she enjoyed a simple everyday life. He let her go and was shaken at how reluctant he was to do so. His arms felt empty, he was bereft not to have her close to him and at the same time horrified at the situation. He fumbled with his camera to obscure his confusion. He couldn't let Kate know his true feelings. It would scare her. She might end up hating him. He hated himself at that moment for he knew he couldn't help himself. He loved Kate with all his being and he didn't have the strength to do the right thing. Which was to stay away from her.

Chapter Seventeen

Denny was bringing out the thirty-strong Friesian herd from pasture for the short journey to the farm for evening milking. He had the aid of the sheepdog, which needed no orders to direct the cows in the right direction and put stragglers back in line. Having just acquired promotion to cowman, a task he was fully capable of, he had left Tom and the rest of the workers in the harvest fields, and he and the women would attend the milking parlour.

To coincide with the new confidence endowed by his position, his body had bulked out in the last few weeks giving him an impressive build. He walked tall, with shoulders as true as a serviceman's, and he had swapped his flat cap and sleeveless jerkin for a Western-style wide-brimmed hat and black waistcoat. To his mind, it gave him a touch of film-star dash, but it had evoked different reactions in others. While he was now coming under the notice of the local girls, and had even lost his virginity, older people were either amused, saying it was his way of growing up, or thought him a bighead or a fool. To the surprise of those at the farm, he had also become moody and remote, not given any more to chit-chat, whistling and innocent pranks. It wasn't the natural progression to manhood. He was sometimes unfriendly. Only Emilia had an idea what was wrong with him but she said nothing, hoping instead that Denny would come round in good time.

Kate met him at the gate, across from the field where she had first encountered Jill. 'Hello, Denny. I've come to give you a hand.' She had a stout stick in readiness to ward off any strays.

'There's no need. I can manage on my own with Dusty,' he muttered, tossing his head in a dismissive manner, then securing the gate. He stared at Kate's feet. 'And you'd only slow us down.'

Kate had felt that his surliness was directed mostly at her for some reason and she had come here to try once again to get back on good terms with him. Before, he had cut off her sentences or left her remarks unanswered, but this time he had chosen a direct insult. She hid her hurt but not her anger. 'That was really nasty! Have I offended you or something? I thought we were friends but now you treat me like an enemy. What's going on?'

He stalked off, using his stick to prod the cows into line. He was ignoring her and she wasn't going to tolerate his animosity any longer. She had to use fast, long steps to keep up with him. 'Denny, for goodness sake, tell me what I've done!'

He strode on, eyeing her sideways, his bottom lip curled in contempt. 'Don't talk to me as if I'm an underling. You carry on as if I'm not good enough for you but you come from a poorer background than I do.'

'What are you talking about? When have I ever made you feel small?' He refused to answer. She could only think of one reason for his attitude. 'Is this because I haven't gone out with you? That's silly. I haven't gone out with anyone. And you're doing all right with the girls, apparently. I really don't understand you.'

'When have you made me feel small? You're so full of your bloody self you don't even know.' Denny couldn't forgive her over the way he'd felt she had shunned him at her birthday party. She had thanked him for his gift then seemed to have immediately forgotten about the ornament, probably thinking it stupid and cheap. Yet she'd squealed like a piglet newly farrowed over Alan Killigrew's expensive silk scarf. Then after the toff Goodyear had come with the news about the Rothwell woman, she'd thrown herself into Jonny Harvey's arms and hung about the hoity swine or Killigrew all evening. She had wanted nothing more to do with him. He was unimportant, nothing to her. 'You think you're everyone's darling. You lap it up when people feel sorry for you and fuss all over you. Your rotten grandmother was a selfish old bitch and you're no better. You're determined to sponge all you can out of the Harveys and Boswelds. But you're nothing special, Kate Viant, and you never will be. You should keep that in mind. The bosses may treat you like you're one of them, but you're not and they'll never forget it. If you're aiming for a husband among their sort you'll be out of luck. No rich man will want to marry a common little cripple, no matter how pretty and sweet you happen to be. And one more thing, watch out for Killigrew. He's only after one thing. He'll not want to marry you either.'

The spitefulness in the tirade, so unfair and all lies, was exactly the sort of thing she'd got from her family, but in this there was biting bitterness too. Not wanting him to see her hurt, she strangled an angry sob in her throat and fell behind.

He looked back, as if crowing over her, like he had won some victory. 'Going to run to Mrs Jill now, are you? Tell her the rotten cowman's upset you?'

This was a ruse and she saw straight through it. There was high colour in his cheeks. He wasn't so brazen and superior now. He was afraid. Afraid a report about his attempt to throw her down in the depths would get him the sack. He was jealous of her and he was pathetic. He had won nothing but her everlasting disrespect. She knew where she stood with those who had given her a home and new purpose. She had their trust and affection, and she had a good friendship with Alan and special closeness to Jonny that no amount of sour grapes could take away from her. The difference between the cowman and Jonny, who was helping with the harvesting today, was worlds wide.

She glared at the boy in the ridiculous cowboy getup. 'You're just a bad loser, Denny James.' She turned and went back to the gate. If she hurried through the fields she would beat him to the milking parlour. She would show him, as she would anyone else who attempted to bring her down, that she couldn't care less what they thought of her.

—

Jonny was ready to leave the darkroom, satisfied with the photographs he had taken in the cornfield. It had been a good day, one of the best, fully justifying his decision to leave the RAF. He had sold a lot of his work locally. Douglas Goodyear had been good enough to recommend him to contacts in the publishing world and he was doing well there too. He was gaining a respected reputation, yet without stepping outside of the county. Although he was looking forward to travelling afar and building up a more diverse portfolio, he was pleased to have two reasons to stay on in Hennaford. There was his part in the village play; rehearsals were to resume after all the farmers had brought the harvest in. A short while afterwards he was to give Louisa away at her wedding. It meant he could remain close to Kate for a while longer. He was being careful not to present how he felt about her or the family would warn him off. Rightly so too – the sheltered existence Kate had led meant she knew too little about life to be sure of her own mind yet where men were concerned. He must proceed with her very slowly. It might be a year or two before he could make an approach to her but she was worth the wait. He asked his heart every day if he really was in love with her and each time it answered that he adored her and his life would be a frightening void without her. Sometimes to him, a man who had vigorously shunned romance, marriage and the rest of it, it seemed ludicrous to have fallen in love at last. But he hadn't known Kate before. Part of his former emptiness must have been his subconscious telling him it was time he found a permanent mate. He had found the one he wanted, and his biggest fear was that someone else, especially Alan Killigrew, would step in and take her away. He had to forge something so strong and special with her that she wouldn't look elsewhere. When he did go away, it wouldn't be for long each time, he'd suggest they keep in touch by letter. He'd write long informative letters to keep him in her mind.

The darkroom opened into the den and he found Emilia and Perry there, sharing the desk and both writing letters. 'We'll be a while yet,' she said. 'Go through and help yourself to a drink, Jonny.'

'Thanks. I thought I'd help out again tomorrow, Aunt Em. All right if I stay over?'

'Of course. We're very grateful of the extra help. We'll join you later for a nightcap.'

His throat was bone dry after heaving sheaves up on the cart for several hours under a blazing hot sun and he needed a glass or two of wine. He was thrilled to find Kate in the sitting room alone, with wireless music playing softly in the background. She must be giving Tom and Jill some space. What could be more perfect? 'Hello, my love. This is a really pleasant surprise.'

She put aside the magazine she was browsing through. 'Hello Jonny. You've had a busy day. Can I get you a cup of tea?'

'No thanks. I'm going to open some white wine. Can I pour you a glass?'

'Just a small one. I'm not used to it. The first time I tasted wine was on my birthday.'

He poured the drinks then sat down beside her on the sofa. He had the ideal excuse. He would show her his latest batch of photographs. 'What do you think?'

'They're excellent, Jonny.' She smiled at him. 'They always are. You'll be really famous one day.'

'I don't know about that. I'm not sure I want that.' I want you, he thought, at my side, always. He leaned in close, pointing out details, breathing in the freshness and sweetness of her, gazing at her more than at the photos. His newfound career was unimportant compared to her. He drank her in. She was wearing a pink and white cotton blouse and trousers. Her silver locket rested against the creamy skin just below her neck. Her complexion was silky and healthy. Her hair framed her exquisite finely sculptured face in glossy auburn waves. He loved her eyes, shining with innocence and promise. He loved her small hands; they were not smooth and manicured, but her fingers tapered and she had a soft touch. She was ethereal and beautiful. It was new to him to admire a woman in other than a sensual way. He desired her, of course, but those deeper feelings could wait.

Kate had got used to his eyes resting on her. She assumed he was sizing up new shots of her. She seemed to be one of his favourite subjects, for she figured greatly in today's photos. She glanced at him. She enjoyed the sight of his gorgeous dark features. She knew every strong angle of his brow, his nose, his high cheekbones, his wide mouth, and every imperfection of the stretched skin of his marred cheek. She could picture him accurately when she lay in bed with her eyes closed in the dark. She liked the strength of him and his heady masculine smell, mixed now with the soap he'd used after taking a bath. He needed a second shave but she liked the dark stubble on his chin. She realized she was staring at him, that would never do. Picking up her glass, she took a sip. 'Mrs Em is writing to Mrs Rothwell again. I think she's feeling guilty about what happened to Abbie.'

'There's no need for that. Abbie was pretty much her own boss. She knew what she was doing when she left here. It was terribly bad luck that Mitchell happened to be there when she was taken ill.'

'But she'd changed after her hopes failed for Mark Fuller. Mrs Em felt she was under her care and that she let her down by not realizing how upset she was. Jill told me about the row they had over me. She feels bad about that. She wanted to see Abbie at the infirmary but only Mrs Em was allowed to go in. You know Mrs Rothwell, Jonny. Do you think she's angry with all of us? She refused Mrs Em's invitation to stay at the farm.'

It was a simple thing to ask and he loved her for it. How enchanting she was. 'No one's angry with you, darling Kate. I got the chance to speak to Honor at the hotel. The only people she blames for hurting Abbie are the beastly Mitchell couple. Thank God they were soon arrested, tracked down for having the nerve to make a bid for the reward money. They'll get a long jail sentence. They deserve to rot there. They left Abbie without a care if she'd die. It was easier for Honor to visit Abbie from the hotel, and as soon as Abbie was able to travel she was eager to take her home and get back to her husband. Archie is not a well man.'

'It's over a month since Abbie was taken home and apparently she hasn't left the house in all that time. She might never get over her awful experiences. I had a tough time, nothing like that, of course, but I know how it can drag you down. I was lucky. I met Jill and was given a new lease of life. Abbie might need something new to help her come to terms with everything. What if it never happens, Jonny?'

Her face was creased with concern and he longed to put comforting arms around her. 'I'm sure something will turn up. Abbie's got her painting. That's sure to take her out and about eventually.'

'I hope so. I'd like to see her, but I don't suppose she'll ever want to come here again.'

'I'm planning on visiting Oak Tree Warren before the year is out. Why don't you come with me?' It would be wonderful to travel with Kate, to show her more of life.

Kate frowned. 'I'd have to see what Jill has to say about that.'

This made Jonny grip her arm. 'Kate, darling, you're your own person. Free to go wherever you like. You don't have to ask anyone's permission. At the very least you're entitled to a holiday. Would you like to go up to Lincolnshire with me?'

'Yes.' There were many things she would like to do, all new experiences, including travelling on a train, and it would be brilliant to go somewhere with Jonny. He was a good friend and… she didn't know what else he was, but she felt differently about him than she did Tom or any other man. She put a hand over his. 'I'd love to.'

'It's a certainty then.' Rapt, he leaned forward and kissed her cheek.

At that moment Perry came into the room. The smile he was wearing disappeared abruptly. 'What's going on?' Jonny shuffled down the other end of the sofa, his face on fire. It was plain what Perry had thought. 'Oh, um, Kate and I were just talking about going up to see the Rothwells.'

'Were you indeed. Jonny, could I have a word? Kate, dear, would you mind going through to the kitchen and making Mrs Em and I some cocoa, please?'

Kate looked from one male face to the other. She could tell Mr Perry was displeased, but she believed it was over them making arrangements without consulting anyone here first. Jonny would put things right. 'Of course, right away.'

Perry closed the door after her. He had disguised his anger and indignation for Kate's sake, she was too naive to know what Jonny's game had been, but now he let rip. 'What the hell do you think you were doing? I could hardly believe my eyes. Your behaviour was outrageous! You can have any woman you like and you usually do, but I find you flirting with Kate. More than that, planning on getting her away so you can seduce her.'

'Perry, it's not how it looked,' Jonny pleaded. He was on his feet.

'I know what I saw, and if Jill and Tom had witnessed it you wouldn't be standing there in one piece. Get to the den, now! I'm telling your aunt about this.'

Emilia was folding her letter when Perry pushed Jonny through the den door. 'What's the matter?'

'Prepare yourself for a shock.' Perry gave Jonny another push, and another, until he was standing before Emilia like a naughty schoolboy.

As Perry spelled it out in disgusted terms, Jonny felt more humiliated than ever before in his life. His love for Kate was being turned into something sordid. 'Let me explain! I was not trying to seduce Kate. Far from it. I'd never do anything to hurt her. I'm in love with her.'

'You're what?' Emilia gasped, coming round the desk to him. 'That's the most ridiculous thing I've ever heard.'

'No it isn't, Aunt Em.' He threw out his hands. 'If you'll just listen to me and try to see things my way…'

'You must be joking,' Perry snapped. 'We know what you're like, remember, Jonny?'

'But I do love her. I didn't think I was capable of falling in love, but I have with Kate. It just happened. I know now what you both share. And Tom and Jill too, and my father and Susan. I love Kate, I really do.'

'Whatever you think you feel for Kate, Jonny,' Emilia said sternly, 'you've got to stop it, for her sake. She's just a child, and even if she was a lot older you've absolutely nothing in common.'

'I've thought about all that, Aunt Em, honestly I have. I admit I shouldn't have kissed her just now, that I should have been more careful, but I wasn't planning on there being anything between us for ages yet. One day the age difference won't matter. After all, Susan is a lot younger than my father.'

'That was different,' Perry said, angry that Jonny should defend himself. 'Susan was a widow in her twenties, with a child, already supporting herself, and not about to get her head filled with fancy notions. Tristan wasn't involved with the social scene you move in. He offered Susan stability, he didn't sweep her off her feet, as you want to do with Kate.'

'But I'm willing to settle down and all the rest of it.' Jonny could almost have cried. Why couldn't he get them to see he was sincere?

'If you're not careful, Jonny, you could ruin the girl's life,' Emilia said, wanting to shake him for causing these complications. 'What if Kate becomes infatuated with you? What if it's already happened? Kate would never be happy living your way of life. You could break her heart. Destroy her.'

'I won't!' Jonny was getting angry now. 'I swear I won't, and if you can bring yourselves not to interfere I'll prove it to you. I don't expect Kate to change for me. I'll be the one to make the changes.'

'You're talking a lot of hot air.' Perry glared at Jonny to make sure he saw that he would not give an inch. 'It's only a matter of time before you'll be sniffing round some high-class piece of skirt.'

'God in heaven, why won't you listen to me?' Jonny screeched. 'It's impossible to hurt someone you love.'

'I think you'd better go home now, Jonny.' Emilia took a deep impatient breath. 'I suggest you back out of the play and keep a low profile until Louisa's wedding. I don't want to talk to you again until you come to your senses. Until you do, if you try to see Kate, then Perry and I will tell Tom and Jill what you've been up to. We'll see you to the front door.'

Jonny gazed a moment at the desk, thinking about its former owner. 'Uncle Alec would have understood. You can turn me out, but if I lose Kate because of you both I'll never forgive you.'

As Emilia closed the front door and Perry reached up to shut the top bolt, Kate came into the passage with two mugs of cocoa on a tray. 'Has Jonny gone?'

'He was needed at home.' Emilia forced a smile.

'I thought I heard raised voices. Is everything all right?' Kate was sure there had been an argument about the proposed trip to Lincolnshire. The Boswelds probably didn't want her to go, but Jonny had made her think. She did have the right to go anywhere she wanted and she really wanted to go with him. She loved his company. He treated her as a grown-up.

Perry took the tray from her and ushered her into the sitting room. 'Everything is fine, sweetheart. We mustn't expect to see Jonny for a while. He's going to be very busy.'

Kate sensed they wanted to change the subject but she wasn't about to oblige them. 'Why?'

'Oh, he thinks he's been neglecting his photography,' Emilia said. 'He has got to earn his living. Well, we'd better not stay up late. We've got another long busy day tomorrow.'

'Actually, I'm a bit tired. If you'll excuse me I think I'll go to bed,' Kate said.

—

Jonny got no further than just below the brow of the hill. In a whirl of anger and frustration that he could be thought of as being so shallow he stopped to light a cigarette. There was no need for his aunt and Perry to have been so harsh. He might not have thought through all the implications of falling in love with Kate but he knew the difference between right and wrong. He might have been a womanizer, and that was an outdated notion, but the women he'd had sex with were all consenting adults who knew their own minds. How could his aunt and Perry believe he had been trying to seduce Kate? He could never do anything to hurt her. All those at Ford Farm were too possessive about her. He supposed he was himself. Now he had no choice but to keep away from her. Kate, and Tom and Jill, would wonder why he was being suddenly aloof. It meant something else he had no choice about. He would have to go away, at least until Louisa's wedding. It would be awful not to be close to Kate but it would give him the chance to show his aunt and Perry that he was capable of 'doing the decent thing'. It would prove he wasn't putting Kate under any sort of pressure or compromising her. He would send postcards to Tom and Jill and put friendly messages on them for Kate, keep himself on her mind. He was a man of strategy. He would play the game carefully and when the time was right Kate would be his. He didn't usually believe in fate and the hand of God working in one's life, but somehow he had known that despite the tremendous odds he would come through the war, and he was as certain as life itself that Kate's trust of him would one day grow into love.

Kate slipped through to the kitchen, saying goodnight to Tilda on the way. Rather than going in to Jill and Tom in their sitting room, she stole outside. She wanted to speak to Jonny. She knew the Boswelds wouldn't approve, she was sure they had quarrelled with him, but she wanted to learn what had happened. She hoped she would be able to catch up with him. Shushing the dogs and sending them away, she went out into the lane and to the brow of the hill. Her heart leapt. Just ahead was the glow of a cigarette. In the light of the moon she made out Jonny's broad outline. She let out a stage whisper. 'Jonny, wait!'

'Kate.' He strode back to her, throwing the cigarette down. He whispered, 'What are you doing out here?'

'I wanted to see you. Did you really have to go home straight away?' It seemed he did not if he was hanging about.

The last thing he had expected was to be facing Kate. He rejoiced in the fact that she cared enough about him to follow him. 'Um, I thought I'd better run along. I'm really tired.'

'Mrs Em said you were needed at home. Was that true? Did you and Mrs Em and Mr Perry exchange angry words? Was it about Lincolnshire? You're my friend, Jonny. You've always been good to me. Do you need to talk? I know it's the busiest time of the year at the farm but I'm sure I could slip away for an hour tomorrow. We could meet in the little spot in Tremore woods by the stream, where we went before.'

More than anything in the world. To be alone with her again where they had spent such an idyllic time was utterly tempting. 'Aunt Em thought you ought to settle down here a little more before you get about, Kate, but I promise you that we will take that trip up to Lincolnshire some day, and other places too. Actually, I'm going away tomorrow, but I'll keep in touch. Shall be back for the wedding, of course.'

'I'll miss you, Jonny.'

Did the moonlight show how much he was smiling at her words? 'I'll miss you too, Kate, very much. You'd better go back in. Tom will be making a last check round the stead in a minute.' He always kissed the women in the family when coming and going. He was sure Kate wouldn't mind if he gave her a peck on the cheek.

As he bent his head towards her, Kate found herself reaching up to kiss him back.

Jonny closed his eyes, making his kiss warm and lasting. It was pure heaven to feel her lips on his cheek. 'I'll see you again very soon, darling Kate.'

'Take good care of yourself, Jonny.' She watched him until he had disappeared in the darkness.

Jonny vowed that now his love for Kate was known he would find a way to make this their last parting.

Chapter Eighteen

For over an hour Abbie had been in the flock-papered morning room of Oak Tree Warren, sitting at her easel, her subject the family Springer spaniel dozing on a fireplace armchair. Her mother had set up her painting gear for a charming study of Jester in his favourite place, to encourage her to resume what had once been her passion. So far she had made only a sketchy outline of the friendly old dog.

'Hello there!' The cheery greeting came from the doorway.

'Oh!' Starting in fright Abbie dropped her paintbrush, the light thud it made on the carpet also making her heart leap. Jester merely opened a lazy eyelid. 'Douglas, for goodness sake!' She was angry with her former brother-in-law for scaring the wits out of her and she was deeply disturbed at how easily she was still panicked. She was in a constant state of jittery nerves. Jester growled at Douglas Goodyear and heaved his clumsy old bones off the chair. Abbie patted him to show there was no cause for him to be alarmed.

Douglas came forward holding out an apologetic hand; in the other he had a bunch of russet and gold chrysanthemums. On his unexciting face the horror that his ploy to lift her spirit had not only failed miserably but had cruelly scared her was plain. 'Forgive me, Abbie. I'm such a dolt. The last thing I wanted was to upset you. I thought I'd drop in again, hope you don't mind. Your mother wondered if you're about ready for a drink. I could fetch it in here, if you'd like.' He pointed to the flowers. 'I brought you these. I'll get the maid to see to them.'

Abbie had clamped a hand to her racing heart. She took several deep breaths to become calmer, watching the guilt and sympathy chewing away at Douglas. She lost her irritation. He was such a dear and a comfort to her. He had supported her parents throughout their ordeal too. 'It's very sweet of you to drop in, Douglas. Yes, I would like a cup of tea in here. And thank you for the chrysanths.' She recognized the flowers as from the gardens of his house, where she had formerly been the mistress. Such a lot had happened to her since she had been widowed.

'May I join you for tea?'

'Of course.' Abbie could tolerate little company nowadays but Douglas never strained her. He and Rupert were as chalk and cheese. Polite to a fault but never boring, he never made assumptions or pushed anyone beyond their capabilities. Under his firm but fair military-style directorship Goodyear Publishers was flourishing. Most important to Abbie, he had never questioned her about her abduction.

'I'll be back in a trice.' A minute or two later he carried in a tray of tea and biscuits.

Abbie was curled up on the big leather winged chair stroking Jester's long curly ears. Douglas smiled at her then looked down as he set the tray beside her on a wine table. Unlike Rupert or Jonny Harvey, he was shy with women. Years ago he had been engaged for a brief time. His fiancée had eloped with another man and Douglas had only dated occasionally since then. 'Thank you, Douglas.'

'My pleasure, Abbie.' He drank his tea on his feet in front of the mantelpiece. Since leaving the Army on Rupert's death to take over the company, his duties in the office had denied him the exercise he enjoyed and he didn't care to sit about. One nice thing about Abbie was that she gave little regard to social niceties and he could relax the need to follow them to the letter. She was a woman he admired greatly, intelligent and gifted and not given to endless titivation or the usual female moods. She had been wasted on his superficial brother. Sadly, she was almost lifeless, and thin and shrunken. Her hair was dull and in need of styling, her skin was winter pale and her eyes weary. She was wearing shapeless lounge pyjamas, a thick wool cardigan and crocheted shawl and furry slippers over bed socks. None of that mattered. She was still a lovely woman.

Abbie saw his concerned expression. She realized that in all the weeks he had been a devoted friend to her she had not asked him how he was. She did so now.

'Oh, I'm very well, thank you, Abbie.'

That was it, he never burdened others with long expositions on his own affairs. It was just one of the things she liked about Douglas. He struck an accomplished figure. Today he was not in one of his bespoke suits but elegant tweeds. He didn't come across as exacting but, as always, pleasingly well groomed.

'It's good to see you painting again, Abbie.'

'I didn't manage very much.'

'That doesn't matter. It's a big step forward for you.'

'Yes, it is. I hadn't looked at it like that. Thank you, Douglas. I'd been feeling a resounding failure.'

'Always happy to help, Abbie. It's quite a pleasant day. Would you consider taking a stroll round the garden? I'm sure Mrs Rothwell wouldn't object if you wrapped up really well.'

Abbie had rarely been outside since her release from the infirmary. All she wanted was to stay where she felt safe. To reassure herself she was out of her horrendous prison and back at home. Every morning she was afraid to open her eyes in case she found herself a captive in that stinking tiny room. She knew she should make the effort to get out and about. She would like to walk on her father's arm but the condition of his lungs meant he daren't breathe in any cold air and his crippled feet made walking difficult. He often used a wheelchair these days. Douglas would make an ideal substitute. 'I think I'd like that. And Jester could do with a walk.'

Abbie changed into several warm layers and wool stockings, then stood like a child in the hall while the maid brought her fur hat and coat, fur-lined boots, gloves and woollen scarf. She allowed her mother to help her into them. She was glad to switch off the present and return to the security of being a pampered little girl.

'There.' Honor viewed her when satisfied she wasn't likely to freeze and succumb to pneumonia. 'Be very sure you don't overtax her, Douglas. Keep her out of the wind.'

'Of course,' he replied, elbow out ready for Abbie's arm. He had put on his overcoat. A checked scarf was knotted expertly to complement his trilby hat and leather gloves.

Two walking sticks tapping along the hall announced the arrival from the drawing room of Archie Rothwell on his tripping steps. A little bent from consistently having to favour his chest, his extreme height was evident nevertheless. He was wearing two cardigans and a thick muffler, thanks to Honor's care and caution, and for warmth his thick white hair was kept rather long. Of quiet dignity, his watchful green eyes gleamed with pride on Abbie. 'Enjoy your walk, darling. When you come in we'll have some hot chicken broth ready for you.'

With the doting audience of her parents, the maid and a faithful friend, Abbie felt a rush of emotion, her strongest positive feelings for some time. She wanted to stay under this protection for ever. 'It's like I'm setting off to school on the very first day.' On the verge of tears, she added quickly, 'Off we go then, Douglas.'

With Jester ambling on ahead along the paved and gravel paths, sniffing at stone walls and grass verges, and making friends with the trunks of various trees, Abbie clasped Douglas's arm with both hands and breathed in the gentle air. There was a benevolent sun in a light grey sky, nothing remotely threatening, and the gardens and sheltering woods were reassuringly familiar. She loved the autumn, the changing colours from lush greens to glorious amber, copper, red, bronze and gold, and she was glad to be alive to enjoy this year's splendour. Glad to be able to call 'Good morning, Jackman' to the gardener raking together fallen leaves, someone she had known all her life.

Pausing and lifting his antiquated cap, the whiskery Jackman called back, ''Tis a pleasure to see you out 'n' about, Miss Abbie.'

'You're enjoying this,' Douglas stated with pleasure.

'I am, thanks to you.' They followed a path that divided the lawn. Abbie stopped and gazed up at a solitary monumental oak tree. As a girl she had thought this tree reached all the way up to heaven. Her favourite story had been one about a magic acorn. A little girl had discovered it was the home of a fairy who granted its finder three wishes. Searching with her eyes for acorns scattered on the ground she wished she could go back in time, wished she had never left Ford Farm in a hurry to take that train. She would have been taken ill with the measles there, and although she would have felt uncomfortable about upsetting Jill, Mrs Em would have willingly nursed her until she was well again. And Jill wouldn't have stayed angry with her for long. She had written a pleasant letter to her, wishing her well, and apologizing for her reaction to the mention of Kate's birthday, saying that she would never forget she owed her life to her. Jill had filled her in on all of Kate's amazing progress from timorous mouse to confident butterfly. Kate had written too, mentioning how she enjoyed riding and that she was missing Jonny away working in the Lake District. Abbie had met near disaster in Cornwall but she couldn't altogether say she regretted going to stay there. She had met some delightful people and her experiences before her abduction had shown she'd needed to take stock and change if she was to avoid further heartbreak and risk losing her friends. She had thought she would never see her parents again, never be here again at Oak Tree Warren. She took comfort that the oak tree now casting a protective shadow over her had matured in this spot for over one hundred years, and would be there for another seven hundred. It wouldn't change in her lifetime or, if she had children, for many, many generations to come.

'I should come outside to paint,' she said. 'Start off in the shelter of the summerhouse.'

'Would you like me to fetch your things there?' Douglas asked, pleased at this next sign of Abbie's recovery.

'No, it's all right. I'll know when it's the right time to work again. After what happened to me, Douglas, it's put everything in a different perspective. My career isn't as important to me now. Only my family and the people who really matter to me.'

Douglas hoped he counted as one of those people. She had opened up to him and he chanced a question. 'Are you nervous about facing the world again, Abbie?'

'Yes. I'm very afraid.'

'I'll always be on hand to help you, you know.'

'Thank you. It's one of my comforts knowing I can rely on you.'

'You do everything in your own good time, Abbie. If you ever want to talk...'

Talk? She didn't even want to think about the vile Mitchells, her incarceration, and the indignities they had heaped on her. How she had nearly died. Thank God, at least, she would not have to give evidence in court. The Mitchells were pleading guilty to all charges, but even that was a selfish ploy to receive lighter sentences. At the beginning they had got her to sign what she had thought was the guesthouse register. They had copied her signature and cleared out her bank account. But she could never clear the fear and suffering out of her mind. The wretched couple had stolen more than her possessions and money. They had stolen several weeks of her life and her peace of mind. And they had put her parents through hell and had planned to rob them too. She hated them. In a voice steeped with pain and venom, she blurted out, 'I hate them, Douglas!'

He put his arms around her. It was awful she should bear new anguish but it was good that she had started to unburden herself. He was more than pleased she had done so to him. Abbie was more to him than a friend. She was precious. 'I'm sure you do, Abbie, and with every good reason. I hate them too for hurting you.'

'Will you take me in now, Douglas?'

'Right away.' He allowed her to stay silent while they went back to the house, sensing it was what she needed.

Abbie was shivering under all her wrappings from the effect of her terrible memories. She was so cold. She had no appetite but she would make herself eat every drop of the chicken broth. She badly needed to build up her strength. If she could become well enough to stay outside for long periods she would feel better and gain some peace, and hopefully sleep better and suffer fewer nightmares and flashbacks. Her body, at one time strong and healthy, was totally out of sync.

It occurred to her that her monthly had not happened for some time. Had she had one before leaving Ford Farm? She couldn't remember. Her mind was cloudy and she had shut out a lot of the details of her ordeal and just about everything else until arriving home. She had lain in her own filth at the end of her drugged imprisonment but there had been no sign of a menstrual flow. It could be that the poor state of her health was responsible for her missing periods. Or… She was seized with panic. Had

Mitchell raped her while she was drugged? She had been examined at the infirmary, and although there had been no apparent signs of sexual interference the doctor had told her something. What was it? Her brow furrowed and her head throbbed with the effort to recall. Then she knew. Dear God, she knew! 'I'm afraid it is my duty to inform you, Miss Rothwell, that you are pregnant.' Pregnant! The word, the fact screamed at her. She had screamed back at the doctor and refused to listen to him any more, and begged him not to tell her mother when she arrived, warning him she would sue him for breach of patient confidentiality if he did. She was pregnant. My God, she was pregnant. Unable to cope in her distress, her mind had blocked out the vile reality. But she had to face it now.

She was squeezing on Douglas's arm, hurting him, and he was aware of her anguish, that she was weakening. 'Abbie, would you like me to carry you the rest of the way?'

'I think I can walk. Take me in quickly, Douglas, and ask my mother to phone the doctor. I need to see him at once.'

–

'Well?' Abbie fearfully prompted Dr Ellerson Fellowes as he closed his medical case. They were in her spacious bedroom. Honor had wanted to be there but Abbie had insisted on seeing the doctor alone. 'How far along am I?'

Ellerson Fellowes, heading towards retirement age, learned and kindly, removed his gold-rimmed spectacles. Abbie was sitting on the bed. He was perched on the dressing-table stool. 'You're sixteen weeks, Abbie. The pregnancy will soon be showing.'

'Sixteen…?' Gripping the counterpane, she forced her mind to operate clearly, making calculations. She let out a tremendous sigh as some of the appalling disgust drained away. 'Then I wasn't raped. Thank God. I had a brief fling with someone from Hennaford.' It was Jonny's baby. They had slipped up. It was still a dreadful thing. 'Dr Fellowes, I don't want this baby. If it had been my abductor's child I wouldn't even have been able to bear the thought of it inside my body. I'd hate it. I'd go mad. I would have ripped it out of me rather than give birth to it. What am I going to do?'

Fellowes went to her and took a firm hold on her imploring hands. 'First of all, Abbie, you need to calm down. Have you lost contact with the father? Did he let you down? Is that why you were suddenly eager to leave Cornwall?'

'No, it was none of those. The father is a good man.' Too weak to stay sitting up, she lay down on the bed and closed her eyes for a few moments. It was Jonny's baby. An accident, but when she thought deeper about it, the child was an innocent factor conceived in lust and joy. It was not something vile and corrupt living inside her. 'It's not so bad now. As long as it wasn't that beastly man's… I can't even remember what he looked like, thank God.'

'Do you think the father would stand by you?'

'He's not the marrying sort but he would stand by me, I'm confident of that.'

'Then may I suggest you get in touch with him as soon as possible. If marriage is on the cards, then the sooner the better. It could be just the new start you need, Abbie. Or another possibility could be to go away and have the baby adopted, then you could put it all in the past.'

'I need to think about it for a while before I do anything, doctor.'

'That is wise, but don't let it be for very long.'

'I don't want my parents to know just yet. Could you tell them I came over all weak? It isn't a lie.' On a thought, Abbie sat up urgently. 'Doctor, I've been malnourished for some time. Will it have damaged the baby?'

'It's a possibility, Abbie, although not necessarily. We would have to monitor your pregnancy more carefully than usual.'

Abbie lay down again and put her hands over her abdomen. Was that a slight swelling she could feel? If she had died her baby would have died too. She had hung on to her life and suddenly the well-being of her baby was important to her. She caressed the place where it was growing and it felt as much a vital part of her being as she was of it. If all went well it would be a handsome child. She would keep this child. She certainly would not marry Jonny. It wouldn't work. She didn't want another failed marriage. Her parents would stand by her. They wouldn't care about the social stigma.

She had survived and been returned to them, they would be delighted to be gaining a grandchild.

She rose from the bed, a little energy flowing through her. 'Actually, Dr Fellowes, I am ready to speak to my parents.' Douglas would be waiting anxiously too. She didn't mind him learning her news. 'Would you like to escort me down?'

Chapter Nineteen

Tony Viant was loafing in his mother's raggedy chair, his feet up on the table, chain smoking and tapping ash on the floor. Things were different now, thanks to him. He had ended his detestable mother's reign. There was no need to plan to escape. He saw Delia differently. She had become haggard and bad tempered. He wanted no personal involvement with her. He would never risk another woman treating him with contempt and keeping him down.

From the other side of the gloomy kitchen Delia glared at him with disgust. Although he hadn't got any jobs today he was in his work clothes. She hadn't been able to get them off him for weeks to launder and she could smell his offensive odours from where she sat at the table, the pages of the *West Briton* spread out on the scrubbed wood for easier reading. This was her only pleasure, to read the local news after the men had all leafed through the weekly newspaper. 'Would you stop doing that, Tony!'

'What?'

'Making the place dirty with ash.'

'What does it matter? Father don't care. He's too busy giving Dulcie Tregaskis a regular seeing-to nowadays. Wouldn't be surprised if he marries that juicy widow and moves out. Hope he does, there'd be more room for the rest of us then. And Sidney don't give a tinker's cuss what happens here.'

'I care! But that counts for nothing, doesn't it?' Her life was better in some ways without Biddy's invidious harping – she got the house to herself most days – but in other ways it was just as bad or worse. 'I was so ashamed when the district nurse called first thing this morning – not that anyone here bothers to ask how I'm progressing. Good job I can get all my treatment free with this new National Health Service. I could have this baby in Redruth Hospital, you know. Wish I could, it would be wonderful to get away from you lot for a few days somewhere nice and properly clean. The nurse must have thought the place a hovel. I went to bed early last night and when I got up I couldn't believe the mess you men had made. Coats on the floor. Fag ends tossed about, crumbs all over the table and dirty crockery because you'd helped yourselves to food, which you had no right to! It isn't you lot who has to stretch the rations and queue up for fresh food or try to eke out the money. And there was beer bottles everywhere, the place stank like a brewery. Worst of all, one of you had been sick!'

'You're turning into a bleddy grouch,' Tony muttered, tossing the stub of his smoke into the black fender.

Delia sighed in frustration. Much more of this and she would give up trying to keep the wretched place clean. 'Well, it's no wonder, is it? You lot treat me as no more than a skivvy. I'm getting near my due date and it's all I can do to get any of you to fetch in a bucket of water. Even you don't bother to help me any more. And I don't get as much as a penny to myself to buy a woman's magazine. If your father moves out there would be one less wage coming in, have you thought of that? Sidney's in a bad mood about money as it is. Now your mother's dead he's taken to going out drinking and he's grumbling there isn't enough coming in because work's been slack for you lately. He never stops moaning about the cost of your mother's funeral because she had no insurance. The undertaker's not been paid yet.'

'Well, he's got a bloody cheek! He's the one who's wasting money. He should act more responsible, with you to support and a kid on the way.'

'Don't say anything like that to him, for God's sake. I'm the one who gets it in the neck when he gets teasy or quarrelsome.' Delia knew a dart of fear. Just like Tony, Sidney had grown swanky now he was no longer ruled by Biddy. He didn't beat her quite so often but sometimes there was a terrible evil look in his eye.

'Don't worry. I know when to keep my mouth shut.' Tony wouldn't confront his brother. He may have killed his mother without a second thought or a moment of guilt since, but Sidney was bigger and stronger and had a brutal way of grinding his fists in when involved in a fight. Tony had no money to go to the pub tonight. The other drink he was partial to was Camp Coffee. 'Make me some coffee.'

'Don't be so lazy! I'm not your slave.'

'All right!' He leapt to his feet. 'I'll do it my bloody self.' He put the kettle on the hob of the slab and went to the larder.

Delia got up when he started pushing things about impatiently on her tidy shelves. 'What are you doing?'

'Where the hell is it? The coffee?'

'There's not much in here. Can't you see for yourself that there's no bottle of coffee?'

'Why the hell didn't you say so in the first place?' he snapped, pushing her aside. 'Why haven't you got no coffee in?'

Sidney, who had been changing upstairs for a trip to the pub, had entered from the stairs door. He had heard Tony's angry complaint and witnessed Delia tottering to keep her balance. He stormed up to Tony and hauled him away from the larder by the front of his shirt. 'You dare speak to my wife like that and shove her around, you bastard! Do something like that again and I'll rip your eyes out. If you want coffee buy it out of your own money, when you can be bothered to earn some that is, you lazy runt.' He thrust Tony away and he fell backwards, hitting his back on the slab and ending up in a huddle on the rush mat.

Pain shot up Tony's spine. Reminded of how he had coldly murdered his mother he was furious and unafraid. He was too winded to get up but he balled his fists and thrust them up. He rasped between laboured breaths, 'You got no right to accuse me. I never stop looking for work. I sometimes bring in more than you do because I don't booze my wages away. And you treat Delia worse than dirt. Does she know you're shagging her younger sister? You'll have two of 'em here soon with big bellies.'

'You dirty, rotten—' Sidney lashed out with his boot at Tony's guts.

Tony howled like an animal and grabbed himself there, doubling over.

Whirling round, Sidney faced Delia. Her eyes were wide in shock and she was clutching the wobbly dresser.

'He's lying. I've been nowhere near your sister. Your father would take his shotgun to me for a start.'

Eager to show she was on his side, afraid she would be the next to suffer violence, Delia nodded. 'I believe you, Sidney. He had no right to say any of that to you.' She took it from Sidney's manner that although he wasn't getting sex off her sister, who wouldn't do such a thing anyway, he was seeing someone else. She didn't care about that. He wasn't bothering her so often in bed now. The baby inside her shifted about, something she hated. She had been disappointed when the district nurse had said all seemed to be going well. Delia couldn't stop hoping the baby would die. She hoped it would be born dead. Then she could get away from this wretched place. It wasn't just a woeful thought. She meant it with all her heart. If the baby was delivered safely she would likely have another the following year and then more, and she would be more and more trapped and dragged down. Sidney straightened his cuffs. 'Did he hurt you?'

'No.'

'I'm off out then.'

Go out and never come back, she thought, as he went to the hooks on the back door and put on his jacket. He put his thumb on the latch.

Simmering with rage, Tony had got up on his knees. Grabbing the poker, he used the arm of the chair to heave himself up. 'You'll pay for what you just done, Sidney. No one bullies me and gets away with it.'

While Delia edged to the stairs door ready to run safely up out of the way, Sidney spun round on his toes. He laughed to see his brother coming towards him brandishing the poker. 'What do you think you're going to do with that, runt?'

'Finish you off, you bastard, that's what. I've done it before!' Tony halted, stepping sideways from foot to foot. His face was a twisted mask of hatred.

'You've what?' Sidney sneered. 'You're not capable of taking sweets off a baby. I admit I let Mother bully me but she had you quaking in your boots!'

'Not at the end she didn't.' Tony tapped the poker on the palm of his hand. 'She fell and was hurt but I made sure she didn't get the chance to torment me ever again.'

Delia gasped. 'What do you mean?'

'Are you saying you killed her?' Sidney demanded. It was laughable, until it struck him something was giving Tony the courage to challenge him like this.

'I pushed her head back against the oven door. The old bitch deserved it.'

The confession made Delia fear for her life. If Tony could commit murder and if he won a fight against Sidney, he might kill them both now they knew about his crime.

Sidney saw the crazed look in Tony's eyes. Normally he'd have no trouble beating him senseless but there was no guarantee of that against the sort of terrible strength and intent Tony had now. He altered his stance and put on a placatory smile. 'You're right there, little brother. The old bitch had it coming to her for years and you were the one brave enough to do it. You've done us all a great favour. Look, there's no need for us to quarrel, is there? You've made life easier for all of us, and we should all thank you. Eh, Delia?'

She nodded, wanting only to get away but too frozen in horror.

'I'm sorry I swiped and kicked you, Tony. Wouldn't have done it if I'd known all the facts. It's worth every penny of the funeral money. And you needn't worry about that. I've got an idea how to get hold of some good hard cash.'

Still expecting his brother to fly at him and try to disarm him, Tony was suspicious. He kept the poker at a hostile height. 'Are you really sorry?'

Sidney spread his hand over his heart. 'On my life. I'm sorry I hurt you, Tony. Let me make it up to you. Why don't you come down the pub with me for a drink and a game of darts? There's a bloke there who deals on the black market. I'll ask him to get some coffee for you. Eh, Tony? Delia will fetch you a clean shirt. What do you say?'

Sense softened Tony's murderous rage. If he killed Sidney violently he wouldn't get away with it like he had his mother's death. 'All right, but I want to be treated with respect from now on.'

'You will be, you have my promise.' Sidney would have tried a handshake but he was worried Tony might strike out at him with the poker. 'We should all make the effort to get along. We're brothers, after all. It was the old woman who caused the strife. She liked to pitch us one against the other. We could all be happy, and the baby will have a better home to grow up in than what we had. Eh, Tony?'

Tony was thinking about Sidney's promises. If all this could be put behind them then perhaps life really could be good. On the other hand his secret was out. Delia was unlikely to tell the police but it made Sidney dangerous. Life would be so much better without him in the picture… 'All right, I'll go with you.'

Delia went up to Tony's tiny room – Kate's old room – wishing her sister-in-law were still here to take the strain off her. She took a white shirt out of the rickety chest of drawers. The new arrangement probably wouldn't go as far as making things better for her. If only the brothers had fought outside and killed each other, that would have been wonderful. Then if her father-in-law remarried and left she would have the place to herself and could take in lodgers for an income.

Tony and Sidney were shuffling round the kitchen, each still wary of the other. 'You mentioned you could get your hands on some money. You planning a robbery?' Tony said. His newly formed confidence made him again consider stealing from old Miss Chiltern.

'Nothing like that. It's strictly legit,' Sidney grinned meanly. 'It involves our little sister.'

Chapter Twenty

Humming contentedly to herself, Kate was grooming Cully after taking an hour's ride. The keen wind had blown drizzly rain against her face but she had enjoyed every invigorating minute. This evening there was the final play rehearsal and she was looking forward to it and the actual performance at the weekend. The cast and support people had remarked that she was a far cry from the shy little maid she had been when they began. The only one missing was Jonny. The father of one of the pupils had taken his part. Alan was a really good actor, his natural wit perfect for the portrayal of a duped Robin Hood as Maid Marian got the better of him at every turn. He would steal the show. He had other pleasant qualities, thoughtfulness and patience just two of them. Kate had noticed he was a ready listener, never cutting off anyone sharing a concern or just an ordinary piece of news.

Dale Patterson had pounced on her one evening. 'The play is a bit short of bystanders, Kate. For the market and the archery contest scenes. Fancy taking a small part in each?'

An instant rise of nerves had made her stammer, 'N–no. I don't think so.'

'Don't be shy.' Alan, who always seemed to be close by her, had thrown in the warmest, most cajoling smile.

'You'll be in costume and you'll feel different then. You'd only have to shout your wares during the market scene and stand about for the other one. I'll be there both times. You'll be fine. Go on, Kate. Give it a go. Anyway, we're all going to be a bit nervous, but you'll love it when it all gets started, honestly.' It was Alan's infectious enthusiasm and his promise to guide her through that made her succumb in the end. She regretted it as soon as she got home, but his arrival at the farm the next, and subsequent, evenings to help her rehearse, quickly soothed away the worst of her nerves. It was good having Alan as a friend, and being with him.

Kate had hung her raincoat and rain hat over the stall door. They were thrown at her feet, making Cully falter and toss her head. 'What the… Denny! How could you be so stupid? You know it's dangerous to suddenly alarm a pony.' This was just the latest nasty trick he had played on her. Jill had noticed his growing animosity towards her and had warned him to behave. Because he was no longer pulling his weight on the farm, Tom had threatened him with the sack.

'I hope you don't expect me to muck out the stables after you.' Denny had taken up smoking and struck a match on the stable wall, cupping his hands while lighting up and tightening the corners of his eyes in what, she supposed, he thought was a macho manner. He looked silly and it made Kate want to laugh. 'You prance around here like you're Lady Muck nowadays. I've got enough to do.'

'It's my afternoon off so I'm not expected to do any work. And don't be so pathetic.' Kate carried on with the currycomb and ignored him, but not for long.

Denny draped an arm over Cully's neck, bringing himself in very close to her. 'How am I being pathetic?' He had added a drawl to his voice, copied off the movies by the sound of it.

Kate sighed with exasperation. He was more of a pest than a horse fly. 'You should just hear yourself. You've turned into a complete idiot.'

'And you've turned into a hoity-toity bitch.' His tone was the same and she wondered why there was no hostility or challenge. One quick glance answered her question. He was eyeing her up. 'But a very pretty one.'

He touched a tendril of damp hair on her forehead and she swiped his hand away. 'Have you gone mad? What do you think you're up to? Get away from me. Go on, clear off. Denny, you're no screen idol, if that's what you think. You're a country bumpkin and not a very good one at that. Stop making a fool of yourself and for goodness sake grow up!'

'You little bitch! Who the hell do you think you are? I'll show you exactly what I am.' Lightning quick, he grabbed her round the waist, trying to thrust his face close to hers to force a kiss. With Cully whinnying and pacing in alarm, Kate fought against him and twisted her face away, but he was strong and managed to get a hand on the back of her neck. He smacked his open mouth on her cheek, dragging a wet trail towards her lips. Gritting her teeth with rage Kate jabbed the currycomb into his side.

Denny bawled out, letting her go and dashing both hands to the bleeding wound. 'You bitch!' he roared, using the foulest swear words. 'You nasty little cripple. You'll pay for that!'

Kate couldn't keep her balance and fell to the ground, terrified Cully would kick out and she would receive a dangerous blow. Scrabbling away from Cully's range, she heard Denny howl and shriek and thought he had received a just punishment from the pony's hooves. She heard a familiar snarl. Then her brother shouting.

'Go near my sister again, boy, and I'll grind you into dust!' Sidney yelled in an ugly voice. Sprawled on the straw, Kate watched in horror as he pounded his fists into Denny's jaw, chest and gut. Denny hit the cobbles, curled up and whimpering. 'You'd better give your notice in here, sonny, or I'll have you up for attempted rape. I won't have you near my sister again. Got it?'

Denny stayed in the foetal position, his arms wrapped round his head, blubbering and sobbing. Sidney used the toe of his steel-capped boot to turn him over roughly. 'Got it!'

'Ye-es,' Denny bawled. 'Yes!'

'Good. Now clear off and never come back.'

Kate got up on shaky legs and settled the fitful Cully. It was horrible to see Denny crawling away on his hands and knees, his clothes wet and fouled, until he found the strength to haul himself up and slink away, still doubled over. Her eyes were wide with shock and disgust when Sidney turned to her. His hard features softened but Kate thought it an act. 'You all right, Kate? Did he hurt you?'

'Why did you come?' she demanded, shutting Cully in her stall and moving off towards the house. The family needed to know what had happened and she needed them around if she was to face her bullying brother. He was wearing his demob suit, overcoat and best cap, and for once was cleanshaven, but his sudden presence here, even though smartened up, could only mean trouble.

Sidney brought her to a halt. 'Kate, I've come with bad news.'

This was unexpected. 'What's happened? Has Delia lost the baby?'

'She's fine. It's Mother. She's dead.'

Her immediate reaction was not grief or sadness but an awful kind of dread and horror. It took her back to the terrible day of her grandmother's death. 'How?'

'An accident. She fell, hit her head and pegged out within minutes. None of us are sorry, Kate. It's a lot pleasanter at home. In fact we're all quite content. Father goes out of an evening now, he's courting the Tregaskis widow.'

'So her death happened a while ago. Why bother to tell me now?' There was obviously a selfish reason.

'Why should you be expected to come to the old woman's send-off after she'd turned you out, we all thought. We had her buried quick, wanted it over and done with. But Delia kept saying she thought you had the right to know. It gives you the chance to pop home now and see the baby if you want to.'

'Why should I want to do that? None of you wanted me, not just Mother.' Kate couldn't keep the bitterness out of her voice.

'Yeh, I admit that.' Sidney looked away, as if ashamed. 'But it was Mother always nagging at us that made us jumpy and argumentative. We men hate to admit it but we was all scared of her.'

'There's no excuse for the way you treated me...' She was stung to fury, still doubtful of his intentions. 'You enjoyed taunting me, hurting me, and you enjoyed telling me I was no longer wanted. Why have you really come? It has to be money. There can be no other reason why you'd bother to come here. You're after money, aren't you?' She started walking again.

Sidney was surprised at how much she had changed from the frightened girl who had begged him not to leave her behind in Hennaford. He would have to be careful. It would be worth it if he could convince her he wanted to play happy families. She was well set up here, she could be pumped for a few quid every now and then and he had just the right ploy. He walked along beside her, hands in his pockets. 'Yeh, I admit it, I did enjoy it. I'm a bit of a hard case, don't s'pose I'll ever change my ways altogether. Father and Tony were just weak, would do anything for a quiet life. It was Mother who made me so shirty. She'd have put two stones to fight. I'm glad you never went that way, Kate. I'll also admit we're finding it hard to meet the funeral expenses. But the main reason I'm here is because of Delia. You and her got along all right. She's lonely. Her family has disowned her because I got her into trouble and she hasn't really got any friends. She's scared about having the baby, not long to go now before the birth, and she's got no woman to give her advice and help her out afterwards. She keeps saying if only Kate was still here. Now I'm not suggesting you move back in, of course. I just thought you might like to see Delia and the baby. After all, it'll be your niece or nephew. What do you say, Kate? Can you help us out with the funeral money and would you like to see Delia?'

There was no way that she would ever trust Sidney. He was rotten to the roots of his soul. But she had been friendly with Delia and the baby was just an innocent little soul. She felt a stirring of interest in her niece or nephew. Yet it was probably unwise to keep in touch with her family. She had to test Sidney's motives. 'Can I think about it?' She expected him to fly into a temper or to try further cajoling. He had always hated not getting his own way at once.

'Yeh, you do that. Thanks for listening to me, Kate. Write to Delia, will you? Tell her what you decide. She'd really like to hear from you. P'raps you'd like to come over one Sunday for tea.' He peered round the yard. No one was about. He was glad of that. He could get off without a confrontation with one or more of Kate's mentors that would perhaps lose him the ground he hoped he'd gained with her. 'I'd better be off. Will that boy give you any more trouble?' Kate could hardly believe his placid attitude, but it didn't mean he wasn't up to something. She had to think about all this but first she wanted him out of the way before he was seen. 'No, I shouldn't think after what you did to Denny he'd dare show his face here again. Give my regards to Delia. Goodbye, Sidney.' She was praying he'd just leave.

'Bye, Kate. I'm sorry about the past.'

He strode away, head up in his usual conceited manner. 'Sorry, my foot,' she muttered. She crept after him, keeping out of sight to make sure he really did leave. In the lane, he lit up a smoke and got on his bicycle, which he'd left propped against the hedge. Would he scowl and go off in a mood? He went off whistling cheerfully, by way of the back lanes. Hopefully, he wouldn't be seen by Tom or anyone else about the property.

Kate trudged back. The ordeal with Denny suddenly taking its toll, and not wanting Jill to see her trembling and flushed, she sat on the bottom step of the goat house. It wasn't wise to stay here on cold wet stone in the steady drizzle. Jill would fuss she'd catch a chill, but she had to clear her thoughts before she went in. She bent her head and brought her hands up to her face. Sidney's timely appearance had saved her from a further struggle with Denny, but why did he have to show up at all? She had hoped to put her family behind her for good. She had no love for her brothers or father and never would have, and who could blame her? But she felt sorry for Delia and couldn't bring herself to dismiss the baby. She knew how it felt to be rejected. Even if conditions were better at Tregony, poor Delia and the baby couldn't look forward to having much of a life. What should she do? Write to Delia? Send some money towards her mother's funeral costs? Did she have a moral obligation to help her family? It would almost certainly open up the way to more money being scrounged off her. She could ignore Sidney's visit and do nothing and hope no one would get in touch again. But what about the poor baby? It was her own flesh and blood. It didn't deserve to be rejected by an aunt who was in better circumstances. She had her grandmother's secret savings and parting with a little of it would cause her no hardship, while it would mean a lot to Delia and the baby.

If Jonny was here she would ask his advice, but she already knew what she would do. She couldn't ignore Delia and the baby. She would tell Jill that Sidney had been here and how he had hurt Denny. And she would have to mention what Denny had done to her. She didn't believe he was trying to rape her, just to hurt and humiliate her. He had definitely lost his job and could be charged with assault. She didn't want that. She would feel the shame, as if it was her fault, and wouldn't be able to face the villagers again, or Alan. She'd hate to forsake her friendship with Alan. Oh God, this had been such a nice day, now it was completely tainted. Thoughts about her mother's death crowded in on her. In her mind she heard her mother screaming. Not because of her accident but at herself throughout her life, as her mother had always done, angry and hateful, shouting and abusing her. She'd had no right to treat her like that. She had been her mother. Mothers were supposed to love and care for their children, not use them like despised worthless slaves.

Then she saw herself back in her grandmother's cottage and Granny Moses was shouting and bawling at her on the day she had died. 'Stupid girl! This soup is scalding hot. I've burnt my mouth. Why didn't you warn me? You're worse than useless. Just like your mother. Neither of you care about me.' Granny Moses banged her soup spoon on the table, again and again. Each time Kate winced and blinked. The soup wasn't too hot, the old woman was complaining again for nothing, just to be beastly, to make her feel small. Her stomach wound itself into knots and she couldn't eat herself, just watch Granny Moses shovel in mouthful after mouthful of soup while stuffing in bread at the same time.

Then Granny Moses was dropping her spoon and clutching at her throat and banging on her chest. Gesticulating wildly with her hands. Kate watched as if seeing it in a dream. Granny Moses was making dreadful noises and trying to spit at her. She was trying to retch, to spit out her food as if accusing Kate of poisoning her. Her face was changing from red to puce to purple. Kate was fascinated with the colours. Fascinated that Granny Moses was actually afraid. And seemingly pleading with her instead of barracking her. With her fingers clawing her throat, Granny Moses thrust back her chair with her legs and shot up, twisting and turning as she came at her. She was like a grotesque monster, terrifying and evil. Kate sprang up and backed away. Granny Moses was going to hurt her. Take her hands from her own throat and put them round hers. Choke the life out of her. Kill her.

Granny Moses was falling, thumping down to the floor, twisting and contorting, her legs thrashing about, her face dark with corruption, her eyes bulging as if about to pop out of their sockets. She stiffened, jerked and became still, her hands flopped down from her throat. In her insanity she had killed herself. It said in the Bible that the wicked would die at their own hands and that was exactly what had happened to Granny Moses.

Long moments passed before Kate realized that her grandmother had been choking to death on too much food and had been pleading for her help. Appalled at how she had shrunk back and left her to battle, terrified, on her own, she edged towards the lump of a body to see if Granny Moses was breathing, then recoiled at the grue-some sight of her misshapen features and clawed hands.

Huddling on the steps of the goat house Kate expe-rienced again every vile shudder of horror and disgust with herself she had felt at the time. She knew that her mind, unable to cope with the terrible truth, had pushed it into a darkly veiled corner, making her forget she had watched the revolting scene without lifting a finger, had even retreated from her grandmother. She had screamed, 'I'll get someone, Granny!' and had fled from the house shouting for help.

Now she knew the source of her nightmares, the reality that had been trying to break through. Oh, God in heaven, it made her a murderer! She could hear her grandmother's accusing voice. 'Murderer. Murderer!' She clamped her hands over her ears and rocked, trying to rid herself of the mocking sound. She took her hands away. There were no voices, except for the usual animal and bird life braying and twittering on the farm. She couldn't stand what she had done, watching and waiting for Granny Moses to die. She sprang up and ran, awkwardly with her limp, stumbling and righting herself, out into the lane and down the hill. She had to get away. She couldn't stay with the kind people who had taken her in when she wasn't the good person they thought she was but a cold-hearted murderer.

Alan had bought a second-hand motor car, a pre-war Morris 8, and had driven it home from the buyer's house at Perranporth. Proud he had saved the purchase price himself, it would give him a reason to go on the extra yards to Ford Farm and show it to Kate. If she agreed to take a ride with him some time, it was just the thing to get her away from the Harveys' ever-watchful eyes, to give him the chance to build up something closer and meaningful with her. It was what he wanted above all else. He was crazy about her. Things were easier now Jonny Harvey had taken himself off. He had been strangely possessive of Kate. Jill and Tom hadn't seemed to notice his inappropriate behaviour towards her. Alan had been about to have a quiet word with Tom and if necessary he would have challenged Harvey. Harvey had better watch out if he started anything of the kind when he got back. He should know better. It was bad form, a gigolo hanging about an inexperienced girl. He wasn't Kate's type nor she his, surely he must know that. Mind you, it was all too easy to fall in love with Kate. He had himself. He wasn't as religious as his mother but he prayed morning and night that the day would soon dawn when she'd return his feelings. He'd wait and hope no matter how long it took.

Kate was hurrying down the hill. It was the wrong direction. She was heading towards the village, and the other way led to Ford House and Keresyk where there was too much of a risk of her being seen. An unfamiliar motor car was crossing the ford. Oh no! It pulled in to the grass verge and someone got out. Through the haze of tears stinging her eyes she made out a man waving to her. This was the last thing she wanted and she veered off for the nearest field. She clambered over the gate, then as best she could squelched through rows of cauliflowers, the wet earth clogging her boots. She slipped and plummeted to her knees, scrabbled to her feet and went on. She was making for the moors, to hide among the scrubby bushes and willow and gorse. It was the only thing in her head, to get away and be alone.

Someone was calling to her but all she could hear was the wind in her ears. She was caught from behind. She was struggling to get away from someone a second time and in her horror and panic she screamed and screamed. 'Let me go! Let me go!'

'Kate! It's all right. I want to help you.'

It was a deep caring voice. 'Jonny!' She went limp. Only he could help her now. She let him turn her round and hold her against him, feeling the shelter of his strong arms.

'It's me, Alan. I was coming to see you to show you my new car. Kate, what's the matter? Why are you running off like this? You can trust me. Whatever's wrong, please let me help you.'

She was disappointed that it wasn't Jonny but Alan was just as trustworthy and understanding. She went quiet and rigid, letting him support her.

'I'll take you home,' he said.

'No! Please not there. I don't want Jill to see me like this.'

'OK. We'll stay here, or I could take you somewhere in the car.'

'No. I don't want to go anywhere. I don't know what to do,' she wailed.

Alan took off his coat and cloaked it round her shoulders. He was frightened for her. What had happened to bring her to this? 'Kate, it's all right. We'll stay here for as long as you like. Tell me why you're so upset. You need to tell someone. I promise it won't go any further.'

She had to tell someone or she'd go mad. 'I've done something terrible, Alan,' she blurted out with a gulping sob.

'I'm sure you haven't, Kate. You couldn't possibly do any such thing. But tell me what you mean.'

'I – I killed my grandmother. There, I've said it. You'll think me terrible now.'

'I'd never think badly of you,' he soothed. 'It wasn't your fault the old lady choked to death, Kate. There's no need to blame yourself. There was nothing you could do.'

'But you don't understand.' She looked up at him from desperate eyes. 'She was choking and at first I just sat at the table watching, then I jumped up and backed away from her. I did nothing to help her, Alan. She was dying and I just let it happen. I killed her.'

'But you didn't kill her. Think about it, really think about it, Kate. What was going through your head at the time?'

'I thought it was a dream. I was scared. I was scared of her. I thought she was coming after me. I forgot all about it until a short time ago, after my brother turned up to tell me my mother had died and it all came flooding back.'

'There you are then. You didn't wish her dead while she was choking, did you? You're not like that, Kate. You're good and kind and wonderful. Your grandmother treated you like a slave yet you kept your patience and did all you could for her. You didn't kill her, Kate, my love. You didn't even hurt her. I read the coroner's report in the *Western Morning News*. She choked on a large mouthful of food. It was wedged in her throat. Even if a doctor had been there he couldn't have saved her. You've done nothing wrong. You don't need to punish yourself with these guilty feelings.'

'But I could have tried to do something to save her, Alan.'

'You were in shock and you were scared. No one could have done anything when they're like that. It was your grandmother's time to die. It's as simple as that. It gave you the chance of a new life. Don't let old memories ruin it for you. Jill and Tom would hate that.' The horror seemed to be leaving her, although doubt was filling her beautiful eyes. It would take a while longer to convince herself she wasn't to blame for the tragedy. 'I'm sorry you've suffered again, Kate, and sorry about your mother. You've had an awful time. Can I take you home now? Jill will understand everything. She'll say exactly the same as I have.'

She nodded. Her home and security was what she wanted now. Thanks to Alan she was ready to go. She pushed her arm through his, needing his help to trudge back through the field and needing him near. 'There's something else.'

'What's that?' he said gently.

She told him about Denny grabbing her and how Sidney had beaten him.

'Oh, Kate, that's terrible.' He put a hand over her hand, making a mental note to have more than a few choice words with Denny James. 'You didn't deserve any of this. Don't worry, I'll help you through it.'

'Thanks, Alan.' Her confidence crushed, she was glad he was with her.

Chapter Twenty-One

Alan enclosed Kate's hand in his. 'You'll be fine, Kate. You can do this,' he whispered. The play was in progress. A castle scene had finished and the scenery was swiftly being changed for the market scene. 'There will be lots of us on stage together.'

Her 'big' moment had nearly arrived and she was trembling a little. She squeezed back on his warm flesh, trying to ignore the jitters in her tummy. Her peasant's costume covered her feet but she wasn't too bothered about her limp. Alan had persuaded her not to duck out of the play. 'Don't let them win, Kate,' he'd said. 'Your family, or Denny. They're not worth it and you are worth so much more. Believe it, believe in yourself. All of us who care about you do.' It had taken an effort for her to reach this point, but here she was, thanks to Alan. She wouldn't allow the past to keep its cruel grip on her life any more. Jonny would have said, 'You have a future. Reach for it.'

'Jill and Tom will be proud of you,' Alan said. 'I'm proud of you, Kate.'

'Thanks.'

'You'll steal the show.'

'No, I won't,' she laughed softly. 'You have already and no one deserves it more.'

A minute later she was facing the seated villagers, with a laden straw basket on her hip. 'Butter and cheese! The very finest!' She'd done it, got her lines out. It was so much easier to repeat them and wander about, helping to make the scene look busy. Alan had been right, once her nerves had settled she got a wonderful high feeling, as if she could do anything in the world. She was eager to return to the stage when it was time for the archery scene.

At the final curtain call, to thunderous applause, Mr Trevean shouted out, 'Well done, Kate! Good to see 'ee up there.' Mr Trevean couldn't have heard very much of the play, but it meant everything to her to receive his good wishes. Many others congratulated her that night. She was a full member of the village now.

—

Dear Jonny,

I hope you are well. Thanks for your message to me on Tom and Jill's postcard. I'm glad you're enjoying taking photos of those big lakes and hills.

It sounds really nice there. I go out riding a lot on Cully. The play went off well. I actually took a small part in it. I was so nervous at first but I really enjoyed it. It's a pity you missed it. Anyway, you will be back for the wedding. It will be nice to see you again.

All the best, from Kate.

Jonny lay on his back in his hotel room re-reading the postcard he had received that morning. He had been hoping Kate would get hold of his address and write to him. It was just a few plain and simple words in her careful writing but as important to him as the breath in his body. It meant she was thinking about him. It was what he needed to ease him off to sleep after the day's long trek capturing the magnificent scenery hereabouts. Wherever he went, on hillside or lake shore, he planned to take Kate some day. Aunt Em and Perry's concerns for Kate were understandable, but he really had changed and he hoped they would see that.

He had shunned all female company here although there had been opportunities for casual sex on this trip. That sort of encounter meant nothing to him now. He had faced up to the seriousness of love. What he felt for Kate wasn't just some temporary fancy. The old days of avoiding a lifetime's commitment with a woman were over. He was pleased about it, relieved, and proud of it. He loved Kate with a force that threatened to consume him. He loved the very hint of her. He could take every single second apart and it was Kate who dominated each of them. From any distance he was able to picture her as if she was in his very presence. She was a living ghost who haunted him. When Kate was a little older, he prayed no one would object to him forming something strong and lasting and wonderful with her.

Tomorrow he would travel on to Lincolnshire and see Abbie, and Archie and Honor, the two close friends from his boyhood. Honor had seemed cautious over the telephone but had said they would be delighted to have him stay for a couple of days, and that Abbie was in much better health. Afterwards, it was back to Cornwall for Louisa's wedding. And back to Kate.

–

The maid showed him into the drawing room at Oak Tree Warren. 'I'll fetch madam from the morning room, sir. Mr Rothwell is in the study.'

Jonny wandered about the long room, approving of its combination of antique seats, tables and paintings with modern lighting and sundries. He took interest in the sepia photographs of Victorian and Edwardian Rothwells. And a monochrome studio portrait of Archie as he'd never seen him before, in naval uniform, upright, vital and distinguished. He admired snaps of Abbie at various stages of growing up. There was a laughing depiction of her that he had taken himself on Perranporth beach, paddling on the shore, the wind in her hair. A free-spirited Abbie then, his lover for a while. How would he find her? He hoped they could resume their former easy friendship.

Hearing the approach of walking sticks he hurried to the door to see Archie. Honor was with him, his faithful and loving mate, guiding him by the elbow. Jonny's intention to cast them an exuberant greeting died away. Seeing them both took him back to the days when he, as a four-year-old, had been wrested away from his mother, struggling to adapt to a new situation during the uncertainties of the Great War. Uncle Alec had seized him from his home and it had taken Jonny a while to realize it had been for the best; then Uncle Alec had become his mentor and his hero. For a second, part of him wanted those days again. He wanted not to see his old friend Archie ageing prematurely, stooped, breathing heavily, shaky on his war-ravaged feet and needing to sit down.

'My dear boy,' Archie said in a gasp. 'I've seen photos of you over the years. It was easy to see you had grown into a fine young man, but you're a sight above my expectations. Isn't he, darling?'

'He is indeed,' Honor replied, her usual pacific smile in evidence. 'Welcome to Oak Tree Warren, Jonny. Would you mind?' She indicated the wheelchair kept in the hall.

'Yes, of course.' He found his voice and feet in a rush and manoeuvred the latest in wheeled conveyances for invalids so that Archie, with some help, could ease himself down in it. Now Archie's hands were free Jonny grasped them firmly. 'It's so good to see you again. I wish I hadn't taken so long in coming here. Honor, you look as lovely as ever. The years haven't passed at all for you.' It was only a slight exaggeration. Her hair was the same maiden-fair, her facial contours still firm, and wrinkles had kindly kept almost entirely at bay.

'Coffee is on the way,' Honor said lightly. 'Shall we go in?'

Once they were settled in the morning room, Jonny asked, 'Where's Abbie? She is here? I've heard she doesn't venture far.'

'You heard right, Jonny,' Honor replied, with a regretful sigh. She had folded her hands on her lap and neatly crossed her ankles. Jonny noticed an agitated working of her mouth and her fingertips pulling at her skirt. She shot a look at Archie.

'Is something wrong?' Jonny frowned. Recalling Honor's edginess over the telephone yesterday, and now this, was there a reason they did not want him to see Abbie? Did Abbie not want to see him?

'Abbie will be here any minute, Jonny,' Archie said. 'With her husband. Douglas Goodyear.'

'Good heavens. Abbie married? That was a bit sudden, wasn't it?' Jonny scratched his forehead. This was the last thing he had expected.

'The thing is—' Honor's words were cut off. Abbie arrived on Douglas's arm. 'Ah, there you both are.' Honor went pink and shifted uncomfortably. 'Jonny's been here a few minutes. I've told him about the wedding.'

Jonny was sure there was more to it. He went to Abbie. She was pale and thin and looked tired. She was wearing a loose dress and cardigan. Should he kiss her cheek or merely shake her hand? Abbie made the decision for him by sticking out her hand. Jonny felt her cold fingers quivering inside his for just a moment. Douglas shook his hand briskly, his salutation on the same brief note. 'Congratulations on your marriage.' Jonny couldn't make his voice bright, it was all too strange.

The coffee was brought in. Honor poured, and while it was handed round there was a tense silence. It was drunk amid awkward small talk, in which only those at Ford Farm were mentioned.

Then Archie cleared his throat in a rumble. 'I think you should tell Jonny the rest of your news, Abbie.'

'Oh, what's that?' Jonny asked coolly. What was going on? The atmosphere was heavy. He felt he wasn't really welcome and that the others were, in some peculiar way, wary of him. He was longing to slip outside for a cigarette.

Abbie glanced at her mother, then her father and then Douglas, before gazing levelly at Jonny. 'Douglas and I were married quickly, just a quiet affair with few guests, because I'm having a baby.'

His immediate inner reaction was, *Well, you don't hang around*. He said, 'Well, this is a surprise. Congratulations again. Good luck to you both.' He saw Abbie bring her hands towards her middle in what seemed a furtive movement. The air was tight with tension. Something was going on, he was certain.

He stared at Abbie and her paleness pinked up considerably. 'I'm about five months along. I was seeing Douglas before I went down to Cornwall. Luckily, my ordeal didn't hurt the baby.'

'Oh. Yes. You were lucky,' Jonny agreed. So this was the reason why everyone seemed cagey. They were all embarrassed by the quick wedding. But it was an unnecessary reaction as far as he was concerned. They must know he wouldn't take a high moral stance. 'Well, that's really good news, isn't it? A baby?' The uneasy silence continued. 'Isn't it? Is there something else?'

'No, of course not,' Abbie said, fiddling with the buttons on her cardigan.

'We're all quite pleased in the circumstances,' Honor said, smiling.

Smiling far too wide, Jonny decided. He glanced at Archie, who dropped his head and shook it a little. And Jonny cottoned on to the truth of this odd situation. He was being deliberately lied to, by prior agreement, and Archie was the only one who had wanted the truth revealed. He shot to his feet, propelled by shock and anger. 'I'm not stupid, Abbie! It's not Goodyear's baby you're carrying, is it? It's mine! How dare you lie to me? I've got the right to know that it's my child. I had the right to know about it before you rushed off and got married.'

He expected anything but the reaction he got. Abbie viewed him, as cool as an autumn stream and as remote as a distant hill. 'I'm sorry, I should have told you the truth, but I don't think I really I owe you anything and nor does my baby. You've never wanted a wife or a child, Jonny. There was no reason to expect you to change your mind for me. You wouldn't want to marry me, admit it. You've slept with so many women you've probably got children all over the place. I don't suppose you've ever looked back to see if you've left any behind. The day that I learned I was pregnant Douglas offered me marriage. I accepted at once. He will make the perfect father for my child. Douglas and I care about each other, we are confident we can make our marriage work. In fact, we're all leaving here to live together abroad, in Monte Carlo, while Father can still bear the travel. The hotter climate will suit his chest. Douglas is selling his shares in the family business and a cousin of mine is to take over Oak Tree Warren. We're all starting afresh. There's nothing else to say.'

'Isn't there?' Jonny was confounded by the finality of her words but he had more demands. 'How am I to keep contact with my child?'

'You're not.' She kept up her unwavering gaze. 'I don't want you to. It's best if you just forget all about it.'

'And how on earth am I supposed to do that? The fact remains that I'm going to be a father, for goodness sake!'

Jonny put his hand up to the back of his neck and shook his head in incredulity. 'You've changed. How can you be so cold?'

'Yes, I have changed, Jonny.' Abbie showed a burst of emotion. 'I had to fight for my life and I see things differently now. My priority is my child. I shall fight in whatever way I see fit to protect it. I'm sorry, but I don't believe it's fair to him or her to be torn between two fathers. I'm sorry you've found out, Jonny. It wasn't what I wanted.'

So am I! Jonny wanted to scream. Of course, he wouldn't have wanted to marry Abbie. It probably wouldn't have worked, especially with her now a distant stranger to him, and it would definitely have meant him having no chance with Kate. But he would have offered to do the decent thing by Abbie if she hadn't decided to shut him out. It was a possibility that he had fathered a child before, but if so, he didn't know about it. He knew about his son or daughter growing inside Abbie's body and he hated the idea of being totally cut out of its life. He swallowed heavily. 'I can see you're determined. Can I at least know the date of its birth and whether it's a boy or a girl?'

'You can learn that when Mother writes in due course to your Aunt Emilia,' Abbie replied. As if suddenly weary she bowed her head and seemed to shrink into the chair.

Jonny could see she wanted to forget all about her time in Cornwall. He felt drained, overcome by a terrible sense of loss. He was doomed to an empty ache in his heart while he wondered about his child for the remainder of his life. He turned to Honor. 'You shouldn't have let me come here. It would have been kinder…'

'I'm sorry,' she said, barely able to meet his gaze.

'We're all very sorry, Jonny,' Archie said, massaging his tight chest. 'I don't know what else to say.'

'There is nothing anyone can say to put this right for me, Archie,' Jonny murmured. 'I've lost three friends and I've lost my child. All that is left for me to do is to leave straight away.'

Chapter Twenty-Two

All was quiet at Acorn Cottage. It was the day of Miss Chiltern's weekly trip into Truro. Having approached the back of the property by the fields, Tony scaled the hedge and crept up to the kitchen window. He was wearing leather gloves and a dark woolly hat, bought specially for the occasion with the last of his cash.

Jobs were getting scarcer for him. He was under no illusions why his services were not recommended any more and it wasn't because he was a poor workman. People had never liked his family, and since his despised mother's death, speculation that she had cruelly thrown Kate out was again a hot rumour. Sidney, who was considered to have 'slocked off' Delia and ruined her life, now had a growing reputation as a hot-tempered, heavy drinker. It was known he had beaten Delia, who, despite her fall from grace, was pitied by most. And there was vociferous disapproval of his father staying overnight at the home of the flighty widow, Dulcie Tregaskis. Tony had decided there was no longer any future at home for him, even more so now he was on rocky ground after admitting he had murdered his mother. He couldn't trust Sidney or Delia not to blab about it. Delia was scared of him but Sidney was not. Sidney was on his guard all the time, potentially a deadly adversary. Even though Kate had written to say she would arrive soon and bring a contribution towards their mother's funeral costs, and Sidney was pleased to think he could bleed her for more money, it wasn't enough to make Tony content. He wanted to get far away and needed a fair amount of money to do it. All being well, Miss Chiltern would provide it.

He had thought it all through. He would be careful, and he had plenty of time to act out his plan. He wouldn't take any ornaments or jewellery which could be traced and incriminate him, the sort of thing that he'd read about – it was what a couple from Truro had done, after abducting some posh woman who had stayed at the same farm where Kate lived. He would search the cottage for money — rich old dears like Miss Chiltern usually had something stashed away somewhere. He was banking on it. He had brought a bag of tools with him. He would break a small pane of glass in the kitchen window and lift the latch and climb in through. Straight away he'd clean up the glass with the brush and pan he had brought from home – when he left he would bury the glass deep in a wooded area and shake out the brush and wash the dustpan in a stream. He would take off his shoes to steal through the house. When he'd found the money, careful to leave everything undisturbed, he would climb out, latch the window and then put in the new pane of glass he'd brought with him.

He knew from detective stories that many a robber was caught by leaving footprints; he'd ensure he left none. He'd bury the gloves and hat with the broken glass and clean his shoes of woodland dirt. If luck was on his side Miss Chiltern wouldn't notice for a few days that the window had been repaired or that her money was missing.

He would be long gone by then, after provoking a noisy quarrel with Sidney and telling the nosy neighbours he'd decided to leave because he couldn't stand the violent atmosphere at home any more.

He got in as planned, and as soon as he had finished in the kitchen he made for the stairs. Any money was sure to be hidden up there somewhere. He had nearly three hours to make a search. Each stair gave an accusing creak under his weight. That didn't matter. On the landing in his stockinged feet he rucked up the carpet runner. Cursing, for it unnerved him, he straightened it. All was meticulously tidy and he made sure the runner was geometrically straight. He became aware of his breathing, thick and nasal and astonishingly noisy. A clock on the wall ticked louder than seemed natural. It chimed on the quarter hour and his heart leapt in fright. He swore under his breath. His confidence was waning and the jitters were setting in. His heart was pounding against his ribs. He was sweating. He could feel drops of it stinging his neck, his back and under his arms, and wetting his palms inside the gloves. He hoped he didn't leave a bad smell behind to alert Miss Chiltern on her return. His limbs felt as if they were in danger of turning to jelly. *Steady. Steady now.* It was natural he was tense and as taut as a spring. He had broken into someone's house and had already committed a crime for which he would receive a prison sentence if caught. There was no going back. *Please let me find some money and get out quickly.*

He had an idea Miss Chiltern slept in the front bedroom above the sitting room. That was the most likely place she would hide money. Thankfully, there were heavy lace curtains at the window so there was no possibility of him being seen from the lane. Wiping his gloved hands down his sides, he took a deep breath, opened the bedroom door and looked in. 'Oh!'

Miss Chiltern was standing facing him, as straight as a woman forty years younger, in her dressing gown and slippers and a sleeping cap on her head. She was tall and slender, and seemed without fear. 'So it's you, Tony Viant, who has seen fit to take liberties in my home. The game is up, as they say.'

Tony cursed himself for not checking that the old lady had actually got on the bus. 'M–Miss Chiltern, I – I can explain.'

'I don't think so. When I heard noises I thought I was dreaming at first, or that I was merely feverish from the cold I've suffered for the last few days. Then I knew beyond doubt that someone was coming up the stairs. I am right in thinking you're after money?' Her cut-glass voice was steeped in nononsense superiority. He had thought her a typical doddering frail old thing. She had never given away that she was made of stalwart stuff.

'L-look…' Tony thought his legs would give out on him. 'I've only b-broken a window. I can mend it. It'll be as good as new. There's no other damage, I swear. Can't we leave it at that? I'll go away from the village today, it's what I intended to do anyway. You'll never see me again. Please, I didn't mean you any harm. I was desperate.'

'Looking for an easy life, more like it. I believe in crime and punishment, Tony Viant.' Each of Miss Chiltern's spiked words reached him as if with a snap in its tail. 'You came here with the intention of stealing my life's savings, without a care about how I would manage for the rest of my life. Move aside, I intend calling the police.'

Fear and panic rent through Tony. There was only a claustrophobic dark cell shared with mean criminals and heavy labour ahead of him. No! He wasn't just going to meekly accept that. This haughty, hard-hearted old bag was glaring at him as if he was nothing but scum. She'd had things cushy all her damned life and didn't care about anyone else. He soared into a rage similar to the one that had made him threaten Sidney with the poker. Dark with fury, balling his fists, he hissed, 'And how does a weak old woman like you think you're going to get the better of me?'

Miss Chiltern was unfazed. 'I'm not foolish enough to keep money under my mattress as you were hoping, and neither am I foolish enough to face an intruder without this.' She brought up her right hand from her side and aimed a small firearm at his chest.

'You're not going to use that,' Tony sneered, too crazed to evaluate this new situation rationally. His hands outstretched he leapt towards her.

'You think not?' Miss Chiltern fired the gun. The bullet went clean through Tony's heart and he tottered backwards. 'You thought wrong.'

The surprise on Tony's face lasted only as long as it took for him to fall to the floor. He was dead before Miss Chiltern stepped round his body to go downstairs to the telephone.

—

'Are you sure you ought to go, darling?' Tom's anxious words echoed inside Jill's head as she made the journey with Kate to Tregony, together on the back seat of Alan's car.

'I just can't let Kate go without proper support, Tom,' was her reply. 'It's very sweet of Alan to offer to take her there but he doesn't know the full story behind the Viants. If Kate gets upset she'll need someone.'

'I agree with all that, Jill, but the Viant men are hard and unfeeling. I'm worried things might get out of hand and you'll get hurt. And the sister-in-law is heavily pregnant. How are you going to feel about that? I wish Kate didn't want to see her family. Why don't you stay home and let my mother go instead? The Viants won't get the better of her.'

'And they won't get the better of me. I'm not a pushover, darling,' Jill stressed. 'I'm sure things won't prove to be too bad now the beastly mother's out of the picture. And Kate's chosen a weekday when all the Viant men should be at work. We'll be fine.'

'Even so, I'm coming with you.'

She had stopped Tom going upstairs to change. 'You need to go to the market, Tom. And I don't want you fussing over me as if I'm too weak to stand up to the lightest breeze. I don't want to end up like Abbie, too nervous to even show my face outside the home. Kate is worried about her sister-in-law. It's right that she goes to see her. She says Delia is a nice person, and the baby, after all, is Kate's niece or nephew. She doesn't feel she can shun an innocent baby. We'll be arriving unexpectedly and Kate can see for herself the truth of how the land lies. We'll only be staying for a short while. We'll meet you in the Red Lion in town for lunch as arranged, I promise.'

Tom had still not been happy about the trip. Nor was Jill now. Facing a pregnant woman, who was carrying a baby that probably didn't have much of a future ahead of it, wasn't going to be easy. Kate was fidgeting and straining to peer ahead. All kinds of thoughts must be going through her mind. Alan drove carefully along the twisting roads. He kept up a cheerful chatter, trying to put Kate at ease. Jill had to smile. This was one good thing, the deepening friendship Kate had with Alan.

A black saloon closed in behind them, the driver honking its horn urgently. 'He's in a hurry,' Jill said, looking out of the back window. A loud ringing started up from the saloon.

'It's the police,' Kate frowned, an ominous feeling invading the pit of her stomach.

Alan pulled in at the next passing place and the Ford zoomed past. 'Packed with detectives, by the look of it. Wonder what's up.'

'Can't remember anything happening like it before,' Kate said, then forgot about it. She had family business to contend with. *Please God, let me be doing the right thing.* She wanted this visit to be over and to be back at the farm. Then hopefully only to hear from anyone from Tregony occasionally, and not because they were after money. She would give Sidney a small amount of money; she didn't want to run the risk of him suspecting she had their grandmother's savings. All she wanted was to see how Delia was faring and how it might be possible to help her and the baby. She certainly wouldn't be making this journey if not for them.

Alan smiled at her reflection in the rear view mirror, something he had done several times. She smiled back, trying to not look grim. It was really good going around with Alan. They had gone to the pictures and visited each other's homes for meals, and to many in the village they were considered to be 'walking out'. Kate wasn't sure about that. Alan made it obvious he'd like to take things further but he didn't pressurize her.

As they closed in on the village, she said, 'It's going to cause quite a stir, me getting out of a car.' And being in the company of a striking-looking, well-dressed young man and a refined young woman. It would be nice to speak to some of her former neighbours but it would be easier if she wasn't seen. That would be unlikely for there was usually someone about. The news of her return, that she had apparently 'gone up in the world', would spread quickly, and if Tony had a job nearby he'd almost certainly get to hear of it and trot home.

'There isn't a back lane or side road we could use to approach the house, is there, Kate?' Alan said.

'No, Alan,' she replied, meeting his smiling eyes in the mirror. She couldn't manage an answering smile. Her tummy was churning with the thought of entering her old home. Her mother might not be there but her presence would likely overshadow the place like a merciless spectre. 'The house is up the hill, not far from the old almshouses.'

The Morris 8 provoked a long, interested stare from a young housewife with two small children. Not recognizing Kate, and with the children tearing ahead, the woman reluctantly went on after them. Alan stopped the car when Kate pointed out her old home. He jumped out to open the rear door for her and Jill. Next to the Viant home, outside the front doorstep, two old men were perched on stools, smoking pipes. It was a familiar sight to Kate. The men, a pair of bachelor brothers, pushed back their flat caps and screwed up their wrinkled, leathery faces at the newcomers to their patch. One of them took on a look of enlightenment as he studied Kate. 'Mornin' to 'ee, maid. 'Tes young Kate Viant, isn't it?'

'Hello Mr Penver.' She gazed down on him, remembering the times the dear old soul and his brother had given her odd halfpennies. 'Yes, it's me.'

'Well, you look a right treat, I must say. Don't she, brother?' The other Mr Penver eyed Kate up and down. 'Ais. But what're 'ee 'doin' back here, young Kate? Betterfit you stayed away. Got new friends, I see. Glad of that for 'ee. But heed my advice, maid, and turn back round 'fore you're seen.'

'I second that.' The first Mr Penver nodded his head. 'You left a miserable place and 'tes no better since your mother went. You be wise and go straight back to where you come from.'

Now Kate was here she wasn't afraid. As if a big dark cloud had lifted she realized her family had no power to hurt her any more. She had new friends, a new position, a new life, and she wasn't going to allow anyone to spoil all that for her. She would tell Jonny this when she saw him, and that would be soon for he had just arrived back at his sister's house in readiness for her wedding. 'I shall be fine,' she told both Mr Penvers.

Alan put his hand on her shoulder. 'Yes, you needn't worry. We're here to make sure Kate will be fine.'

Delia had been making her father-in-law's bed. Hearing a motor car stop outside she had gone to the window to view this rare occurrence. With the first excitement she'd had in ages she threw the bottom section up on its creaking sashes. 'Kate! Hello. Come in, come in. I'll be right down.' She made a hasty check on her appearance in the tarnished wash-stand mirror. She was ash-pale and her complexion was spotty but otherwise she didn't look too bad. Since Kate had written, Sidney, rubbing his greedy hands in glee, had not been so contentious. While staying wary of Tony, he had ordered the other two men to keep the house tidier, that they must all take their boots off outside and take turns fetching in the water. All to impress Kate. Life was a little easier for Delia, at least for the time being. She was able to keep the place more in order, as she liked to, so she would feel less ashamed of Kate seeing it. She wished Kate hadn't brought these people with her though. They must be posh to have such a nice motor car. At least Sidney had got hold of some extra tea so she would be able to offer them a decent drink.

Kate, Jill and Alan were waiting in the kitchen when Delia came through the door at the bottom of the stairs. Witnessing Delia's nervousness, Kate was taken back to that bleak day in her empty grandmother's cottage when she had been faced with Tom, Jonny and Abbie Rothwell. Her heart flew to Delia's cause. It was awful to see her wan and hollow-eyed, her swollen belly stretching a faded smock that someone must have handed down to her. She looked ten years older than she should. Kate felt the urge to take her away from all this. She went to Delia with open hands.

Delia knew that if Kate had come alone she would have collapsed in her arms and sobbed out her despair, but she was embarrassed in front of the two strangers. She stayed stiff and allowed Kate to kiss her cheek, whispering, with a choke in her throat, 'Thanks for coming.' How she envied Kate her good clothes, her glowing health, her better circumstances.

'This is Mrs Jill Harvey, who kindly gave me a home,' Kate explained. 'And this is Alan Killigrew, also from Hennaford, who kindly drove us here.'

'We're pleased to meet you, Mrs Viant,' Jill said, full of pity for Delia. The sight of her almost grotesque bump tore at her. By the evidence all around the poor child inside her belly had little to look forward to. How was it fair that children were born into such harsh circumstances while she and Tom had lost their child, who would never have known a day without love and with excellent prospects ahead of it?

'Well, s-sit down everyone. Or w-would you like to go through to the front room?' Delia stammered.

'We'll be fine here,' Kate smiled, hoping to lessen Delia's discomfiture. She saw her mother's chair and flicked her eyes away. The crochet blanket had gone and a different patch cushion was placed there, but Biddy Viant's throne filled her with distaste. Next she faced the spot where Sidney had said she had plunged to her death. She had a terrible picture of that in her mind, just as she did the last haunting image of her dead grandmother. The double dread made her shudder. Alan was behind her and she shot her head round to him. He would know that the old bleakness was on her again. She had told no one but him about her grandmother's last moments. He rubbed reassuring knuckles on her arm. Kate smiled at him to convey she wouldn't let the haunting go on affecting her. Jill noticed. She had seen Alan make this gesture before and wondered again what it was he shared with Kate.

'We've brought some things from the farm, Mrs Viant,' Jill said, placing a wicker basket on the table. 'That Kate thought you'd like.'

'You take a look, Delia,' Kate said. 'While I put the kettle on.'

Feeling it would be better to leave the women alone, Alan excused himself to take a smoke in the back garden.

'Is he your young man, Kate?' Delia paused from spreading the table with what to her was pure luxury; enough bacon to last a week, eggs, butter, cream and jars and bottles of preserves. There was a batch of scones and even a cake.

Jill glanced at Kate to see what the answer would be.

Kate took cups and saucers, all odd ones, off the dresser shelf. 'Yes, I suppose he is.' The admission rolled off her tongue, surprising her. She'd think it through more thoroughly in private moments.

Jill was utterly pleased. Alan suited Kate perfectly. Mrs Em and Perry would be pleased too. Although Tom considered Kate still too young for romantic attachments, they seemed eager for Kate to become closer to Alan.

'He seems very nice,' Delia said. 'Good-looking too. I'm glad you've done well for yourself, Kate, and that you're out of here. Bring some plates and knives. It's not the afternoon but we can have a proper cream tea.' She was relishing the promised taste of the treat on her tongue.

'How about you, Delia?' Kate asked, placing the teapot on the table. 'How are you really? Don't be afraid to say in front of Jill. She's been a tremendous help to me, as you can see. We're here to help you if you'll allow us to.'

'Things could be worse, I suppose,' she shrugged. 'I must accept my lot. We all have to.' She would keep her pride in front of Jill Harvey. At least the extra food and the hope that more would be provided in the future would ease the financial strain. Going red in the face, she went on, 'I hope you don't mind me asking, Kate, did you bring something towards your mother's funeral? Sidney keeps going on about it.' He would be as teasy as hell if Kate hadn't and he would take it out on her.

Kate took an envelope out of her handbag. 'I've managed to save seven pounds and five shillings. You're welcome to it, for your sake, Delia. There's also two pounds inside for you. Put it somewhere safe.'

Breaking from spooning raspberry jam onto halved scones, Delia expelled a mighty sigh of relief. 'I can't thank you enough. The undertaker's been hounding us. He said we could pay ten shillings a week. This will show him we're in good faith to clear the bill. You're a good girl, Kate.' She slipped the two pounds into her apron pocket to secrete away the minute Kate left.

'I wish I could do more for you, Delia.' Kate felt blood swirl about her face in guilt that she had so much more in savings, but then decided that was silly. She could secretly feed Delia a little money at a time. 'I'm knitting something for the baby. Have you got much put by?'

'A few odds and ends.' Delia was off-hand. She didn't want to talk about the baby. God forgive her, she thought of it only as an unwanted creature inside her. It would be an effort to love it.

Jill had hardly been able to take her eyes off the woman's protruding stomach. With an ache in her heart, she asked, 'What do you need? For the baby?'

Delia saw the terrible sadness lurking behind Jill's eyes. 'Just about everything. Um, have you got any children, Mrs Harvey?'

'No. I lost a baby a few months ago. If not for Kate I would have died.'

'Oh, I'm sorry. Ironic, isn't it?'

'What is?' Jill asked.

Delia didn't get the chance to explain. The village constable burst in through the back door, making her shriek in alarm. 'Here, Bert Blewett! What do you think you're upon? Have you never heard of knocking?'

'What is it?' Kate demanded. Something must be wrong for the usually mild-mannered, burly policeman to enter this way. 'Has there been an accident?' Alan came inside to see if there was trouble, going straight to Kate.

For a dark moment Delia hoped it was Sidney that PC Blewett had come about, that he'd been killed in an accident. It would be wonderful to be free of the brute, free not to have any more children. She'd certainly not marry again. She could just about bear her life then.

'There's been no accident.' PC Blewett took off his helmet, puffing from the harried bicycle ride he'd had. 'But it's terrible news for you just the same.' He pulled himself up straight and became officious. 'I'm sorry to have to inform you that your brother-in-law – and your brother, Miss Viant – Anthony Viant is dead. He was shot in self-defence while perpetrating a burglary. Shot by old Miss Chiltern. He had forced an entry into her cottage and put Miss Chiltern, who was ill at home, in fear of her life. She's in shock, the doctor's been sent for – although, to his mind, the old lady seemed to have a strong grip on herself. The detectives are at the cottage. I've been sent to tell you not to go near Anthony Viant's bedroom or to touch any of his things. You'll be asked to make a statement later, on what time he left the house and if you had noticed anything unusual about his behaviour. Where

249

are your father-in-law and husband working today? They need to be sent for.'

During the constable's speech Kate had gone to Delia, taking the spreading knife from her frozen hand. Delia had turned rigid. Now she was shaking. She let out a terrible howl and Kate felt her folding in a faint. 'Alan, help me to get her to a chair! '

Together he and Kate eased her backwards to the chair Jill brought up behind her. 'Don't just stand there,' Jill barked at the constable. 'Get some water.'

'In the bucket by the door!' Kate snapped at him. 'You could have at least got her to sit down first before coming out with the news.' Tony was dead, killed as a criminal. Grief mixed with the shame of what it meant to her family name. She cradled Delia round the shoulders while Jill wet her handkerchief in the water, fetched in the tin mug PC Blewett had found on the draining board, and dabbed at Delia's burning cheeks. She put the mug to her lips. 'Delia, try to sip some water.'

'It'll be all right, Delia,' Kate crooned. 'We'll look after you.'

Alan asked, 'Do you think she needs the doctor?' He shot a glare at the constable. 'It was a terrible shock for a pregnant woman.'

'I'm sorry, honest I am,' PC Blewett blustered. 'Didn't know what I was thinking of. Do you want me to help you get her upstairs?'

'We'll see,' Kate said, as Delia stirred and moaned.

'Look, I'm sorry, but I have a job to do. Kate, do you know where your father and brother are?'

She trawled through the family routine. 'Um, it's Wednesday… yes, they'll be delivering at St Mawes.'

'Right. I'll get them home. I'll run along then. Sorry about Mrs Viant. I'll apologize to her prop'ly later.' Putting on his helmet, he left.

The door was opened again at once and in came the neighbours, Mrs Peam and both Mr Penvers. 'We heard the maid scream,' Mrs Peam said, avidly searching faces. 'Has something bad happened? Is it Sidney?'

'No,' Kate replied. 'It's Tony who's dead. You might as well know the truth. It will get around quickly enough. He was shot. By Miss Chiltern. He was trying to rob her.'

Before more questions were uttered, Delia came to with a sickening wail. She clung to Kate in a panic, clutching at her cardigan. 'I can't stand it! I don't want to stay here! I'll go mad. I'm scared. I wish I was dead. I don't want to go on. I don't want this baby. I just want to die.' She broke down in anguished sobs.

Kate was finding it hard not to cry herself as she rocked Delia like an infant. 'Don't worry, don't worry. I'm here. I won't leave you, I promise.' She glanced at Jill. 'It's all too much for her. I can't leave her.'

'I don't want you to stay on here, Kate,' Jill said, afraid Kate would never get away from this wretched place again.

'Is there somewhere Mrs Viant could go?' Alan said, sharing Jill's concerns.

'She didn't ought to stay here at all.' Mrs Peam drew in on them. 'I've heard Sidney beating and threatening her. If he takes on an ugly mood she could be in danger, and that poor child that's due any day.'

'Ais, 'tes no place for a woman in her condition,' one Mr Penver declared.

'Could be the end of her and the child,' said his brother. 'Never seen someone in such a state.'

Kate looked at Jill. 'We have to do something. Well, I do. It's my responsibility.'

'I've seen enough. We'll take her to the farm for a few days,' Jill said without hesitation. 'If Tom were here he'd say the same thing.'

Kate was mightily relieved and grateful at the offer, that Delia would be getting away from the terrible situation of Tony's justifiable manslaughter, but she felt it was only fair to point out, 'She could give birth during that time.'

'All that matters is she's safe and well. Kate, pack some things for her. We'll leave a note for your brother explaining Delia was taken ill and we thought it was for the best. Hopefully, he'll understand. I don't suppose he'll want the care of her anyway.'

'Thank you,' Kate said. 'If you and Alan get her into the car, I'll pop upstairs.' She was in no doubt that Sidney wouldn't look after Delia properly. He was unlikely to cause trouble, seeing this new situation as a way to further his own ends. But if he did get violent with Delia or anyone at the farm, somehow she would see him off herself.

Chapter Twenty-Three

As he entered the farmyard it bothered Jonny that he should be feeling awkward. As much as he loved and respected his Aunt Emilia, this had been his uncle's property before hers, damn it. He should be able to come and go without feeling he was up to no good. Aunt Emilia wasn't his blood relative, and Perry was just her second husband. They'd had no right to banish him from Kate as if he was some sexual predator. He had declared he loved Kate and they should have taken him at his word. They were not Kate's stand-in parents, and nor were Tom and Jill. They were friends who should allow her the dignity of living her life her way. He could offer Kate the absolute that a man was capable of giving a woman. No one would stop him from seeing her. If Kate wanted him too, that was how it was going to be.

The day before he had turned up on Louisa's doorstep, in Truro. 'This is a lovely surprise, Jonny. I wasn't expecting you for a couple of days. What's the matter?' Her delighted greeting had died away; she had noticed his shadowed expression. He was raw to the bone after the events in Lincolnshire but had convinced Louisa he was feeling low because he'd found Abbie unwelcoming and was tired after travelling. The only person he could ever tell about his baby, the child he would never see and never know he existed, was Kate. When the time was right, as his friend or future bride, he would confide his aching secret to her. And his bride she would be, even if it meant he had to fight off the most relentless opposition. The fact that he might have to, so unnecessary and ridiculous, filled him with anger. First he must commiserate with Kate over the dreadful news he'd read in today's *Western Morning News* about her brother's death.

He strode towards Tom's door. He was going straight to Kate.

'Jonny!' She was behind him, in work clothes and boots, coming from the piggery. Dropping a pail she hurried to him with her lopsided gait.

'Kate!' He ran, arms reaching for her. She was a gorgeous vision. Her hair was shining in its glorious red tints and her eyes and skin were glowing with loveliness and health. She wasn't a girl any more. In his absence she had claimed her woman's rights and she was a creature of blossoming sensuous beauty. He loved her more than his senses and nature deemed possible.

Her arms lifted to meet his embrace but he didn't just hug her. He lifted her off her feet and clutched her to his body and fixed a loving kiss on her soft warm cheeks. 'Darling Kate, how I've missed you. It's wonderful to see you, to be with you again.' He could hardly contain the thousand other things he wanted to declare to her.

She laughed into his eyes and kissed him back. 'I've missed you too, Jonny. It seems you've been away for ages.'

He had been worried he would find her dispirited through the bereavement but she seemed confident and purposeful. He could feel the energy flowing through her.

Her eyes were shimmering with tenderness. He wanted to gaze at her for ever. 'You look gorgeous, Kate.'

Kate placed her face against his neck for a second. It was a marvellous surprise that Jonny was here. He was part of her new life and things hadn't seemed complete without him around.

Reluctantly, he put her down but wound his arm round her tiny waist.

She lifted her arm to do the same to him. Without saying so, they wanted to stay alone and walked to the seclusion of the goat house steps. Perched side by side, they linked together once more.

'I was sorry to learn about your latest trouble, Kate. How your brother died. What he did. Louisa phoned Aunt Em and she filled her in on the details. How terrible that you and Jill were there, but it was a good thing for your sister-in-law. You seem to be taking it well, but how are you, deep down?'

She rested her face against the side of his arm. Her worries for Delia had taken precedence over her own feelings but the reality behind Tony's death hit her with a dark force. 'It was a dreadful shock. I'm upset, of course, but I don't seem able to grieve as much as I should. I can't help thinking that if the old lady didn't have that gun then Tony might have hurt her instead, or worse. At least it's got Delia away from the place for a while. She's still in a dreadful state. Keeps saying she doesn't want the baby. We got the doctor to her and he had to sedate her. He says she's very weak and needs to build up her strength if she's to come safely through her labour. Jill and I will make sure she will. She sleeps most of the time, thank goodness. We left the telephone number for Sidney but so far he hasn't bothered to ring to ask how she is. That's typical of him. Not that we want him here. He's a heartless brute. Delia's scared of him. She'd be better off without him. I can't help thinking she wishes it was Sidney and not Tony who'd died.'

'I'm so sorry you've had to put up with all this. Is there anything I can do to help? Anything at all?'

'I might need help in getting Delia away from Sidney for good. I don't want her to go back to him. He'd only be cruel to her and the baby.' She had been trying to work out ways for Delia to gain this freedom. Her grandmother's money could be used to give Delia a new start, but she needed to go somewhere far enough away where Sidney was unlikely to find her.

'I've got contacts all over the country. I'm sure I could find a suitable place for her. As soon as your sister-in-law has given birth, we'll get her away together.'

Kate met Jonny's avid gaze. 'That's an enormous relief. Delia will be so grateful. Strange, isn't it? How so many of us haven't had a traditional family life. I was despised and thrown out by my mother. You partly grew up here, and then you were taken to Watergate Bay where you had a stepmother and stepsister. Jill was brought up by her grandmother, and Tom, and his brother and sister, had Mr Perry for a stepfather from a young age. When Alan and his sister were orphaned, Mrs Killigrew took them in before she was married, then she and Mr Killigrew adopted them. Your sister Louisa was adopted and her past kept a secret for many years. Mr Fuller's wife abandoned their little girl, and Jana will soon be getting Louisa for a stepmother. And now my little niece or nephew is facing the future without its father.'

Jonny's brow had shot up at her familiar mention of Alan Killigrew. Was he hanging about her? If so, he'd soon see him off.

'You've just come back from seeing Abbie. She was good to me. Do you think the Rothwells could find a nice little home and part-time job for Delia?'

Jonny couldn't help drawing in a hurt breath at the mention of Abbie and Oak Tree Warren.

'Sorry.' Kate touched his arm. 'Here's me rambling on about my concerns when I haven't even asked you about yourself. Wasn't it a good meeting with the Rothwells? You don't look quite yourself, Jonny. Something was wrong before you went away. Do you regret leaving the air force? I keep worrying that you think you've made a big mistake. I suppose you could always join up again. Isn't the photography going as well as you'd hoped?'

He smiled deep in her eyes, putting a hand firmly over hers, softly rubbing her fingers with the pad of his thumb. 'My career is going just fine, Kate. I'm beginning to make a bit of a name for myself.'

'I'd like to hear all about it.'

'You will,' he promised. 'I could take you out for dinner or we could steal an afternoon to ride together. The thing is, I had a bad experience when I was away, Kate.' He told her about the tense time in Lincolnshire. 'I was so looking forward to seeing Archie, my old friend. It was all very awkward.'

'And Abbie was pregnant all the time she was here. Gosh! No wonder Mr Goodyear came down straight away when she disappeared. And now they're planning a new life abroad. Do you think she was cold towards you because you remind her of what she went through?'

Jonny took a deep steadying breath. He couldn't allow Kate to believe a lie and perhaps despise him later when the truth emerged. 'Kate, please don't think too badly of me. Actually, the baby is mine. I would have offered to do the right thing, but Abbie felt Douglas Goodyear would make a better father than me, offer the baby a more settled life. She's quite determined that it will never know who its real father is. My child will be one more growing up without both its rightful parents. Abbie is over-protective towards it. The child could be smothered by love. It's all a bit of a mess really.' He searched her eyes, praying she wasn't shrinking away from him.

Too many sordid things had happened in Kate's life for her to be judgemental about others, and she was touched that Jonny had confided in her. 'I'm sorry, Jonny. It hardly seems fair to you. Life's never simple, is it?'

He gave an ironic laugh. 'I suppose if it was we'd all be complaining we were bored. Kate, I must ask you to keep this to yourself for ever. There's no point in going against Abbie's wishes. I haven't even told Louisa, but I had to tell you. You see, I care for you very much.'

'I'm glad you see me as a special friend. You're special to me too. Well, I'd better go in. Delia is in the house alone. Come with me? I'd like to hear all about the Lakes.'

Jonny went with her, staying close. On the flagstones outside her kitchen was Emilia, with her arms folded and a grim expression. He didn't care about his aunt's disapproval. She had followed her heart twice in her life and she wasn't going to stop him from following his.

-

Jill took up Delia's supper. 'Hello, Kate's with Alan and Tom's cousin, Jonny, who's showing them some photos. It's a little baked fish. Let me help you sit up, then see what you can manage to eat. The doctor wants you to build up your strength. Your body has an important task ahead very soon.'

Groggy and lethargic, unwilling to open her eyes, Delia allowed herself to be tugged gently until she was sitting up. 'I'm sorry,' she murmured, too depressed to raise her voice above a dry whisper. 'I'm such a bother to you.'

'No you're not.' Jill put on jolly tones to prove she was telling the truth. 'We're happy to help.'

'But it's not as if I'm a blood relative of Kate's.'

Jill set the legs of the tray either side of Delia, just below her bump. 'Try to eat up. Kate cooked it especially for you.'

She stayed in the room. Delia needed to be coaxed to eat her meals. She brought up a chair.

The food was cut into small manageable pieces to eat with a spoon. Delia had no appetite but the first taste stimulated her tongue and she got a few spoonfuls down. 'It's nice.' She rewarded Jill with a wan smile, before lying back breathless.

'That's the ticket. Shall I help you with the rest?' Minutes later, 'An empty plate. Kate will be pleased. Would you like to try some apple pie?'

Delia shook her head. Jill took the tray away. 'Do you need the bathroom?'

'I'd better go.'

'A short walk will get the blood flowing. Make you feel better.' It was necessary to escort Delia in case the sudden exercise made her feel dizzy. On the way back, Jill said,

'When you're up to it you can take a bath. The district nurse is coming tomorrow to give you a blanket bath.'

'I've never been in a proper bath before. Everyone's so kind,' Delia said, when tucked up in bed. 'I didn't know before that people could be kind.'

Jill resumed her seat, getting the feeling Delia wanted to talk. 'That's very sad. Kate said you didn't have a particularly good life at home before you married.'

'No, I didn't. My parents were very strict and always suspicious of others. The first time I looked at a boy they called me a whore. I resent the way I was brought up. If I'd been taught about proper relationships, to look up in life, I wouldn't have been tempted to meet secretly with one of the village ruffians. If Sidney didn't marry me when I got pregnant they'd have thrown me out anyway, not caring if me and the baby died in the gutter. I hate them for it.' The more she went on the more upset she got, until large bitter tears fell down her washed-out face and dripped off her chin. Jill passed her a hanky then perched on the bed and rubbed her arm in sympathy. 'This baby won't have any doting grandparents. It's got nothing really. It'll have a life of going without. And a father who'll only be rotten to it, who's already seeing other women. And a mother who doesn't want it.' Kate had promised she'd get her away from Sidney but Delia wasn't looking forward to anything. Right now it would be a blessing if she closed her eyes and never woke up.

'But you'll want the baby when it's born. When you're holding it in your arms. It will be different then.'

'No it won't!' Delia cried great wracking sobs. 'I don't feel anything for it. I don't feel anything at all. I've had everything cursed and beaten out of me. You'll think me terrible, you losing a baby that you badly wanted, but I just want it to be all over and I don't ever want to see this baby. I hate the very thought of it there inside me. I don't want it. I don't want it!'

Jill moved her hands to Deha's trembling shoulders. Poor girl, she wasn't much older than Kate, and had the bleakness of never knowing security and peace. 'It'll be all right, Delia, I promise you. Neither Kate, nor I and Tom will allow you to go back to your old life. It's natural what you're feeling after all the terrible things that have happened to you. But you're here now and you're safe. Try not to get so upset. All you need to do is to rest and get stronger. When the baby comes you will get all the help you need. Does that make you feel better?'

Delia stopped sobbing, mopped her eyes and grew serious. 'You're trying to say the right things, bless you for that. But you can't really understand how I feel. Whatever happens, Sidney will cause trouble. He's planning on sponging off Kate for money. If she refuses he'll get ugly about it. And no matter what you say, I don't want this baby. Even if Sidney was no longer part of my life. I wouldn't want it because it's part of him, part of his rotten parents and his murdering brother. I'm going to tell you something now, God knows I need to tell someone, but I don't want you to ever tell Kate. It's better she never knows. She's got a chance of happiness with that Alan and I don't want nothing to spoil it for her. Tony admitted to me and Sidney that he murdered his mother. That after she fell he deliberately rammed her head back against the oven door to make sure she died. I'd lived in fear of Tony ever since. So you see, I want to get away from the Viants and everything that reminds me of them. Otherwise I'll go mad. I'll never make a good mother to this baby. It doesn't deserve that. Have I convinced you at last?'

Jill fell quiet, shoulders hunched. She felt as if the breath had been knocked out of her. It was a lot to take in. 'But what do you think you can do with the baby?'

'It's obvious. Give it away. Have it adopted. You can have it, if you want it. You've told me the odds are against you having your own children. You can have this child. That way it'll get all the love it needs and I'll be really free.'

Jill felt her heart leap. She and Tom had talked about adoption. Was she looking at the perfect solution? Delia seemed to mean all she had said. She wanted to deliver the baby and disappear, go away and start a new life. She could be given the funds to do so, and if Sidney Viant caused a problem he could almost certainly be bought off. It was unlikely he really wanted his child – money seemed to be his only priority. Legal papers could be drawn up and the baby would be hers and Tom's. *Her baby.* The thought made her long for it. Its biological parentage didn't matter. But she would have to be cautious. Delia had suffered a lot of trauma but she might bond with the baby and change her mind. Jill knew she mustn't build up her hopes only to have them dashed. First she must speak to Tom. She told Delia this.

Delia had grown calmer as she'd watched Jill in her thoughtful silence. She had not been able to see a way out before unless she abandoned the baby. There was hope at last.

Alan was determined to linger at the farm until Jonny Harvey left for an overnight stay at Tremore. It was getting late and Jill and Tom couldn't understand why Jonny seemed so unwilling to leave. 'Time you were getting along, isn't it?' Tom said. He was referring only to Jonny, happy to allow Kate a few minutes alone to say goodnight to her boyfriend. Jill had taken Tom aside and told him about Delia's unexpected offer, saying they wanted to go up to bed and talk it over more thoroughly.

'I suppose so,' Jonny replied reluctantly, assuming the dismissal included Alan Killigrew, who had irritatingly hung on but whom he had firmly kept at a distance from Kate. 'I'll say goodnight then. Goodnight, Kate. I'll see you very soon.' He didn't care to walk down the road with Killigrew and went on ahead, not bothered that it would be considered rude.

'We'll go on up, Kate,' Jill said, eager to return to the business of the possible adoption. 'Goodnight, Alan.'

'Goodnight, Jill, Tom,' Alan said, releasing his exasperation with a sigh that he was alone with Kate at last. He hadn't been able to get near her all evening. He did so now.

'Lock up in ten minutes, Kate,' Tom said pointedly, then Jill dragged him out of the room. She didn't mind how long it took the younger couple to say goodnight.

'Kate, why did Jonny Harvey come back if he'd already been here today?' Alan said, as if he didn't know, trying to keep the jealousy and annoyance out of his tone. 'You'd think he'd want to spend more time with his family. He monopolized the whole evening. His snaps were good but when you've seen one you've seen them all. He's got a wedding to go to on Friday, he should put his energies into that.'

'Don't be grumpy. Jonny likes our company at the farm.' Kate's mind was on Delia. Her welfare and the baby's were her priority. Jill had said she had perked up a little. That was hopeful news.

'He likes your company, more like.'

'What?' Kate emerged from her thoughts.

'Jonny Harvey. He's after you, didn't you notice? Well, he can't have you. You're my girl. Aren't you, Kate?' Alan gently pushed a tress of her hair behind her ear. 'We've got something going, haven't we?'

She didn't need to be faced with this right now. 'I'm not sure, Alan. I like you very much but…'

There was a drag in Alan's stomach. His hopes slipping away? How could he compare with Harvey's expertise and sophistication? He'd fight for Kate though, even physically if need be. Kate was worth any amount of pain. 'But you like Jonny Harvey too? I can see all the qualities that attract women to him, Kate, but he's too old for you.'

'Are you seriously saying Jonny's after me?' It made Kate want to laugh.

'He thinks he's in love with you. It's written all over him. If Jill and Tom had their eyes open tonight they would have seen it too.'

Kate shook her head. Jonny was in love with her? No. It was impossible. Of all the women he knew, had been with, she was the exact opposite. He saw her as a special friend. Very special, to have confided in her alone about Abbie Goodyear expecting his baby. If he did love her and if he had been sending out those kind of signals she had been as blind to them as Jill and Tom. She recalled his greeting today. He had been glad to see her, really glad, as a friend would be. But he had clung on to her and touched her a lot. Alan was right about him taking over the evening and lavishing her with attention. Jonny had also seemed to resent Alan's presence. He'd been like that with Denny James too. She hadn't stopped to think back then how strange his behaviour had been. So perhaps Jonny really did have feelings for her. She couldn't take this in.

'Do you care about him too?' Alan said, feeling her long silence verified his dread.

'No, of course not.' She wasn't in love with anyone. She wasn't ready for that sort of thing. She was too set on finding her own identity to want to tie herself to someone for the rest of her life yet. She liked Jonny very much. She enjoyed being in his company. Alan's too. She had told Delia that Alan was her young man but she had never behaved as if he was. This was all getting too much.

Alan exhaled in relief. The thought alone of losing Kate filled him with a dark hollowness. He loved her so much, more with every minute. He longed to tell her but that would be unwise. 'Then there's hope for me?' He couldn't stop his feet from moving in closer to her.

Kate turned her head away. 'Look, Alan, things are complicated right now. I've got Delia and the baby to consider. I haven't got time to think about what I want.'

'OK,' he said quickly, praying he hadn't blown every-thing, putting the space back between them to show he wouldn't pressure her. 'We can go on as before?'

'Yes,' she replied at once. She didn't want to lose anyone from her life.

'Great. I'll pop along tomorrow evening. I'll say good-night then.' He bent his head to kiss her goodbye as usual.

Kate leaned her cheek for his kiss, glad to be going off to her bed. But she was taken over by the knowledge that the instant he left she would feel appallingly empty. She didn't want him to go. She just didn't. She found herself stepping towards him and her arms reaching up to encircle his neck. She was following her instincts and it felt completely natural. 'Stay a while longer.' The words flowed from her lips.

'Oh Kate.' Alan drew her in to him, snuggling his face against her neck.

Kate wrapped herself against his body tighter and tighter. She had been in Jonny's embrace today but this was entirely different. Not brotherly, as she'd thought the contact with Jonny had been, and so very much more than warm and comforting. It was heady and exciting. It was wonderful and amazing. It consumed her in the most blissful way. She put her energy into drawing all she could from him while returning the same intense offering. Kisses. They just happened, on their lips and their eyes and their necks. Warm velvety sensations, new experiences she demanded more and more of.

Alan took his mouth away from hers. 'You're so lovely, Kate. I've wanted this for so long.' He was in raptures. Enfolding her even deeper in his arms his next kiss was a lover's kiss. Kate yielded to it and answered it. They both revelled in it, taking every thrill and every scrap of sweetness out of it. Forgetting everything and everyone else.

Chapter Twenty-Four

'It was a lovely wedding, Jonny,' Emilia said. With Perry, they had just waved Louisa and Mark off on their honeymoon. They were in the drawing room of Louisa's house in Kenwyn Church Road, where the reception had been held, after a civil wedding and a church blessing. All the guests except those from Ford Farm had left. 'You must be very pleased to see Louisa happy and settled again.'

'Of course,' he replied stiffly. Handsome and elegant in his RAF dress uniform, he wished Kate had been able to attend today but she was at home caring for her sister-in-law. 'I've never found it necessary to have any reservations about her and Mark.'

'As I and Perry have about you and Kate, is that what you mean?' For a short time Emilia had once been Jonny's foster mother, she cared deeply for him and hated these bad feelings. 'Jonny, we are right to be concerned, even more so now. We have something to tell you.'

He stared at her, then shifted his eyes above her head. She was interfering again. 'What?'

'Please don't be sharp, Jonny. You haven't been to the farm for a couple of days, busy with the last arrangements for the wedding. During that time Kate and Alan have become a steady couple.'

Jonny's reaction was the need to swear. 'I don't believe you. You'll try anything to build a barrier between Kate and me. Well it won't work. Nothing will. You might as well give up.'

Perry came forward. 'It's not a lie, Jonny. Your aunt is telling you this to save you making a fool of yourself and we're both eager that you do nothing to upset Kate.'

Jonny felt his guts hit the floor. He had no choice but to believe them. Just two days' absence and Kate had stepped into a relationship with Killigrew. For heaven's sake, why? She'd showed him no special favour that last evening. What made her suddenly fall into his arms? Perhaps it was the anxiety over her sister-in-law. Kate had needed someone and because he himself wasn't there, she'd turned to Killigrew. That must be why.

'Alan is perfect for Kate,' Emilia went on, full of pity for Jonny. All life had gone out of him. She saw again the bewildered small boy he had been when Alec, just her employer then, had brought him to the farm. Jonny really did love Kate. What a terrible fate for him to fall in love at last but with someone whom was unlikely to feel the same way. Kate wasn't immune to being swept off her feet by Jonny, the same as other women had in his life, but she was a realist. She would know their worlds couldn't mix. Jonny couldn't settle in one place while Kate was looking for stability, to build something worth working at or fighting for in a familiar place. Emilia was anxious. 'You won't do anything to cause problems, will you? Say you won't, Jonny.'

He couldn't look at his aunt. He couldn't bear to see her sympathetic expression. But he had hope. Killigrew was Kate's first boyfriend and first boyfriends didn't usually last. She'd be more receptive to him when it was over, and no one could say she didn't have experience in that direction. He would not give up on Kate. 'I'd never, never do anything to hurt Kate.'

Emilia touched his arm. 'What will you do now, Jonny? I mean, have you got plans?'

He had a meeting with a small local publisher next week, with the view to putting together some local scenes and historical facts. There was a ready market for a series with the holiday trade and many local people would be interested too. Now Louisa was moving into Keresyk with Mark he was thinking of buying this house from her. It would be his first home. And, he hoped, his and Kate's home, a haven to return to, close to her friends and his family. Where he could invite Kate to, where he'd make sure they were alone, where he could ease her away from the boy Killigrew and make him seem no more than a playmate to her.

'Yes, Aunt Em, I've got plans.' The main one was to see Kate, to work out how things were between her and Killigrew and the right strategy to separate them. 'I'd like to be alone now.'

'I'm sorry, Jonny, about everything,' Emilia said quietly. 'We'll gather Tom and Jill and go home.'

Tom and Jill were looking at the wedding presents. Jill had been eager to leave for some time. 'I'll be glad to get back. Delia's not getting any stronger. Her labour could start any minute. It's a lot of responsibility for Kate alone.'

'Tilda's there,' Tom pointed out.

'Tilda panics too easily. She'd be no good during that sort of thing.'

'I suppose you're right, darling. We'll be off soon anyway, try not to worry.'

'But I can't help it, Tom. If anything was to go wrong…'

'It won't. You must stay calm, darling.' Tom had grasped at the possibility of adopting Delia's baby as eagerly as she had. At the very least he'd thought it worth considering. It was fraught with problems, not least the fact that the father had the right to his say in the baby's future. They were trying not to build up unrealistic hopes, but the offer had been made and as each hour passed it meant more and more to them. How could they not want this baby when Jill might not be able to conceive children of their own? Having given Delia refuge under their roof, Jill had witnessed her distress and was emotionally involved. Disappointment now would be heartbreaking for her. Tom had spoken to Delia, expressing the doubts and all the issues to her, encouraging her to think that she might love her baby, that things would be easier now she had friends on her side. Delia had remained adamant she did not want the child, and had grown frantic that she might be forced to take it with her when she left the farm. He and Jill had reassured her that they were willing to adopt the baby if that was what she still wanted and they would see she had a fresh start wherever she wanted to go. They had consulted a solicitor to act for them when, pray God, the time actually came. They had told no one of these plans. First, they wanted to wait and see what Delia's reaction would be after the confinement. It didn't occur to either of them that Kate might be making plans for her sister-in-law and niece or nephew. Kate was courting with Alan. Why should she have more than that on her mind once Delia was away and settled?

'Perhaps we should think about Delia going into a nursing home where she would have medical staff on hand,' Jill said. 'There would be less danger to her and the baby then.'

'That's a good idea,' Tom replied. 'We'll put it to her when we get back, but if she wants to stay put, we'll let her. You should stay close to the house from now on, darling. If the baby is to be ours we've got too much at stake to take any risks.'

'What are you two whispering about?' Emilia came their way.

'Nothing,' Tom blurted out. 'We were, um... it was a nice wedding, Mum. Have you noticed how different Jonny is today? He usually jokes at a wedding that he'll never be caught as a groom.'

Emilia shot a glance at Jonny across the room. He was side-on to her, staring down at his open wallet in the palm of his hand, touching it with his fused fingers. Tracing an outline. A photograph, no doubt of Kate. She groaned inwardly. Jonny wasn't about to step out of Kate's life. He was a fighter, a survivor. Someone, perhaps more than one person, was going to get hurt. Interfering couldn't prevent it. All she could do was to stand back and pick up the pieces.

–

Kate had her feet up in the kitchen, knitting a bonnet for Delia's baby. She was halfway through a full layette, but she only knitted in her room or when Jill was out, sensitive not to upset her. Jill and Delia had formed a close friendship

271

and Jill often mentioned the baby. It was a pity Delia had to go far away to be safely rid of Sidney, otherwise Kate would have suggested Jill should be a godmother to the baby. It would have been some way towards allowing Jill some input into a child's life.

Tilda came bursting through from the other part of the house.

'Ah, come for some tea?' Kate said, hoping she wasn't in an unnecessary flap.

'No, 'tisn't that,' Tilda puffed, ruffling her apron, something she did when alarmed. 'Your brother's coming through the yard. There's not one of them blessed dogs about to see him off if he's come to cause trouble. I've locked Mrs Em's doors. Do you want to lock Mr Tom's?'

'No. I'll go out to him. Don't worry, Tilda. He was bound to come here sometime. I'll sort out what he wants. Can you stay here till I come back in?'

'Course. But you be careful, maid. If I hear shouting or swearing I'll ring for the constable.'

Kate confronted Sidney on the flagstones. 'Have you come to see Delia? She's resting, asleep.'

'I've come for no such thing.' He was scowling to the inner reaches of his hard face. He had his best clothes on, bicycle clips round his trouser bottoms. There was a dark red mark above one of his eyes. 'I've only come to tell you that I'm off.'

'Off? What do you mean?'

'What I said. I'm leaving home. And seeing as you took it upon yourself to take my wife away, I'll have you know there's now no home for her to return to. So you can have the pleasure of the responsibility of the bitch from now on. I've got no way of supporting her and the brat anyway. Things were said about Tony at the coal yard and I got into a fight. I was sacked. Weren't bleddy fair, but that's how it is. Father's moving in with the Tregaskis woman, marrying her as soon as can be. So I'm making a clean break. Tell Delia not to try to find me. She can divorce me in a few years for desertion.'

Kate could almost have laughed at his gloating face. He thought he was burdening her and that Delia would be upset about being abandoned, but it was what they both wanted. Best of all, Delia didn't need to go away. She could live in a little place in Hennaford and look forward to a peaceful life, with care and support close by. 'I see,' she said grimly, disguising her pleasure. 'There's nothing more to be said then.'

Sidney eyed her coldly, then as if hating to say so, 'Never thought you'd have turned out to be so pretty. You've done well for yourself.'

'Are you jealous?' It was her turn to be smug.

He muttered something under his breath but she heard the foul swear words in it. 'Got any money you can let me have? I'm owed wages but I'm not likely to ever get it.'

'Only a pound or two.'

'That'll do. See me on my way a little.'

'Wait there.' She went back inside and ran upstairs to fetch her purse.

'Kate!' Delia called from her room. 'I thought I heard Sidney's voice. Is he here?'

'No, it's the baker. You just rest, Delia.'

She hadn't reached the stairs before Tilda shouted, 'Kate! Kate! Come quick!' Damn it. Sidney had come inside the house. She hurried down to the kitchen. 'I told you to wait outside.'

Tilda had retreated to the far reaches of the room. Sidney's eyes were searching shelves and the mantelshelf. 'These fancy friends of yours must have some money lying about, Kate. I'm sure they wouldn't mind sparing me some as a favour to you.'

'There's no one else here!' Tilda shrieked.

Kate's heart fell. That was a stupid thing for Tilda to reveal.

'Aha.' Sidney's eyes gleamed with greed. 'I thought it was quiet. Come on, Kate. Surely someone's got a few notes stashed away in an old teapot or something. What about you?' Sidney snarled at Tilda, obviously enjoying her fright.

Tilda gulped and a plump hand flew to her bosom. Kate was afraid she might faint or become hysterical, then Tilda glanced at her and seemed to gain control. 'Yes! I keep some savings in my room. Nearly forty pounds for my old age, but you can have that if you promise never to darken these doors again.'

'That's better.' Sidney moved his bulky shoulders in a swanky manner. 'Go and get it. I'll stay here and see what Kate can do for me.'

Tilda glanced at Kate again. Kate knew she would scurry to Mrs Em's den and phone for help in case Sidney didn't leave quietly. She had no idea if Tilda had any cash in the house or whether she would hand any over to Sidney. If Sidney got really stroppy she would tell him he could have their grandmother's savings and hope that would see the back of him. She tossed her purse to Sidney and he caught it in a deft hand. She said, 'Jill keeps a little money in an old tin for emergencies. You can take that.' Going slowly to the dresser – Tilda needed time – she leaned down to the cupboard and drew out a flat toffee tin.

'It was worth me calling.' Sidney gave a mocking laugh and snatched the tin from her. His coal-dust darkened fingers tore off the lid and scrabbled to take out a ten-shilling note and some change.

'You're despicable.'

He laughed again. 'Learning big words, eh, little sis? You've got in with some young toff, I hear. His car was the talk of the village, almost as much as Tony's death. Going to marry him?'

'That's none of your business.'

'More fool you if you don't. You going to Tony's funeral when the cops release his body? It'll be a quiet affair. God knows where the money for that is going to come from.'

'Well, it won't come from me. I don't suppose Mother's funeral will ever get paid for. That's Father's responsibility.'

'Kate! Kate!' The calls came from above.

'Ah, that's my darling wife. Think I'll say goodbye to her. Tell her she never was much good to me.'

'No, Sidney! Leave her be,' Kate pleaded. 'Delia's suffered enough. Just take what you've come for and go.'

'All right. But where's that old woman?' Sidney went after Tilda, stopping at the foot of Jill's stairs. Delia had dragged herself to the top of them. He took in the luxurious borrowed nightdress and bed jacket she was wearing and it angered him. 'So there you are! Thought you'd go after Kate and see what you could get out of these rich buggers too! Never gave a thought about me.'

'That's not fair, Sidney.' Kate tried to pull him away. 'Just—'

Kate's words were cut off by Delia's screams. 'I'm not going back with you! Go away! Go away!'

'You're my wife and you'll do what I say!' Sidney roared in evil pleasure, stomping up the first few steps. He'd show her one last time he was in control.

'It's all right, Delia. He hasn't come for you. He's going for good.'

Kate's pleas were lost on Delia. She was in frenzy.

'Sidney, come back down and go outside!' Kate yanked on his arm.

He wrenched himself away from her, pushing her so hard she was sent stumbling towards the wall.

'I hate you!' Delia shrieked at Sidney. 'Don't you dare come near me!' At the top of the stairs on the wall was a heavy barometer. She backed up and ripped it off the wall, then returning to the top of the stairs made to hurl it down at him.

'Delia, don't!' Kate screamed.

Delia threw down the barometer and Sidney grabbed the handrail and ducked. The force of the throw pitched Delia forward and the next instant she was falling, coming down at speed, head first.

Kate screamed and screamed. 'Delia!'

Delia's fall was broken as she hit Sidney's body. Crouching, he yelled out in pain as he was struck on the back by her top half. Without forethought or humanity, instead of making a grab to hold her he thrust up his arms and heaved her away. Like a rag doll, Delia was flung upwards and back, coming down to hit her spine on the stairs. She had cried out at the beginning of the plunge, now she yelled in agony, a terrible animal sound.

Sidney shuffled, cursing loudly, until he was staring down at his wife. Kate pushed past him to Delia, sprawled on the stairs, her head lolling backwards. The breath and perhaps the life had been knocked out of her and she was still, her eyes staring upwards. Sidney hastily headed back to the kitchen. 'Where are you going?'

'I'm not hanging about here.'

'But you can't just go. Delia's hurt!'

'And she might be dead and I couldn't care less. I'm off.' He disappeared, banging the doors as he charged outside.

Delia groaned. Leaning over her, Kate supported her head.

Tilda came through from the other part of the house, a small tin cash box with a tiny key on a blue ribbon in her hands. 'Oh, dear God, dear God. I've rung the constable and for Tom and Jill to come back home.'

'Ring for the doctor,' Kate cried. 'Hurry!'

Delia focused her eyes on Kate. 'We're getting help,' Kate told her soothingly. 'Keep still. You'll be all right.'

Delia's lips were moving and Kate put her ear close to hear her whisper. 'Jill… Jill… the baby.'

'She's on her way home. Don't worry. Sidney's gone for good. We'll look after you. Everything will be fine from now on.'

Deha's eyes were closing and before she lost consciousness, she whispered again, 'Jill…'

Chapter Twenty-Five

'Of all the days for your brother to have come, Kate, with all the rest of us out.' Jill wrung her hands. She couldn't bear it if this led to the loss of the baby, and Delia was in poor shape too. 'You shouldn't have allowed Delia to get out of bed.'

Kate didn't answer. Jill had never been sharp with her before, but with the terrifying incident replaying itself inside her head it didn't matter. And she understood Jill's point of view. Jill had willingly helped her during her time of deepest need and she had done the same for Delia. This next sordid incident had happened in Jill's home. It was not surprising she was angry and upset.

It had been an agonizing time for Kate waiting for help to arrive. The village constable, after helping Dr Edward Greaves carry Delia up to her room, had subjected Kate to endless questions, and she had received another barrage when the family, including Jonny, had rushed in from the wedding reception. The constable had left satisfied that Sidney was not directly responsible for Delia's injuries, and as no one wanted to press charges against him, wanting only to be rid of him for ever, had considered no more police activity need be involved. There was still the anxious wait for the doctor's report. He had decided Sidney had taken the brunt of Delia's fall, and he was now biding his time to consider whether Delia should stay here and continue with bed rest or be admitted to hospital.

'You can't blame Kate for what happened. She's been through an awful time too.' Jonny was appalled at Jill's stance. It was hard not to go to Kate and throw his arms around her, say something to ease her dejection. Every so often she trembled in shock. 'Sounds to me that she controlled the situation very bravely, and Tilda had the presence of mind to summon help. It could have been a lot worse.'

Kate was grateful for his support. The others had sent her head into a whirl of confusion but Jonny was calm and had not added to the pressure. He had come in quietly, as a concerned friend, nothing more, she was sure. Alan had been mistaken about him falling in love with her. Alan had seen things that way out of jealousy, fearing he had a rival. Each time she thought about it the idea of Jonny falling for her seemed more unlikely, even ridiculous. She and Jonny were very close, they shared an affection, but they lived on a different rise, with different outlooks and dreams, there could be nothing else between them. She met his eyes and lingered on his steady gentle gaze. He was secretly telling her that whatever happened he was one hundred per cent behind her, as a good friend would be. Opinions and advice about Delia's care flew round the room, but Delia was her relative, and apart from the baby, Kate was all she had left. If Delia wasn't up to making decisions then she would make them on her behalf.

'Yes, of course. I'm sorry, Kate. That wasn't fair of me,' Jill said, finally going to her, aware that her priorities had shifted. In any other case Kate would have been her first concern. 'At least Sidney will never trouble Delia or you again.'

'All being well.' Emilia glanced up at the ceiling. 'Delia will be able to start out fresh when the baby is born.' She was worried about how Delia would come through her labour when the time came. Dr Greaves had said he would feel happier if she was in the infirmary but he didn't think it particularly wise for her to travel. He was a busy man. He must be greatly concerned to be spending so much time with Delia. She was worried about Jill too. She was edgy. She couldn't keep still and was rising up and down on her toes. How was she going to cope if the baby was born under her roof when she had been so looking forward to her own baby's first cries here?

Jill twisted her bottom lip and glanced at Tom. She couldn't stand the strain and deserted Kate to seek his shelter.

Perry put a fatherly arm round Kate. 'I'm sure everything will be all right, my love.'

The bedroom door above was opened. 'Ah.' Tilda leapt towards the range. Her nervousness had returned and she needed to be active. 'Here's the doctor at last. I'll put the kettle on again.'

'Mr and Mrs Harvey, can you come?' Dr Greaves called urgently down the stairs.

Jill and Tom shot out of the kitchen and Emilia, Perry and Tilda were on their heels.

'He should have called for me,' Kate complained to Jonny as they brought up the rear.

'Don't worry, I'm here for you.' He pushed her through to the front of those gazing up the stairs.

'I need someone to call the district nurse,' Dr Greaves, young, stocky, with thinning hair, directed in his precise, clipped manner. 'The baby's heartbeat is weakening. I fear the fall may have caused placental abruption, in which case the baby needs to be delivered quickly. Tell the nurse not to delay. I'll need to do a Caesarean. Mrs Viant was in a lot of pain from the accident and I've already sedated her. You should prepare yourselves for possible bad news where the baby is concerned.'

'Oh no!' Jill cried out. Tom took her away. Emilia and Perry hurried to the telephone. Tilda went off trembling to make tea. Kate stayed put, clenching her fists. Damn Sidney, damn her vile evil brother. He had traumatized and hurt Delia again. Getting her away from home had not been enough to protect her. Now he might be responsible for the death of his own child, and for even more pain and heartbreak for Delia. And for Jill too. Jill didn't deserve this.

'I'm sure everything will be fine, Kate,' Jonny said gently.

'You can't promise that, Jonny. It's not how things work. Excuse me, I want to make a phone call.'

The district nurse was tracked down and got to the farm within twenty minutes. Another nail-biting vigil began. Jill and Tom couldn't tear themselves away from the house, but Kate couldn't bear to stay inside it. She went out to the back garden, where she could listen for sounds from Delia's bedroom. All she could hear was the occasional muffled voice of the doctor or nurse. Jonny joined her. She was pleased to have his company. He circled an arm round her and she rested in his comfort. 'I'm so scared for them.'

He placed the side of his face on her head. 'You're right, I can't promise they'll both come through safely. But I can promise I won't leave you.' Not ever, there was no need to. The proof was Kate needed him and was responding to his embrace.

'Thanks, Jonny. It means so much.'

That proved it too. Alan Killigrew was of no real account to her.

Time went by and then some more. How long did the operation take? It seemed hours. Then, as if Kate's inner senses had received a signal, she reached for Jonny's hand. 'It's time to go in.'

They found Jill and Tom huddled at the foot of the stairs, a pathetic sight in their wedding clothes. They seemed to be really hurting. It was so good of them to be deeply concerned for a woman they hadn't known until a few days ago.

Fear-stricken that her worst nightmare had come true, Jill peered at Kate. 'I'm sure something's happened.' Something bad, she meant. 'I thought I heard a baby's tiny cry then it went quiet.'

Tom knocked on his mother's door, and Emilia and Perry and Tilda filed through in a funereal hush.

Dr Greaves appeared up above them in his suit and tie. He was a highly professional sort and his expression was blank. 'I'm coming down.'

All went into Jill and Tom's kitchen. Jonny spoke up. 'Whatever you've come to say, doctor, you should address it to Miss Viant first.'

'Quite, quite,' Dr Greaves replied, with the gravity of a judge. 'You have a nephew, Miss Viant. It was an effort to get him to breathe but he seems to be holding his own for now. Could someone ring for an ambulance? He's underweight and needs more care than can be given here.'

'But he stands a chance?' Kate said. Jill was with her, clutching at her hand. This must be a terrible reminder for her.

'I'm hopeful. With all her experience with babies the nurse is hopeful too.' Dr Greaves pulled at his starched shirt cuffs. 'Now, to get to Mrs Viant. It's a different story, I'm afraid. I'm very sorry, she was too frail to survive the operation. As you already know, her health wasn't anywhere near as good as I'd hope to find in an expectant mother. The accident was too much for her. Her heart actually stopped just before I'd got the baby out. Do take comfort in the fact that she didn't suffer. The ambulance can take her body away. I'll inform the coroner.'

'Oh, my God! Not this!' Jill exclaimed, dashing her hands to her face. She had been hoping Delia wouldn't change her mind about keeping the baby but now she would never have the chance to.

Kate felt a rushing in her ears and her legs began to buckle, but taking a deep determined breath she held her ground. Her voice shook. 'Delia dead. Poor Delia. Thanks for all your efforts, doctor. Can I hold the baby and stay with Delia alone for a while?'

'Of course. Just give the nurse and me a little more time.'

Delia looked as if she was sleeping, at peace, back to her true age of just twenty years. It was this that made Kate break down and cry and tore her heart to pieces. She sat at the bedside, cradling her tiny nephew swathed in a warm blanket, and held Delia's marble-cold hand. 'My family made me suffer too but at this moment I'm ashamed to be a Viant. I think this is what you wanted, Delia. To die. To be out of it. I don't blame you for that. You never had the good fortune of meeting someone like Jill earlier in your life like I did. Rest in peace, you deserve it. Here's a promise you can take with you. You never knew your little boy, but I promise you that I will do everything in my power to see he has a good life. I will never, ever forsake him.'

Chapter Twenty-Six

'Tom and I will take you to follow on after the ambulance,'
Jill said when Kate came downstairs. The district nurse
was behind her carrying down the little bundle, and Jill
strained to see the baby she was hoping would become
her son. She and Tom would look for the right moment
to broach the matter to Kate of Delia's wish for the baby,
their passionate wish too.

Kate nodded, too bereft to talk.

Jonny was longing to kiss the tears from her face, to
give her his solace, his strength.

Kate went to the kitchen window. She saw what she
was hoping for from the result of her telephone call, what
she really needed. 'There's no need, Jill. Alan's here. He'll
take me.' She was out of the door before anyone could
react.

Jill glanced anxiously at Tom, hoping they weren't
about to be cut out of the baby's life. Kate was his next
of kin and had the right to say what happened to him.
What if she wanted to settle down with Alan and bring
him up herself? They could hardly go to her and tell her
about Delia's wish. And Delia would have likely offered
her child to Kate if she had thought she was about to get
married.

Jonny's heart and hopes plummeted as violently as his plane had plunged into the sea. He was a casualty again. This time the pain was almost too much to bear. Still, he rushed outside after Kate. Only to freeze in horror, watching as if in some terrible dream while Kate flung herself into Alan's arms and sobbed against him. He saw the desire of his life being taken into the other man's loving embrace, a man who whispered soothing words to her, caressed her, cared for her in the way that he was denied. Then Kate looked up at Alan and in her eyes was the look of a woman in love. A love not given in the first flush of womanhood, but the strong and enduring sort of love that lasts for ever.

All this time Kate had seen him as no more than a friend, not even so close a friend as to mention she was in love with someone. It was as plain and as devastating as that to Jonny. He had to get away. He couldn't bear for Kate to see his desolation.

Someone touched him. 'Come with me, Jonny.' It was Emilia.

'I've got no other option, have I, Aunt Em?'

'I'm afraid not.' She led him away to a quiet spot.

'You can't help me,' he said, wiping the tears from his eyes. 'No one can mend a heart broken in this many pieces. I was wrong, terribly wrong. I thought I could make Kate fall in love with me. You were right. There's too much of a gap between us to ever have been bridged. I'll go back to Louisa's house. I need to be alone.'

'I'm sure you'll find love again one day, Jonny. There's bound to be someone out there for you. You know what it is like to be in love now.'

He shook his head, the searing pain of what could never be nearly blinding him. The intolerable loneliness was already settling in. 'I can't imagine loving anyone but Kate.'

'I know it's wretched for you right now but you'll never regret loving her, Jonny.'

'No, I won't. Never that. I can't stay round here. I'll say goodbye at Tremore tomorrow. Tell Kate I've gone away on an assignment. Bye, Aunt Em.' He dragged his feet out into the lane, leaving Kate behind for ever. He'd lost everything but somehow he'd survive. He was that sort of man. The world and its sights and even perhaps some of its pleasures beckoned him, but without Kate it wouldn't be the same.

–

Tom helped Jill restore to its former state the room Delia had died in. 'There's a feeling of peace in here, don't you think?' he said, weighed down with sadness. What terrible suffering Delia had endured. 'I mean, Delia doesn't seem to be lingering. I think she's at peace.'

Jill had been using her underlying senses too, wondering if there was anything of Delia's pain and woe still in the room. 'I think you're right. Do you think it was a happy release? Poor Delia went through so much. I feel guilty now about longing to have her baby.'

'Try not to fret about it, darling. I don't think Delia would have wanted that.' Huddled together, they stared at the empty bed. 'At least she knew some consolation at the end of her life. She might never have come to terms with all the torment she went through, she might have spent the rest of her life in misery.'

'Yes, that would have been very likely, but how terrible when death is the only way out. Kate seems to be coping quite well. She's got Alan. Nothing could be better for her. We can only pray the baby will be strong enough to pull through. I can't help wondering what she'll decide about him.'

'Me too. She may not decide anything for days.' Tom sighed heavily. 'The waiting is awful.'

'We'll just have to be patient.'

'Yes. I can't help...'

'What?'

'Thinking about names for him. Can you?'

'I wanted Thomas if we'd had a boy. That's what I'd like this time, all being well.'

'I'd like Alec, after my father. The next Alec Harvey at Ford Farm. Alec Thomas, if that's all right with you, darling. If we get the chance...'

'If we do. I wonder what's going through Kate's mind. Yes, darling, the waiting is awful.'

–

'Can we stop for a while, Kate?' Alan said on the way back from the infirmary. 'We need to talk.'

'That's what I want too,' Kate said, smiling at his outline in the dark confines of the car.

He pulled off the road in a field gateway. They snuggled together, holding hands. He said, 'Four deaths in such a short time, my poor love. I'll help you get through it all. And I'll help with the arrangements for Delia. Have you any ideas what you'd like to do for her?'

'Her family won't want to get involved. I'll have her buried in the churchyard, that way she'll always be near her little boy. I think she'd want that.'

'The doctors are sure the baby will pull through, thank God. When he's released, will you take him to the farm? Will he be welcome there?'

'More than welcome.' Kate smiled to herself. While she had waited for the baby to be examined by a paediatrician she had seriously considered what was best for his future.

'I'm glad you're confident of that. Darling, if you want, we could get married, provide a home for him.'

She interlocked her fingers through his and kissed his chin. How like Alan to make such an unselfish gesture. 'It's wonderful of you to offer, darling, but I've a better idea.'

'Better?' he said doubtfully, kissing her hair. 'What's that?'

'After Delia fell, when she was lying on the stairs, she tried to tell me something. I'm certain I know what it was. She knew she would die and she wanted Jill to take her baby. It was Delia's last wish.'

'Maybe so, Kate, but what if Jill doesn't want the baby? Or Tom?'

'They do, I know they do. I saw it all over their faces. I've a feeling that after the number of times Delia said she didn't want the baby – couldn't cope with it was what she meant – she had actually mentioned it to them. And even if she hadn't, I know them so well it would be on their minds anyway. It's the perfect thing. The baby will have two loving parents, a whole new family, and me as his doting aunty.'

'And an uncle too. If that's what you want, Kate. Will you marry me, get engaged?' Alan held her tight. 'I love you so much.'

'I love you more than anything, Alan,' she returned the tenderness. 'Yes, I'd love to marry you one day. Getting engaged will be fine for now.'

They joined in a passionate kiss to seal the promise, more needful and with more offering than before. Putting her grief for Delia aside, she had never thought she could be this happy. Everything had changed so much for her in the last few months. She had changed so much too. She had gained freedom from soul-destroying servitude and now lived a life worth living. She had thought to stay unattached for a very long time but already she had joined herself to the man who would be the greater part of her life from now on. There was no need to seek 'herself'. She had found all that in Alan. She had found love, the meaning for her being alive. She couldn't imagine not being with him. He made her complete. There was nothing as good and fine and fulfilling as to be his and to be this happy. She wanted the couple who were almost as close to her to know this wonderful wholeness too, to have what they wanted more than anything.

'Shall we go on and tell Jill and Tom their good news?' She smiled up at Alan. 'They must be desperate for us to get back.'

'Yes, let's do that and put them out of their misery.'

'And at the same time tell them our wonderful news.'

As they expected, Jill and Tom were peeping out of the window watching for their return and came rushing outside to meet them.